SINS
REVEALED

SINS
REVEALED

A
Joe Erickson Mystery

Lynn-Steven Johanson

LEVEL
BEST BOOKS

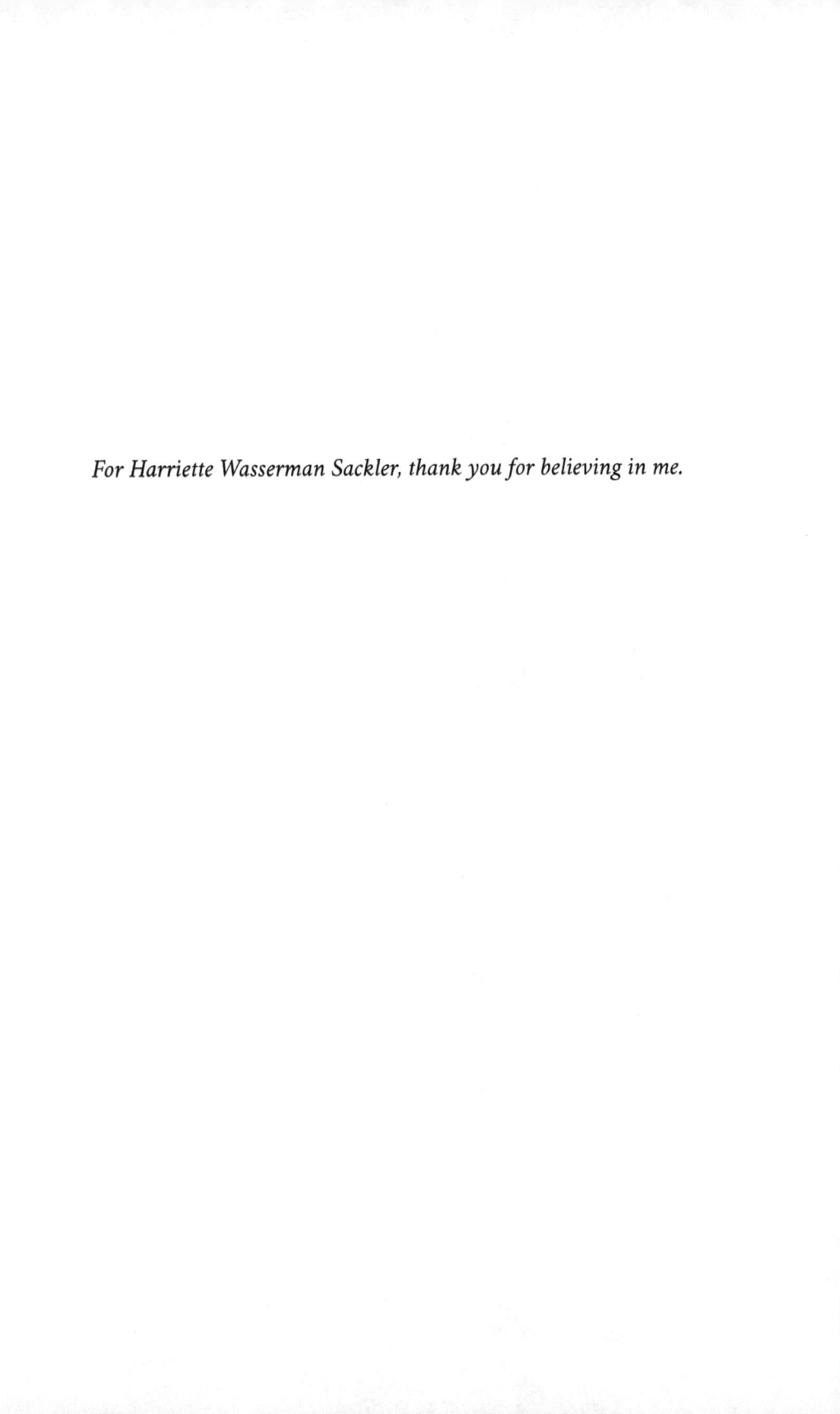

For Harriette Wasserman Sackler, thank you for believing in me.

Praise for Sins Revealed

"Lynn-Steven Johanson's novel *Sins Revealed* is the eagerly awaited fifth outing in his Chicago Detective Joe Erickson's series of police procedurals. It's an intricately plotted, fast-paced investigative mystery where nothing is as it seems. Johanson's straightforward writing style smoothly propels us forward through a complex story of family betrayal, tortured relationships, and murder."—J. Woollcott, award-winning author of *A Nice Place to Die* and *Blood Relations*, the DS Ryan McBride Belfast Murder series

"Johanson leads readers down a murky, serpentine path full of unexpected turns, as Joe Erickson unearths layer after layer of dark deeds and deception, proving that some sins can never be buried long enough or deep enough."—J.R. Sanders, author of the Nate Ross novels

Chapter One

Never in his wildest dreams did he think himself capable of killing a person, much less two. He kept asking himself how the hell he could have done this as he drove on, his hands trembling as he gripped the steering wheel.

At 2:30 a.m., traffic was light on Western Avenue as he steered the old Chevy pickup toward the park, knowing it would be quiet and sure it would be devoid of people. Slowing to a crawl to let a lone vehicle pass, he shut off his lights, pulled into the park, and drove through the grass. Locating a place well inside the park sheltered by trees on three sides, he stopped the pickup and got out.

His first task involved surveying the area, checking for anyone who could be wandering through the park. Satisfied he was alone, he tossed a package near a tree, walked to the pickup bed, removed a two-gallon gasoline can, and set it down. Then he pulled up the tarp, removed the first body, and placed it inside the truck's cab. Next, he pulled out the second body, set it in the cab next to the first, and rolled down the door's window.

Stepping to the gasoline can, he unscrewed the cap to the spout and began dousing both bodies with gasoline. Moving to the driver's side, he leaned in and continued dousing until the bodies were thoroughly soaked. He shut the doors carefully, not wanting to create a spark by closing them too hard.

Moving to the truck's fuel cap, he unscrewed it, stuck in his handkerchief, and wet it with gasoline. Then, the last gasoline in the can was poured over the outer part of the pickup, starting from the front of the hood, progressing to the roof, and onto the bed and tailgate. After emptying the can, he placed it in the bed along with the gas cap. Reaching in his pocket, he removed a matchbook, lit it on fire, tossed it through the cab's open window, and quickly jumped back. The gasoline ignited with a loud "whoosh." Flames quickly engulfed the old pickup.

He retrieved the package he had tossed near the tree and ran out of the park as fast as he could, not knowing if and when someone would notice the fire. The old clothes and cap he was wearing and the package he was carrying would suggest he was a homeless person, so he would not draw undue attention to himself walking down a sidewalk at this time in the morning.

Out of shape for running, it took him some time to catch his breath after he made it out of neighboring Rosehill Cemetery and onto Ravenswood Avenue. After he had walked for a good twenty minutes, a light rain began to fall. Spotting an alley with a dumpster covered by a small roof extension, he ducked in behind it. Sheltered from the rain, he sat back against the brick wall and closed his eyes in an attempt to sleep.

Sometime after sunrise, he awoke. The rain had stopped. He looked at his watch—almost six o'clock. He stood, opened the package, and removed a new set of clothes. Changing out of the old clothing he wore the night before, he donned a golf shirt and a pair of khakis. Tossing the old clothes and cap into the dumpster, he stepped out of the alley and began walking down the sidewalk. Half an hour later, he entered a diner where he ordered toast and coffee.

Using the restroom, he washed his face and scrubbed his hands and arms to get rid of the residual odor of gasoline. Usually, he ate a hearty breakfast, but he had little appetite this morning. However, he was in desperate need of coffee. After eating two slices of toast and downing several cups of black coffee, he settled his bill and left, feeling awake and focused.

Flagging down a taxi, he had himself dropped five blocks from where his car was parked. He walked the rest of the way. Once he reached his car, he got inside and took a deep breath, closing his eyes and laying his head against the back of the seat. It was done. After a minute, he opened his eyes and focused. Driving away, he felt confident there was no way anyone could tie him to the previous night's events. Any evidence was now in ashes.

He drove home, observing speed limits all the way. Eventually, he walked through the door of his house. After pouring himself a healthy glass of Jack Daniels, he turned on his big-screen TV, settled into his recliner, and began watching a movie. Not long after finishing his whiskey, he was fast asleep.

Chapter Two

Detective Joe Erickson was driving to work in a new black Camaro. He had been without a car for over a year. His previous Camaro was blown to bits by a car bomb planted at the direction of mobster Vincent Scalise. Using Uber rides to and from work became inconvenient and expensive. Since Scalise was now in prison, and since no one had made another attempt on his life, he felt it was safe to get another car.

Two months ago, his friend, Dennis Scott, located this Camaro. Dennis's shop helped Joe complete all the modifications on his previous Camaro. The original owner of this two-year-old black beauty had made many of the same modifications Joe had made. Unfortunately, the owner died in a skiing accident in Colorado, and his widow asked if Dennis could help her find a buyer. He knew Joe was looking, and a deal was made.

Five minutes from the Area 3 Detective Division where he worked, Joe received a phone call from the duty sergeant directing him to West Ridge Nature Park. Not wanting to take time to stop at Area 3 to acquire a squad car and wait for his partner to arrive, Joe pulled out a portable blue light, placed it on his roof, and drove to the crime scene.

The West Ridge Nature Park is a twenty-acre park recently developed into an impressive natural space filled with native plants, boardwalks, and a fishing area. Joe and his life partner, Destiny Alexander, had been there several times. Today, he would be returning to that peaceful space because someone had been killed.

The Medical Examiner's van was already there. A uniformed officer directed him to the crime scene. As he came upon the taped-off area, he saw the familiar form of Kendra Solitsky at work next to the burned-out hulk of a pickup truck.

Joe presented his ID to Officer Johnson, who was supervising the crime scene.

"What have we got?"

"Looks like a victim inside the truck. Burned beyond recognition. It's not something I'd care to see more than once. Freakin' ugly, man."

"Who called it in?"

"A coupla joggers. They run in the park several times weekly and noticed the burned-out wreck. One of them walked over to check it out and saw the remains."

"Where are the joggers now?"

"Sitting in my squad car. The site of the victim was pretty upsetting."

"No doubt. I'll want to talk to them in a few minutes."

Joe looked toward the pickup truck and saw Kendra waving to him. Joe waited at the edge of the crime scene tape as Kendra removed her Tyvek hood and mask and walked toward him.

"I'd say 'good morning,' but I'd be lying," said Joe as Kendra got close.

"More like, 'Helluva morning,' if you want to know the truth."

"What have we got?"

"Two victims—"

"Two?"

"Two. When I got here, the officer on the scene told me one, but evidently, he was too freaked out to look closely. There are definitely two charred bodies. The fire burned them so badly, I can't even tell their gender until I do an autopsy."

"No accident."

"No. No-no. No accident."

"Can you tell if they were killed before the fire?"

"I can't tell hardly anything from this scene. I can smell an accelerant. It was used to burn the victims and the vehicle."

Joe looked around at the scorched grass and said, "It's lucky it didn't burn more grass and catch trees on fire."

"It rained early this morning. It probably kept the fire from spreading."

"How do you do an autopsy on bodies so badly burned?"

"PMCT."

"Excuse me?"

"Post-mortem computed topography. CT scans, in other words."

"I see."

"The victims will have to be identified by dental records. And the scans will show abnormalities that can lead to cause of death. We'll be taking DNA samples and sampling fluids. You won't have to attend these autopsies, Joe. Won't be your typical autopsy procedures."

"Okay."

"I'll need to wait for the Evidence Techs to get here before I can go any further," said Kendra as she stepped under the crime scene tape. "Removing the bodies will take some time."

"Since it rained, I suppose that compromises additional evidence."

"It didn't help."

As they walked away, Kendra handed Joe a note. "You may be able to use this. The truck was burned all to hell, but I could make out the number on the license plate."

"Thanks. This gives us something to go on."

As Joe walked back toward the squad car with the two joggers, he saw his partner, Sam Renaldo, walking toward him.

"What have we got?" asked Sam.

"Two bodies burned beyond recognition in what's left of a pickup truck. Torched sometime last night."

"Oh, man."

"I'm about to interview the two joggers who found the remains this morning. Come on."

The joggers were sitting with the doors open for ventilation.

"You can get out if you want," said Joe to the joggers. "After we ask you a few questions, you can go."

"It's about time," said the middle-aged man. "We've been sitting here for almost an hour."

"We apologize for the wait. But this is a criminal investigation, and we have to observe certain protocols."

"It's all right," said the woman. She was a good ten years younger than the man and had the lean body of a runner. "Guess I'll have something to talk about at work."

The man scoffed, "Make sure you tell them how you puked."

"I couldn't help it."

After getting their names and addresses, Joe asked, "What time did you come across the vehicle?"

The man, James Renfro, replied, "About six o'clock or so."

"Yeah, about six," confirmed Wendy Sutherland.

"Who called it in?" asked Sam.

"I did," said Renfro. "Wendy was too busy throwing up."

"Knock it off!" objected Sutherland. "I couldn't help it. It was gross. And the smell..."

"Understandable," said Sam. "It takes a strong stomach to deal with something like that, especially for the first time."

"Hopefully, the last time. I don't want to see something like that ever again."

"How often do you jog in the park?" asked Joe.

"Nearly every day," said Renfro.

"And did you jog here yesterday?"

"Yeah."

"And you didn't notice the pickup yesterday?"

"No, it wasn't here yesterday. We would have noticed it."

"Did you see anyone else in the park this morning?" asked Sam.

"No."

"No, I didn't see anybody else," concurred Sutherland.

"You didn't touch the truck or anything, did you?" asked Joe.

They both shook their heads no.

Joe looked at Renfro. "Did you upchuck, too?"

"Are you kidding?" replied Renfro with disdain.

"He was too afraid to look inside," said Sutherland, getting a dig in.

Renfro was about to respond when Joe interrupted him. "We had to ask for forensic purposes." Joe looked over at Sam and read his expression. "I think we have what we need. If you think of anything else, you can call me." Then he handed each one of them his card. "Thank you both for your time, and we appreciate you calling this in."

"You're free to go," said Sam.

Without saying anything, Renfro and Sutherland started jogging out of the park.

"Somebody wanted those two people dead and didn't want their identities known," said Joe.

"Looks like a mob hit to me. What do you think?" asked Sam.

"If it was a mob hit, they would've been smart enough to remove the license plates before torching the truck. Looks like an amateur's mistake."

"License plate?"

"Yeah. Kendra wrote down the plate number for me. It was scorched, but she could make out the numbers. Illinois plate. Let's run it when we're done here. It may be the only clue to the victims' identities."

"Probably reported stolen."

"Think positive, Sam. Think positive."

Chapter Three

The first thing Joe did when he returned to his Area 3 office was to run the plate number Kendra had given him. The plate matched a 1985 Chevrolet C10 pickup registered to Perry Gardiner, whose address was listed on West Victoria Street in the Edgewater neighborhood. He looked for Gardiner in the driver's license database and saw he was twenty-six years old with the same address listed as a home address. Locating a landline phone number, he called it and found it was no longer in service. Not surprising. In the age of cell phones, landline use has been steadily declining.

Joe's background check on Gardiner revealed he was unmarried and unemployed. He was honorably discharged from the US Coast Guard eighteen months ago, serving as a Damage Controlman for four years. Joe checked the nature of the job, and it involved individuals who were experts in the building trades, firefighting, and flood control.

His mother, Phyllis Gardiner, is a retired teacher, last working at Warren G. Harding Elementary School. Her address showed she is living in Rogers Park. His only sibling, an older sister, is a speech pathologist who also resides in the city. His mother is divorced from his father, William Gardiner, who lives in Florida.

Out of the corner of his eye, Joe saw Sam walking to his desk. As he passed, he asked, "Think it's time to check out Perry Gardiner's residence?

"Yeah, I do. Let's drive up there and see if anybody's home."

The West Victoria Street residence was a two-story white house with an unattached garage. The features suggested the house was built at the turn of the twentieth century. It appeared structurally solid but needed some basic maintenance and updating. The two-car garage looked to be constructed at a later date.

Joe and Sam stepped onto the porch and rang the doorbell several times but got no answer.

"Let's look around," said Joe. "I'll take the house if you want to take the garage."

"Sounds good," said Sam. As he turned to go, his foot nearly went through a rotten board near the steps.

Joe looked through windows as he moved around the house. None of the windows on the first floor had blinds or curtains pulled so he could see inside. The house's contents were spartan. The rooms had basics but lacked the usual décor a person would add to make a place feel like a home. New sheetrock had been hung in the dining room, but it had not been taped and finished. The banister railing and steps to the second floor had been stripped of their finish. Clearly, the occupants were attempting to renovate the interior.

As Joe returned to the front, Sam was sitting on the porch steps.

"Not much in the garage. From what I could see through the windows, a few garden tools, a lawn mower, and some basic hand tools hung from a peg board. What about the house?"

"Someone's living there, but it's been furnished with what looks like Salvation Army stuff. No personal items anywhere."

"Did you see the rectangular patch dug up in the backyard?"

"Yeah. Think it was being dug up for a garden?" asked Joe.

"Looks like it. It's fairly recent. Dirt's still in the grass around the edges."

"Something to look into later. Let's check with the neighbors. See if they can tell us anything."

"Okay. You want the house on the left or the right?" asked Sam.

"Doesn't matter."

"Okay, I'll take the one on the left."

Joe walked to the house on the right, a blue and white Victorian with a wrap-around porch. He rang the doorbell. After a moment, a woman's voice came through the video doorbell speaker.

"Can help you?"

Joe held up his ID and said, "Yes, I'm Detective Joe Erickson with Chicago PD. I want to ask you some questions about your next-door neighbor."

"Just a minute."

After a few moments, the door opened, and an attractive silver-haired woman in her late forties stepped out onto the porch. Joe held up his ID so she could see it. She glanced at it and then looked him over.

"Detective, huh?" she asked in a sultry voice.

"Uh-huh."

"You'll have to excuse me. I just got out of the bath," she said as she tightened the belt on her robe.

"You're excused."

"Well…exactly which one of my neighbors are you investigating?"

"Perry Gardiner."

"Ah."

"What can you tell me about him?"

"Well, not much really. He lives there in his great-uncle's house. It was passed down to his father and now to Perry, it seems. His father's job took him out of state, but he kept hold of the house. When Perry came back from the service, he moved in.

"What about Perry's mother?"

"Oh. She moved out during the divorce. A long time ago."

"I see. Do you know if Perry lives there by himself?"

"He lives there with a girl. I don't know who she is. They come and go, but they don't seem to work regular jobs. Maybe they work online from home, like I do. They're a strange pair."

"What makes you say that?"

She hesitated and moved closer to Joe as if she was relaying something confidential. "Well, Detective, this is just my impression. It's not like I know them or anything. I haven't even talked with either of them since they moved in."

Joe wanted to reassure her because he needed her information. "Look…I'm sorry. "What's your name?"

"Jane. Jane Myerson."

"Look, Ms. Myerson, your impressions are important. So, feel free to say what you sense about them."

"I sit out on my porch and have a glass of wine or two occasionally, so I see them now and then. It's not like I'm spying on them or anything. You can't help but notice. She seems so meek and walks around with her head down most of the time. He orders her around, and she seems to obey. It's weird."

"I see."

"Now, that's just my observation. Who knows? She may act differently inside the house."

Noticing a wedding ring on her finger, Joe asked, "Has your husband ever spoken to them?"

"Oh, no. My husband passed away three years ago."

"I'm sorry," said Joe.

"Thank you. I live here by myself. My boyfriend says they remind him of hippies from the sixties. The way they dress and act and all."

"Can you tell me what kind of vehicle Perry drives?"

"An old pickup. Light blue and white."

"Only the pickup? No other vehicles?"

"Only the pickup, as far as I know. Why? Is Perry in some kind of trouble?"

"We don't know. We're still investigating. If he does come back, would you give me a call?" He handed her his card.

"I certainly will."

"Thank you, Ms. Myerson—"

"Call me Jane," she smiled, toying with the belt on her robe.

"Thank you, Jane."

"You're welcome," she said, giving him a wink. "I have fresh coffee inside. If you're interested."

"Sorry, but my partner's waiting."

"That's too bad. Another time, maybe?"

Her provocative response caused Joe to crack a smile and say, "Maybe." He turned and stepped off her porch.

"Bye, now."

Wow! He could feel her eyes on him as he walked to the squad car. A minute later, Sam walked over from the other house.

"What did you find out?" asked Joe.

"The guy I talked to said Perry's mother and father divorced around ten years ago or so when Perry was a teenager. Perry continued to live with his father until he graduated from high school. His father, Bill, remained in the house until his company transferred him a few years ago. This guy only had one brief interaction with Perry when he moved into the house. He said he barely recognized him. His appearance changed so much. Said he lives there with some girl."

Joe filled in a few gaps he learned from his conversation with the oversexed widow next door.

"I think it's time we talk to Perry Gardiner's mother about our suspicions," said Sam. "Find out who the girl is."

"Yeah. And request the name of Perry's dentist."

"Unfortunately."

That evening, Joe went home to an empty house. Destiny was in Canada attending an International Psychology Conference. He was alone for the week. Cooking wasn't a problem since he was a great cook. And he planned to prepare certain dishes she would not eat since she was a vegetarian. Steak Diane, Shrimp Diavolo, and other dishes were on the menu. He would need to jog a little farther each morning to burn off the excess calories—a small price to pay for culinary excellence.

Chapter Four

The next morning, Joe and Sam drove to Rogers Park, a neighborhood on the far north side of Chicago that borders the city of Evanston to the north and Lake Michigan to the east. Phyllis Gardiner's condominium was located on West Farewell Avenue.

Joe pulled their Taurus squad car into an available parking space in front of a brown brick building complex. Its style suggested it was built sometime in the early years of the twentieth century, like many buildings found in Rogers Park. At close to a hundred years old, the building had been renovated into condominiums at some point.

After being buzzed in, they took the elevator to the second floor and rang the doorbell to Apartment 2C. An attractive, petite woman opened the door as far as the chain allowed.

"Yes?"

"Phyllis Gardiner?" asked Joe.

"Yes."

Joe held up his ID and said, "I'm Detective Joe Erickson, Chicago PD. This is my partner, Sam Renaldo. We need to speak with you."

"Is something wrong?"

"Possibly. Could we come in?"

With some trepidation, she removed the chain and opened the door, allowing them to enter her condo. Phyllis Gardiner, who appeared to be in her early fifties, took good care of herself. Her hair and makeup were done, and she was dressed in black slacks and a gray and white tailored blouse, something Destiny would wear. Joe wondered if she looked like this every

14

day or if she was planning to go somewhere.

They walked into a tastefully decorated living room dominated by a gray sofa and matching chair, both adorned with colorful throws and pillows.

"Have a seat," she said. "Now, what's going on?" she asked, clearly concerned.

"Have you spoken to your son, Perry, today?" asked Joe.

"No."

"When's the last time you spoke to him?

"Oh…a month ago or so. Why?"

"Well, we have a situation. Yesterday morning, we were called to the scene of a vehicle fire. The fire had consumed a pickup truck sometime early that morning. Two bodies which could not be identified were found inside the cab. The number on the pickup's license plate matched the one registered to your son, Perry."

Phyllis sat there, seemingly stunned. After a few seconds, Joe decided to continue.

"We don't know for sure if one of the victims is your son. We went to his home but didn't find anyone there. Do you know if he traveled out of town? It's possible his vehicle was stolen, and the victims were—"

"You said the victims could not be identified?" she asked.

Joe looked at Sam. He didn't want to get into the gruesome aspects of the crime scene with her, so Sam decided to speak up.

"I'm sorry to say the victims…they were badly burned, and no personal identification items were left to determine who they were."

Phyllis, who had been fidgeting with her hands, looked toward Joe and Sam. After a moment, she took a deep breath and spoke.

"So…so, what you're telling me is Perry and my niece could be dead? That's what you're saying?" Her intense dark eyes darted back and forth from Joe to Sam.

"I think we have to consider that possibility," replied Joe.

"Could you give us the name of your niece?" asked Sam.

"Gina. Gina Whitmore. She's my brother's daughter."

"Maybe we can reach her through her cell phone. There's a possibility

Perry could be with her. Do you have her cell number?" asked Joe.

"Uh, yes. I do. Let me get my phone." Phyllis rose and picked up her phone from the dining room table. Sitting back down, she began pushing buttons. "Her number is 312-555-8183. You want me to call her?"

"No," replied Joe. "Don't try to call her. We'll take care of it. Do you know where she works?"

"She used to work as an early childhood teacher in Chicago Public Schools, but I don't know if she still does."

"Does she have parents here in the city?"

"No. They live in Indiana."

"Where in Indiana?"

"Muncie."

"What are their names?"

"Mark and Carol Whitmore."

"Thank you," said Joe as he wrote down their names and location. "Is there any way you can tell if the victim is Perry?"

"Let's see if we can contact Gina and check if Perry may be with her," said Sam. "But it may help if you can give us the name of his dentist."

"Dentist." Phyllis paused. "That bad, is it?" she asked, tears forming in her eyes.

"Just in case," added Joe, reassuring her as kindly as he could. "Just in case."

"Well, then...It's...our family dentist. Dr. Browning. Edward J. Browning."

"Thank you."

Joe saw the look on Phyllis' face and tried to let her down gently. "I know this is disturbing for you, but we need to narrow down our search and determine the victims' identities the best way we can."

"We'll be in touch once we know more," said Sam.

Joe and Sam stood, preparing to leave.

"I'm sorry we had to give you this kind of news," said Joe. "I hate leaving it up in the air like this. I think, at this point, we should hope for the best."

"I understand," replied Phyllis.

Joe gave her his card. "You can call me if you have any questions or any other information for us. Is there a phone number you'd like us to use to contact you?"

She gave them her cell phone number and led them to the door. As they entered the hall, she said, "It's Perry. I know it...I just know it." Her voice trailed off in tears as she closed the door.

As Joe and Sam walked out of the building, Sam said, "Forensics collected the remains of two cell phones in that burned-out pickup, right?"

"Yeah."

"Want me to try calling the number she gave us?"

"May as well."

After going through the entrance doors, they stopped, and Sam called the number Phyllis gave them. After a moment, he looked at Joe and said, "It's dead."

"Like its owner, I'll bet."

"Yeah. Afraid so."

"When we get back, I'll call Kendra with the name of Perry's dentist. Maybe she can make a positive ID with the dental X-rays."

As Sam drove them back to Area 3, Joe got a call on his cell phone from an unidentified caller.

"Detective Joe Erickson."

"This is Julianne Hendricks, Phyllis Gardiner's daughter. Were you at my mother's home telling her my brother might be dead?"

Joe could detect the anger in her voice, and he responded as non-confrontationally as possible. "That's correct, Ms. Hendricks. We have evidence pointing to that possibility."

"Well, my mother called me very upset."

"I can assure you we approached this matter as delicately as possible. But there is a good chance your brother and his cousin are the victims of a homicide."

"A good chance?"

"Yes."

"You mean you don't know?"

"Ms. Hendricks, there's no pleasant way to put this, but the two victims in question were burned beyond recognition. The only way an identification can be made is through dental records or DNA comparison. We're in the process of making a positive ID, but it will take some time. But given the pickup belonged to your brother, and your brother is nowhere to be found, we are fairly convinced he is one of the victims. Now, you're welcome to try to contact him yourself if you wish."

Silence on the other end. Then she spoke. By the tone of her voice, her anger had abated somewhat. "I understand. My mother is retired from teaching but works as a tutor for young children with reading issues. I don't want her so upset she can't work. From now on, I prefer all information about my brother to come through me first rather than my mother. Is that acceptable?"

"Certainly. We can do that. Give me your phone number and your contact information, and we'll communicate through you from now on."

After Hendricks complied, the call ended. Joe looked at Sam and said, "I think I got her calmed down a little. We'll need to interview her once the ID has been made."

"You should have been a diplomat, Joe."

"With my past experience with politicians, they'd give me a post in Siberia."

Chapter Five

That afternoon, Joe called the Office of the Medical Examiner and told Kendra that Perry Gardiner's dentist was Dr. Edward Browning.

"Do you happen to get a phone number for his office?" asked Kendra.

"No," replied Joe. "I didn't want to task his mother with any more questions, given the circumstances and her state of mind."

"I understand. Did you find out anything about the second individual?"

"Yeah. There's a good chance the person is his cousin who was living with him. Her name is Gina Whitmore. She was previously working for the Chicago Public Schools as an early childhood teacher. But I don't have the name of her dentist if she has one in the city."

"I can find out since she worked in the public schools," said Kendra.

"If not, I have her parents' names and the city in Indiana where they live. We could go through them if we have to."

"Let me do some checking with her insurance company first, and I'll let you know if we need to contact the parents. Hopefully, I can find a dentist."

"Okay. When are you conducting the autopsy?"

"Tomorrow. I'm swamped with regular autopsies today. Given the specialized nature of the scans, I'll need to take some time with them. I've already taken DNA samples, but I'll have to have something to compare them with. I could send in Evidence Techs, but it's not critical they collect it. You could do the collection if you're willing."

"What do you need?" asked Joe.

"If you could locate items like toothbrushes, hairbrushes, razors, used glasses, forks, spoons. Bag them individually, label everything, and bring them in. Be sure to wear gloves and masks when you do the collecting."

"Got it. I'll go to their house and collect samples today."

"Good. You're not so bad for a cop, you know that?"

Joe laughed. "You're not so bad, yourself. Talk to you later." Joe ended the call and walked to Sam's desk. Sam was finishing a search for Gina Whitmore's social media. He turned in his chair when Joe walked up.

"Kendra wants us to collect some DNA samples from Gardiner's house."

"Okay. When you want to do it?"

"How about now?"

"Now?"

"Why? Do you have something pressing?" asked Joe.

"Nothing that can't wait."

"Good. I'll get some evidence bags if you want to get the squad car."

A few minutes later, Joe and Sam were on their way to West Victoria Street and the Gardiner house. When they pulled up to the house, they saw a woman on the porch attempting to unlock the front door.

Joe and Sam bailed out of their squad car and ran toward the house.

"Stop!" yelled Sam.

"Stay where you are," yelled Joe.

Both men climbed the steps to the porch as the dark-haired woman turned to them, holding a set of keys. Pointing a pepper spray cannister at them, she warned, "Don't come any closer!"

Sam had his ID out first. "Sam Renaldo, Chicago PD!"

"Detective Joe Erickson," said Joe, holding up his ID. "Who are you?"

"Julianne Hendricks," said the woman, still holding the pepper spray on them. "My father owns this house."

"I suggest you put the pepper spray away, Ms. Hendricks," said Sam. "It would be a serious mistake to spray us."

After a moment, Hendricks put her pepper spray back in her purse. "I had no idea who you were. What are you doing here?" she asked.

"We should be asking you the same thing. Don't you see the yellow crime scene tape on the door?" asked Joe. "It means you can't enter."

"All I want is my Kindle. Perry took it and didn't give it back."

"Doesn't matter," said Sam. "You can't go in."

"I just want my Kindle back."

"You can't have it."

"Why?"

"It could be evidence. May have fingerprints or DNA on it."

"I want to know if it's there or whether it was burned up in his truck. If it was destroyed, I need to replace it."

"Look," said Joe. "We have official police business here. If you're willing to wait and we see your Kindle, I think we can tell you if it's in there. Okay? Would that be satisfactory?"

She let out a frustrated sigh. "I suppose."

"Why don't you wait in your car while we do our job," suggested Sam.

Hendricks left the porch in a huff, and Joe and Sam entered the house as she walked to her car. They gloved up and put on masks.

"You want the kitchen or the bathroom?" asked Joe.

"Kitchen," replied Sam. "What am I looking for?"

"Anything that might have DNA. Glasses and silverware they may have used."

"Got it."

"Bag each piece individually." He handed Sam several evidence bags and then made his way to the bathroom.

Joe bagged two toothbrushes, a nasal inhaler, hairs from the bathtub drain, a men's razor, a pink disposable razor, a lipstick, a hairbrush, and a makeup sponge.

He moved to the bedroom, pulled back the covers on the bed, and took swabs from each side, thinking he may pick up shedded skin cells. After completing his DNA collection, he put everything into a brown paper bag and walked downstairs. He spotted a Kindle on the table as he moved through the dining room to the kitchen.

When he saw Joe walk into the kitchen, Sam pointed to sealed bags and said, "They didn't clean up after their last meal, so I found unwashed dishes. I got silverware and glasses."

"Done?" asked Joe.

"Yeah."

"I spotted a Kindle on the dining room table. Here." Handing Sam a brown paper bag to hold all his evidence bags, Joe walked into the dining room and looked over the Kindle for Hendricks. Then they walked out of the house to their squad car, where they dropped their gloves, masks, and evidence bags in the trunk.

Hendricks got out of her car and walked to them. "Did you find it?" she asked.

After placing the paper bag on the floor of the back seat, Joe turned and asked, "What color is your Kindle?"

Her eyes lit up, and she looked at Joe with anticipation and said, "It has a deep blue leather cover. Perry wasn't giving it back to me."

"Is this it?" asked Joe, producing the Kindle for her to see.

"Yes! That's it."

He handed it to her. "You mean I can have it?"

"I don't think your Kindle is evidence-worthy."

"Oh, thank you."

"We may need to speak to you about your brother at some point," said Sam.

"So, you think he's dead?"

"At this time, we don't know for sure. But circumstantial evidence is pointing in that direction," said Joe. "But we don't have anything conclusive. At least, not yet."

"But you'll go through me if you do find conclusive evidence, right," Hendricks asked, seeking confirmation of what was agreed upon over the phone.

"Right. We'll make sure all communications go through you rather than your mom."

"Good."

"Maybe you could tell me something. Does Gina Whitmore have any relatives here in Chicago?"

"Oh, yeah. Her brother. David. He lives here. Her parents live in Indiana, but David works here in the city."

"Do you have a phone number for him?"

"Yeah." Hendricks looked up his number on her phone. It's 312-555-0203.

"If you need something inside the house, next time, call me," said Sam as he handed her his card.

"Okay. I'll do that."

"Oh, one more thing. You wouldn't happen to know what Perry was doing for a living, would you?"

"I have no idea. It's hard to tell what Perry's been up to. I've only talked to him a few times since he's been back."

Joe re-attached the crime scene tape across the door as Hendricks drove away. As they drove to the Office of the Medical Examiner, Joe said, "I'm not getting a very positive picture of Perry Gardiner. How about you?"

"Sounds like no one wanted to be in close touch with him. His sister, his mother, his neighbors..."

"Yeah. I think we need to learn a lot more about him to see what could have motivated someone to kill him and his cousin. It's one thing to kill them. But to incinerate them afterward...that's what's got me puzzled."

"Sounds like he must have really pissed somebody off."

"Could be."

Joe and Sam drove the collected items to the Office of the Medical Examiner, and Kendra took official possession, establishing the chain of custody. Kendra looked over the individually collected items and how Joe and Sam bagged them, and she noted how they tagged, labeled, and marked each one.

"Not bad, you guys," said Kendra. "Very professional."

"We aim to please," said Joe.

"You never know when something might wind up in court," added Sam.

"Well, this probably won't. But for future reference, your methods for ID comparison purposes would probably hold up. Now, I need to get to work on this stuff."

"How long do you think this will take?" asked Sam.

"DNA, it's slow. The backlog in this state sucks. But as soon as I get dental records, I can make the ID one way or the other the same day. I'll let you know as soon as I know."

"Thanks, Kendra," said Joe.

"Hasta la vista," said Sam.

"Get back to work, you two!"

Chapter Six

J oe and Sam put their heads together the next day and determined they needed to interview Gina Whitmore's brother, David. While Sam tracked down his place of business, Joe conducted a background check on him.

David Leon Whitmore was born in Iowa City, Iowa, and grew up in Muncie, Indiana, a city of 65,000. His father owns an accounting firm in that city. David is the second of three children, with Gina being the youngest. He graduated from Indiana State University with a degree in business administration and worked in sales at several automobile dealerships in Indiana and Illinois. He presently works for a BMW dealership. A divorced father of two, he is currently unmarried. No arrests. His home is located in the Uptown neighborhood, and his annual income exceeds $375,000. *Must be one helluva salesman*, thought Joe.

Sam emailed Joe a website link to BMW Sales of Chicago. Joe clicked on the link, which brought up the dealership's website. He looked at the top of the page and clicked on About Us and then Meet Our Staff. He scrolled through the staff names until he came to "Dave Whitmore." Joe clicked on Whitmore's name, and his smiling photo appeared, showing him dressed in a company polo shirt. A short bio listed him as one of their top salespersons who had been with BMW for five years.

Joe wrote down Whitmore's contact information and decided to call him to set up a meeting rather than pop in on him at the dealership. He might not appreciate the police showing up if he was in the middle of negotiating a sale.

Joe made the call, and a woman answered. "BMW of Chicago."

"I need to speak with one of your salespersons. David Whitmore."

"May I say who's calling?"

"It's Detective Joe Erickson, Chicago PD."

"Oh. Is this about a sale?"

"I'm afraid not."

"Hold, please."

After listening to BMW advertising for about a minute, a man's voice came on the line. "This is Dave Whitmore."

"Mr. Whitmore, this is Detective Joe Erickson, Chicago PD. I need to speak to you about a case we're investigating."

"It doesn't involve one of my kids, does it?"

"No."

"Then, I don't understand."

"We didn't want to intrude on your place of business. But we need to speak with you about an incident we're investigating. Is there a place and time we can meet with you?"

"Well, I could meet with you this afternoon, say 3:30?"

"That works for us," replied Joe. "Where?"

"I don't know. What's good for you?"

"You could come to our Area 3 office. We have a room where we can talk. It's not far from where your dealership is located."

Joe gave him the address, and they agreed to meet at 3:30. Afterward, Joe grabbed his lunch of leftover Shrimp Diavolo from the refrigerator and warmed it in the microwave. One of the younger detectives walked in as he was eating and remarked, "Smells good! What restaurant did you get that from?"

"No restaurant, Davis. I made this for my dinner last night."

"You made that? Damn! I should hire you to cook for me."

"You couldn't afford me."

As Joe was eating, he thought about what Perry Gardiner could have done to get himself killed. Drug dealing gone bad, stealing from the mob, double-crossing a crime boss, killing or raping someone connected, snitching.

Almost all of them lead back to organized crime in one way or another. That's where his mind was going as he searched for a motive.

When Sam came back from lunch, Joe told him about the 3:30 meeting he set up with David Whitmore. Joe also thought it would be a good idea to contact one of his acquaintances in the Narcotics Unit to see if Perry Gardiner's name would turn up. His reasoning was if Perry did not have a job, he may have made money trafficking drugs. Sam agreed the homicide had the look of an organized crime death despite the fact the license plate was still attached to the vehicle. Then again, not all hitmen are smart or experienced.

When 3:30 rolled around, David Whitmore had not appeared. Ten minutes later, Joe got a call saying Whitmore was waiting at the public access area.

Whitmore was a man in his mid-thirties but looked older. Evidently, the high stress of making sales had aged him. His dark hair had grayed through the temples, and forehead lines and crow's feet were prominent. His demeanor was cordial but with serious overtones.

"Not a very pleasant waiting room you have here," said Whitmore.

Joe knew it wasn't and answered, "I know. It is what it is."

Joe ushered him into the interrogation room and introduced him to Sam.

"I have to tell you I'm at a loss as to why I'm here," said Whitmore.

"Have a seat," said Sam. They all sat, and Joe began.

"Have you spoken to your sister in the past couple of days?"

"No, why?"

"We were called to the scene of a car fire two days ago. The pickup had been totally engulfed in flames, and the two individuals inside the cab were burned beyond recognition. The pickup belonged to Perry Gardiner."

After a moment, Whitmore said, "Oh, Jesus."

"We've tried to locate your sister and Mr. Gardiner, but to no avail," said Sam.

"We haven't been able to make a positive identification yet," said Joe, "but we believe there's a good chance the victims are Perry and Gina. I'm sorry."

"That son-of-a-bitch!" growled Whitmore. "I knew something like this would happen."

Joe and Sam remained silent. Whitmore's face reddened, and his hands grew into fists. After a few moments, he looked at the two detectives and said, "He as good as killed her."

"What do you mean?" asked Joe.

"She moved in with Perry to save money. She gave up her apartment because she didn't have a job for the coming year yet. She lost her position due to budget cuts. She told me she was moving into my uncle's house because Perry wouldn't charge her rent if she helped him with the renovations he was doing."

"That sounds like a pretty good deal for her," said Sam.

"Yeah, on the surface. But he must have turned her on to dope or something because she changed. Perry turned into some kind of freak."

"Care to explain," asked Joe.

"Perry used to be an affable guy. Really smart, sense of humor, clean-cut.Took good care of himself, you know. But when he came back after serving in the Coast Guard, I couldn't believe it. A complete turnaround. He looked like a bum. Long hair and beard. And his personality changed, too. He was confrontational, intense, unreasonable. I called, and he wouldn't even let me talk to Gina. I finally stopped by the house, and he wouldn't let me in. She finally appeared behind him at the door and said she didn't want to see me. But when I talked to her, I could tell she wasn't herself at all."

"You suspect drugs may have had something to do with it?" asked Sam.

"What else could it be? She was like a zombie."

"A zombie?"

"Yeah. She looked down, wouldn't make eye contact, barely spoke loud enough to be heard. He had to have done something to her."

"So, what did you do?" asked Joe.

Joe could see the anger in his eyes, and as he looked at Whitmore's hands, he could see the white knuckles of his fists. "Ooh…I wanted to belt him." Then Whitmore paused and took a breath. "But I didn't. I left."

"And you never saw either one of them afterwards?"

"No."

"Did you speak with your parents about her?"

"No. Why upset them? I mean, what could they do about it besides worry?"

Whitmore's answers had grown increasingly hostile, and Joe and Sam realized they needed to calm him down.

After a moment, Sam asked, "David, what's the best way to contact you in case we need to talk to you again?"

"You can call my cell phone. Leave a message if I'm not available, and I'll call you back. Don't call me at work. I'm either on the phone or with a customer." He gave Joe and Sam his cell phone number, and Joe handed him his card.

"You can call me if you have any questions or remember anything you think might be important," said Joe. "I know this is upsetting, and we'll keep in touch once we have more definitive answers."

"Yeah." As he rose to leave, Whitmore turned and said, "I want you to know that my sister's a wonderful person. She's kind and respectful, and she loves kids and books, and her family's really important to her." Tears welled up in his eyes as he described her, and his emotions got the best of him as he tried to continue. "I can't...I don't know what...what he did to her. I...sorry."

"It's our job to find out," said Sam.

"We'll do our best," added Joe. "Thanks for coming in."

After Whitmore had gone, Sam said, "It sounds like Perry had some kind of mind control over his cousin."

"It does," concurred Joe. "Abuse or Svengali Syndrome, maybe."

"What's that?"

"Look it up. It's a form of mind control. Combine that with drugs, and you have a compliant follower. It's a possibility."

"How do you know about that?"

"I recall it from an advanced psych class I took in college. Weird stuff sticks with me for some reason."

"Weird stuff," smiled Sam. "Okay, I'll check it out."

"I may ask my shrink about it if we get more evidence pointing in that direction. I have a session scheduled next week."

"What about Destiny? She's had a lot of training in this sort of thing, hasn't she?"

"Yeah, she has. She's in Canada at a conference right now. But she should be back this weekend. I'll run it past her when we talk tonight and get her take on it."

After dinner, he called Destiny. They had talked every night since she had been in Montreal at the conference. His call went to voicemail, so he left a message. Half an hour later, she returned his call.

"Sorry, I missed your call. I was having an early dinner with one of my old FBI colleagues."

"Male or female?" joked Joe.

Destiny laughed. "Female, and she's not my type."

"I'm glad," chuckled Joe. "How was the conference today?"

"There was a great speaker on advanced research on moral development this morning. Fascinating presentation."

"Moral development. Understanding failure in moral development could come in handy in my line of work."

"No doubt."

"Probably begins with bad parenting, doesn't it."

"In a lot of cases. But there's more to it than that. A child can have great parents and still have moral development issues."

"Mm. Say, I've got a question for you. What do you know about Svengali Syndrome?"

"Svengali Syndrome?" said Destiny, more of a surprise reaction than a question.

"Yeah."

"You think you have a case of Svengali Syndrome rather than abuse?"

"Possibly."

"Wow. Well, I know what it is, but I don't know a lot about it. I've never encountered it in the field."

"I may know more by the time you get home."

"Maybe you should consult Dr. Lemke."

"I'm planning on it. I have a session with her next week. If it turns out this murder victim had Svengali Syndrome, it could play into an M.O. for his killer."

"Tell you what. I'll ask around. I'm sure someone here will know more about it than I do. Who knows? I may even find an expert on the subject."

"That would be great. Thanks for checking."

"You've got me curious, now."

After the call, Joe went online to research Svengali Syndrome, but there wasn't much written about it. Only a few links proved helpful, and neither went into any detail. *Must be a rare condition*, he thought. *I may have to rely on Dr. Lemke's insight if she's familiar with it. Then, of course, I could be wrong, and all this speculation could be for naught.*

Setting his laptop aside, he got up and grabbed a bottle of water from the refrigerator. He returned to the couch, switched on the TV, and saw *The Girl with a Dragon Tattoo* was starting. It was one of his favorite films. Not a bad way to spend the evening and take his mind off work.

Chapter Seven

When Joe was working at his desk late the next morning, he received a phone call from Kendra. He had been hoping she would call with the results of her autopsies on the charred remains so identification would finally be conclusive.

"Good morning, Joe," said Kendra. Her voice was perky, so Joe assumed she had results on the autopsies.

"Do you have good news for me, or did you get lucky last night?" asked Joe, knowing his quip would be met with an equally irreverent response.

"Both, for your information. But I'm only going into details about one."

"Okay."

"I was able to make positive identifications on your two victims. Based on dental records, the remains are Perry Gardiner and Gina Whitmore."

"I was afraid of that."

"When the DNA results come back, I'm sure they'll confirm my findings. I also determined cause of death for each one. You want to hear that, too?"

"Please."

"Perry Gardiner died of blunt force trauma to the head. There was a fracture to the temporal region on the left side of the skull. Given the condition of the body, I wasn't able to tell anything about what may have been used. But it was heavy enough and used with enough force to fracture his skull."

"I see. What about Gina?"

"She was strangled. Her hyoid bone was fractured."

"And that couldn't have been caused by the fire?"

"No. No way the fire would have done that."

"So, they were both dead prior to being burned?" asked Joe, seeking confirmation.

"That's correct. I'll send the official report along in a few days, but I thought you would appreciate a heads-up."

"Thanks, Kendra."

Since the identities had now been confirmed, they needed to notify Perry's sister of her brother's death.

Julianne Hendricks worked as a speech pathologist at Rush University Children's Hospital. Joe called and found she was working today. He and Sam drove to the hospital's location on West Harrison Street. A receptionist directed them to the location of her department within the confines of the large hospital.

They found the Speech Pathology Department and presented their IDs to the receptionist. After introducing themselves, they asked to see Julianne Hendricks, clarifying she was not in any trouble.

"I'm afraid she's seeing clients all morning. She's booked pretty solid most of the day," said the receptionist after consulting Hendricks' schedule.

Joe gave her his card. "Have her call me when she gets a chance, will you please? It's very important we speak with her."

"I'll be sure to do that."

As they turned to leave, Julianne Hendricks came walking down the hall. When she saw Joe and Sam, she hesitated slightly but kept on walking, coming to a stop before them.

"I assume you're here because you have some information about my brother?" she asked.

"We do," said Joe.

"I have a few minutes before my next client, so why don't you come to my office?"

Joe and Sam followed her down a hall, where she unlocked a door and let them into a small office. She closed the door behind them, walked behind her desk, and dropped a file folder on it.

Before Joe or Sam could speak, she said, "It's Perry, isn't it? The body, I mean."

"It is," said Sam. "My condolences."

She didn't show much emotion, given it was her brother. She simply let out a breath and said, "I figured it was. My cousin, Gina..."

"Yeah," said Joe. "She was the other victim."

"My god. Do you know what happened? Was it some kind of accident? Or some weird suicide pact?"

Her suggestion of a suicide pact surprised Joe, and he wanted to know why she would suggest such a thing. But now was not the time or the place to go into it.

"They were killed before the fire," said Sam.

"We're treating it as a double homicide," added Joe. "I know this isn't the time or the place, but we'd like to set up an interview with you. We'd like to learn all we can about your brother, your cousin, their living situation, friends, and so on."

"I understand."

"Do my aunt and uncle know? About Gina?"

"Not yet," said Joe. "I'm going to make a call to the police in Muncie so they can notify your aunt and uncle once I get back to the office. I wanted to let you know first so you could tell your mother. So, she wouldn't get a phone call from your aunt and uncle before she was notified."

Nodding, Hendricks said, "I appreciate that, Detective."

"We're sorry it turned out this way," said Sam.

"Thank you."

Getting ready to leave, Joe said, "You have my card. If you need anything...."

"Looks like I'll have to cancel my appointments for the rest of the day. If you're going to notify my aunt and uncle, my mom will be getting a call from my aunt. They're pretty close. Mom will need to know right away."

Hendricks followed them out of her office and made a beeline to the receptionist while Joe and Sam walked toward the elevator.

"Think we'll be hearing from David Whitmore?" asked Sam.

"I think we can count on it," replied Joe.

Back at his desk, Joe phoned the Muncie Police Department and informed appropriate personnel of Gina Whitmore's death and the need to notify her parents, Mark and Carol Whitmore. He did not give any details regarding her death other than that she died in Chicago, but he provided his contact information should they wish to speak with him. He knew he would be getting a phone call from the grieving parents at some point, and he wasn't looking forward to explaining that their daughter was a victim of foul play, strangled and then burned beyond recognition.

Chapter Eight

Destiny returned early Sunday evening, the first of Joe's two days off. When her flight arrived, she called him from O'Hare so he knew when to expect her home.

"I hope you're hungry," he said.

"I'm famished. Have you been cooking?" she asked.

"I have."

"You're the best!"

He had prepped all the ingredients for one of her favorite dishes, Mushroom Bolognese, so it wouldn't take as long to cook it once he knew she had arrived. Usually, the prep and cooking time would be an hour, but if he timed it right, it should be ready shortly after she got home. Unless…Unless the airline lost her luggage and she had to deal with that. Then, he could have a culinary disappointment on his hands!

An hour later, Destiny walked through the door, dropped her suitcase, and remarked, "Oh, my! What is that delicious aroma? Is it…"

"Uh-huh. Your favorite," smiled Joe.

"Ohhh. That was so nice of you." She put her arms around him and gave him a kiss.

"Welcome home," he said, returning the kiss.

"Thank you."

"Care for a glass of wine?"

"Please."

Joe poured her a glass of Cabernet Sauvignon, a nice pairing to the Mushroom Bolognese since it was one of its ingredients.

After dinner, they adjourned to the living room, where Destiny brought up the subject of Svengali Syndrome.

"I'm curious," she said. "Did you find out anything more that leads you to think you may have a case of Svengali Syndrome rather than simple abuse?"

"Not yet. We have more interviews to do before it can go beyond mere suspicion."

"Well, the reason I ask is because I found an expert on the subject at the conference. Dr. Myron Blumenthal. He practices psychiatry in St. Louis, and I was able to speak with him for about half an hour about it. I came away with a good understanding about how it works."

"This could be all for naught. I mean, this could turn out to be nothing more than suspicion on my part. You could have been wasting your time."

"Not at all," assured Destiny. "It was fascinating to learn about it. You never know when I might be able to employ it in my work. I may be profiling someone with this syndrome one day."

"There wasn't much online about it. Basics, really."

"It's not that common. The thing about Svengali types is they're master manipulators of others. They have a keen sense to recognize and zero in on a given person's vulnerability and exploit it in order to gain control over them."

"What kind of control?"

"It can range from control of their finances to complete control over their lives."

"Can drugs come into play?"

"Certainly, but it's often a case of gradually gaining psychological dominance and securing a kind of mind control. The victim can't do anything without the Svengali's permission. Total and complete obedience is the result."

"Does violence play a part in the relationship?"

"In some cases, but more often than not, it's intimidation—the threat of violence that's ever present."

Joe thought for a moment and then looked back to Destiny. "It's frightening to think someone could be so vulnerable and succumb to something like that."

"I know. But it happens. Unfortunately, it often goes undetected, and it's only discovered in criminal cases like financial fraud or domestic abuse."

"Mm."

"Let's talk about happier things. What did you do while I was gone?"

"Well, I had to take my hairshirt to the cleaners this morning and my scourge to a repair shop."

"I admire your discipline."

"Confucius say, 'Control your mind or your mind will control you.'"

"Really?" Destiny chuckled.

"Actually, I think it was Horace."

"Well, I'm home now, so you won't need those things anymore."

Joe's phone rang, and he looked at the number. His mood immediately sunk. The call was from an Indiana area code that included Muncie.

"I'm sorry. I have to take this."

Destiny saw the look on his face and knew it was serious. She got up from the couch and walked into the kitchen as Joe answered his phone.

"Detective Joe Erickson."

"Detective Erickson, this is Mark Whitmore. Gina Whitmore's father." His voice was quiet, and he was barely controlling his emotions. Joe needed to make this call as easy on him as possible.

"I was expecting your call, Mr. Whitmore. My sincere condolences."

"I'm on speaker phone so my wife can hear. The police here in Muncie didn't give us any details. Can you tell us what happened?"

"I can. I'm the lead detective on this case, Mr. and Mrs. Whitmore. I want to warn you. What I'm going to tell you is going to be disturbing."

"What could be more disturbing than our daughter's death?" asked Mrs. Whitmore.

"Your daughter Gina and her cousin, Perry Gardiner, were the victims of a homicide."

Joe could hear the air intake and the trembling breath on the other end as Whitmore and his wife grappled with the news.

"We found the victims in a burned-out pickup truck belonging to Perry

Gardiner."

"They...They were murdered?" asked Whitmore.

"They were."

Silence. Joe could hear the Whitmores mumbling something in the background.

"I don't understand," said Mrs. Whitmore, fighting back tears. "Why would she have been murdered? She never..."

Silence.

"You said a burned-out pickup?" asked Whitmore. "Was she...Were they... ?"

Joe tried to couch this as delicately as he knew how. "I regret to say that both victims sustained extreme injuries...Very extreme."

"Oh, god...How bad? You can tell me."

"The medical examiner had to employ dental records to make the identifications. I'm sorry."

Joe could hear Mrs. Whitmore sobbing and Mr. Whitmore comforting her and suggesting she pour herself a drink.

In a low voice, Whitmore asked, "So, what you're saying is, we should plan to have her cremated...to finish the job?"

"If it were my daughter, I would consider it. Yes."

"Thank you, Detective. I appreciate your candor."

"I'm sorry I had to give you such unpleasant news, Mr. Whitmore. I can tell you, we're doing everything in our power to find out what happened to your daughter and apprehend those responsible."

"You'll keep us updated? When you make an arrest?"

"I will."

After the call ended, Joe sat back against the couch, took in a deep breath, and let it out. It was a load off his mind, and at the same time, he felt so bad for Gina's parents.

Destiny came into the room carrying another glass of wine and handed it to him. She sat beside him.

"After that call, you deserve a second glass. I couldn't help but overhear. That was rough."

"I wasn't looking forward to their call, but I knew it was coming. They needed to know."

"You handled it well." She leaned over and kissed him on the cheek. "Very sensitive."

"It's one thing to inform someone of a person's death. But when the details are not only violent but grotesque…" Joe took a drink of his wine.

"Maybe they will have some sense of closure when you catch the one who killed them."

"Maybe."

"Put your wine down."

"Okay," said Joe, sitting his glass on the coffee table.

Destiny leaned over and gave him a long, passionate kiss as her hand moved slowly from his knee up his thigh. Then she whispered in his ear.

"Right here?" he asked.

Destiny simply smiled and kissed him again.

Chapter Nine

Joe called Julianne Hendricks and arranged an interview to discuss her brother. She agreed to a meeting for the next day at two o'clock in her office. In the meantime, Joe and Sam decided to split their focus in order to cover more ground. Sam would begin interviewing former colleagues of Gina Whitmore, while Joe would focus on people who knew Perry Gardiner.

Joe decided to research Julianne Hendricks before he met with her the next day. Hendricks was born in Chicago thirty-two years ago, the oldest of two children of William Lee and Phyllis Rae Whitmore Gardiner. She holds bachelor's and master's degrees from the University of Illinois at Urbana-Champaign. She has been employed by Rush University Children's Hospital as a speech pathologist for the past four years. Recently divorced from Brent Charles Hendricks, she lives on North Avenue in Old Town, a trendy area for a young, single person. No arrests. DMV shows a two-year-old Prius registered in her name. According to FOID (Firearm Owner Identification) search, she does not own a registered firearm. For all intents and purposes, Julianne Hendricks appears to be an upstanding citizen.

Joe traveled to Rush University Children's Hospital the next day to meet with Hendricks. He was ten minutes early, so he killed some time looking around the hospital before finding Hendricks' office and knocking on her door. There was no answer. He tried the door, and it was locked. Looking at his watch, it was exactly two o'clock. He decided to wait, thinking she might be running behind if she had a session booked.

A few minutes later, he saw Hendricks rushing down the hall toward him.

As she drew close, she gasped, "I'm so sorry. The consultation with my client's parents ran a little late."

"I wasn't waiting long," said Joe, attempting to put her at ease.

Unlocking her door, she invited him in. She placed the files she was carrying in a tray on her desk and then asked him to sit.

"So, what would you like to know, Detective?" she asked as she seated herself.

Joe got straight to the point. "According to other people we've interviewed, Perry had changed by the time he moved back to Chicago. Can you enlighten me about what you observed regarding his behavior?"

"Oh, god. Where to start," she sighed.

"Anywhere you like."

"Perry was a good kid growing up. Smart, good grades in school. Personable. A good athlete—excelled in baseball. He went to college for a year—thought about majoring in journalism. But after a year, he had misgivings and wasn't sure about what he wanted to do with his life. So, he joined the Coast Guard."

"He like it?"

"He'd come home on leave and say serving was okay, but he looked forward to getting out. I don't think he liked the Coast Guard, to tell you the truth."

"You know what he did? What his job was?"

"He was a Boatswain's Mate, whatever that is. Said he did all sorts of stuff."

"I see. Go on."

He served his four years, and after his discharge, he landed in San Francisco. We didn't hear from him for almost two years until he contacted Dad, said he was coming back to Chicago, and asked if he could live in the old house."

"So, your dad lived elsewhere, right?"

"His job took him to Florida, but he never sold the house. It originally belonged to his uncle, and he thought maybe he would return to Chicago at some point. So, given Perry's construction experience in the Coast Guard, he let Perry live there if he would make needed repairs. That way, he wouldn't have to pay someone to look after it."

"So, getting back to my original question, I heard Perry had changed a lot when he returned."

"God! I barely knew him."

"How so?"

"He was always neat and clean. But he came back with a full beard and long hair. And his whole personality had changed. It was like he'd completely lost his filter. He'd say anything that came into his head, no matter how unpleasant. Insulting, belligerent. And his language. Zheesh. It was 'f-this, f-that.' I mean, I'm no Puritan. But...I couldn't stand to be around him."

"What about your mother?"

"She was so upset. She cried after seeing him. Sickened by what he'd become."

"You think it was drug-related?"

"I have no idea. How do you know what might have happened when he was living in San Francisco? Something changed him."

"What can you tell me about your cousin, Gina Whitmore? She'd been living with him."

"I know. And I don't get it. She was sweet, kind, soft-spoken. It wasn't much of a leap for her to become an early childhood teacher. She loved little kids, always reading some research about that age group when I saw her. The nicest person."

"When was the last time you saw her?"

"A couple of years or so. I didn't see her much. She wasn't around when I saw Perry. Sad to say, I only saw Perry three times when he came back here. Once when I brought Mom over to the house to see him. That was a disaster. And another other time shortly afterward, when he came by and asked if I had a Kindle he could use for a few days. That was when I told him not to see Mom anymore. And one more time, when I tried to get my Kindle back."

"How did he react to you telling him not to see his mother anymore?"

"He didn't care. Told me she ruined his life, anyway. Nothing could have been further from the truth," she barked. "I don't know where he got that idea."

"So, you don't know why Gina might have moved in with him?"

"No. Sorry."

"Do you know if Perry worked somewhere?"

"I don't know that either. He never mentioned anything when Mom and I met with him. He must have had some kind of income."

Joe decided to pursue another line of questioning, hoping he could locate another witness who may have had contact with Perry and Gina.

"Do you know any of Perry's friends, those he may have had here in the city? Friends who may have contacted him if they knew he was back in town?"

"Oh, boy. Let's see...Well, there's Harley. Harlan McManus. Harley and Perry hung out together in high school, and Harley always came over to Mom's when Perry was home on leave. He was an EMT last I heard."

"I assume there's going to be a funeral service for Perry?" asked Joe. "Has one been scheduled?"

"We're having a memorial service at ten-thirty tomorrow morning. At the Winston-Day Funeral Chapel. We're waiting for Dad to get in from Florida. He should be arriving later this afternoon. I'm waiting for a text."

"You think Harley will be there?"

"Probably."

"I'll plan on being there. I didn't know your brother," said Joe, "but I'd like to let your mother know that Chicago PD cares about the families of victims. And...I'd like to speak with Harley and any other friends of Perry's who may be attending. Maybe you could point him out if he's there?"

"Certainly. I can do that."

Chapter Ten

Joe drove onto Fullerton Avenue and arrived at the Winston-Day Funeral Chapel fifteen minutes prior to the ten-thirty start of Perry Gardiner's memorial service. He wanted to greet the family and also get eyes on Harley McManus, whom he needed to contact for an interview.

Upon entering the large brick building, he was greeted by a highly polished wooden floor and soft gray walls. He walked past a carpeted lounge area and into the chapel that was set with folding chairs. About two dozen people had gathered for the service. Perry's mother and daughter, Julianne, were standing in front near a table with flowers surrounding a ceramic box containing the cremains and an 8X10 framed photo of Perry in his blue Coast Guard uniform. He was a good-looking young man with a smile on his face, quite different from the description provided by those who had seen him following his return to Chicago.

A man in his mid-fifties stood next to Julianne. Joe assumed he was Perry's father. He was a good-looking man with a full head of dark hair with only hints of gray. Joe walked toward Perry's mother, who was talking with an older woman using a walker.

After the woman moved on, Joe stepped forward. "Mrs. Gardiner," said Joe, shaking her hand. "My condolences. I'm sorry for your loss. I'm here to let you know that Chicago PD is doing everything it can to solve this crime."

"Thank you, Detective. Nice of you to come."

Joe moved on to Julianne and shook her hand, saying, "My condolences, Ms. Hendricks. If I can be of service, please feel free to contact me."

"Thank you." Referring to the man next to her, Hendricks said, "Detective

Erickson, this is my dad, Bill Gardiner. Dad, Detective Erickson. He's investigating Perry's case."

Joe sensed Gardiner was surprised by his presence, and after a moment, he shook Joe's hand. Then Gardiner said, "I didn't know investigating officers attended funerals. Seems strange to me."

An odd thing to say, thought Joe. But given the circumstances and how awkward the death of a loved one could be, Joe let it slide. "We do, sometimes. To show that police care about victim's families. My condolences, Mr. Gardiner. It must be hard to lose a son."

Mr. Gardiner nodded his response but said nothing more.

Joe glanced to his left and saw Liz, Destiny's friend, next to him in line. She greeted Mr. Gardiner and said, "I'm sorry Jared couldn't be here. He had business in Florida and couldn't get away."

Joe heard Mr. Gardiner respond with only an "Mm" and nothing more. Not even a thank you. Uncomfortable moment. He looked at Gardiner, who looked down. Joe intended to speak with Liz, but she stepped away, and he needed to speak with someone else."

Joe stepped back to Hendricks and asked, "Harley?"

"Oh, he's here," said Henricks. "He's the one in the purple paisley tie."

"Thanks."

Joe turned and walked slowly back toward the rear of the chapel, scanning the guests. His eyes suddenly fell on a young man with a neatly trimmed goatee and mustache. He was dressed in a black blazer, gray pants, and a multi-colored purple paisley tie. He was standing alone in the back.

Joe walked up to him and said, "Hello. Are you Harley McManus?"

McManus looked startled. "Yeah, I am."

"I'm Detective Joe Erickson, Chicago PD. I'm investigating Perry's death. I wonder if I could have a word with you after the service?"

"I suppose."

"Thanks," said Joe. Then he turned and chose a seat as close to the exit as possible. A few minutes later, the minister, the Reverend Randall Weller, moved to the front, and everyone began taking their seats.

The minister conducted the service, which lasted about half an hour. The obituary was read, extolling Perry's virtues as a loving son, a fine athlete, and one who honorably served his country in the US Coast Guard. It painted the picture of an All-American Son. Three classic hymns Joe recognized were sung with piano accompaniment: "The Old Rugged Cross," "Amazing Grace," and "How Great Thou Art," the words of which had been laid out on the chairs.

When the final prayer was said, and the service concluded, Joe stood near the door so the reluctant McManus could not slip past before Joe could speak with him. After a dozen people filed out, McManus approached him.

"You said you wanted to speak to me?"

"I do," replied Joe. "I'd like to interview you about Perry. Did you see him after he returned from San Francisco?"

"Yeah."

"When's a good time when we can sit down and talk?"

"I'm pretty busy. I took today off so I could attend the service, so..."

"This afternoon?"

"How about now? Get it out of the way."

"Fine with me," said Joe. "Where?"

"Let's find a place where I can get a drink."

"A bit early, don't you think?"

"Given what I've got to tell you? I'll need some fortification."

"Okay...Uh...There's a Serbian restaurant I know of on North Lincoln Avenue. They open at eleven.

"The Whiskey Café?"

"You know it?"

"Yeah. I go there often."

"Great. I can drive if you want."

"Sounds good."

Joe drove McManus to the Whiskey Café and asked for a booth toward the back. The hostess accommodated them, and a server was at their table a minute later. Joe ordered a cup of coffee while McManus ordered a Jack Daniels on the rocks.

They spoke about the weather until their drinks arrived, and then Joe began questioning.

"How long were you friends with Perry Gardiner?"

"Since high school. We played baseball together. He pitched, and I played third base. We were inseparable. Best friends all through school. If I wasn't over at his place, he was over at mine. We were like brothers."

"So, after high school, what happened?"

"Well, we went off in different directions. He went to college downstate at Western Illinois University. I went to community college here and decided to become an EMT. He thought he wanted to be a journalist, but during that year, something made him question all that. He kinda lost direction, I think, and didn't know what he wanted to do anymore. So, he decided to join the Coast Guard. Thought maybe serving in the military would help him figure it out, you know?"

"Did it?"

"I don't know. He'd come home on leave, and I'd come over to his dad's place to see him. He seemed a little distant. We'd have a few laughs and go out to places where we could drink and have a good time. It wasn't the same. Then, he started coming home on leave less and less."

"Did you lose contact with him?"

"Not at first. We still texted and emailed each other. Called once in a while. But that tapered off, too. When he got discharged, I stopped hearing from him altogether. Tried contacting him, but nothing."

"But you saw him when he moved back here, right?"

"Yeah. Once," said McManus, shaking his head slightly. "I heard he'd come back to Chicago and was living in his dad's house, so I decided to go over for a visit. I was eager to see him after all this time." He stopped and took a healthy gulp from his drink.

"And?"

"I couldn't believe it. A totally different person came back, physically and mentally. Long hair, beard. Dressed in old jeans and a work shirt. Sloppy. Not the neat person I knew. He told me he'd been living in San Francisco, hustling, and living by his wits."

He took another drink and then continued.

"He said, 'Ever sleep with a man, Harley?' I was shocked. Claimed he'd dropped LSD out in California, said it opened his mind to all sorts of stuff. Jesus! I didn't know what to think."

"Was his cousin, Gina, living with him then?" asked Joe.

"Oh, yeah. Oh, yeah. God!"

"Care to explain?"

"She was like some kind of slave. I mean…He said to me, 'She'll do whatever I want.' I said, 'What do you mean?' 'Watch,' he says. And he said to her, 'Strip!' and right there, she took off all her clothes. Right in front of me. Just like that! I mean, she stood there buck-naked. 'You can have her if you want,' he tells me. Those weren't his exact words. I won't repeat the ones he used. I must have said 'no,' I can't remember. Then he says to her, 'Lay down.' And she lays down on the floor, and he drops his pants and starts…oh, god. I…I got up and left. I couldn't believe my eyes. Right in front of me, he… This guy used to be my best friend, for god's sakes!"

McManus had tears welling up in his eyes. He reached for his glass of Jack Daniels and killed what was left. Afterward, he let out a deep breath and stared at his glass.

Joe gave him a few moments and then asked, "Gina didn't say anything?"

"No. She did whatever he said. Like she was his robot slave following his every command. I can't imagine the things that must have gone on in that house."

"Was there any indication either of them was under the influence of drugs?"

"Perry? Not that I could tell. Gina? Well, something was sure as hell up with her. No normal person acts that way or would do the things she did."

Harley tipped up his glass again as if he was trying to get the last drop.

"You want a refill?" asked Joe.

"Yeah, I could use one."

Joe signaled the waitress to bring him another drink. When it came, he asked for menus. The least he could do is buy this guy lunch.

"Can I buy you lunch, Mr. McManus?"

"Call me 'Harley,' if you don't mind."

"Okay, Harley."

"Yeah, I guess you can buy me lunch."

"Good," said Joe. "Because I usually eat about this time. I appreciate you talking with me so candidly."

"It feels good to get that off my chest."

"I can imagine."

"I want to tell you something. This whole thing with Perry is a hellish nightmare. To see your best friend return as a vulgar, disgusting piece of human garbage...it's heartbreaking. I hate to say this, but...maybe whoever killed him did the world a favor. You know what I mean?"

Joe paused momentarily and then asked, "If what he became bothered you so much, why'd you come to the memorial service today?"

McManus didn't take time to think of an answer. "To honor the friend I used to know. To let his mom and dad know I care. It was clear to me Perry'd become some kind of psycho. I doubt if the old Perry was still in there somewhere. I don't know if therapy could've brought back someone that far gone."

"Any idea who could have wished him harm?"

"No one. Everyone. I have no clue. But I hope you find whoever the hell did it. No one deserves to die like he did."

"Agreed," said Joe. He finished his coffee and then asked, "Did Perry have any other friends who still live in the city? Friends who may have wanted to visit him, knowing he'd come home?"

"Not offhand. There may be some college friends I don't know about. There were some people at the service today I didn't know."

The waitress returned with menus, a tray with Perry's drink, and another cup of coffee. Later, after taking their orders, Joe probed more, but he didn't learn anything that proved useful.

After a lunch of Karadjordjeva, a Serbian specialty consisting of baked veal steak wrapped around Serbian cheese, Joe concluded his interview. He asked McManus if he could drop him off at his apartment complex. McManus declined and said he needed a long walk after "spilling my guts" about Perry. Joe understood and headed back to Area 3, where he planned to tell Sam all he had learned today about their victim. He was more convinced than ever that Svengali Syndrome could be at the heart of Perry and Gina's relationship. But what, if anything, did it have to do with their deaths?

Chapter Eleven

Back at Area 3, Joe relayed the control and abuse issues exhibited by Perry Gardiner to Sam, who wasn't shocked easily. Still, even he was taken aback by information provided by Harley McManus.

"He was doing that kind of stuff, and she...just let him?"

"Can you imagine the kind of stuff that must have gone on in that house?" asked Joe.

"I don't want to think about it."

Then, Sam told Joe he had tracked down and spoken with Bianca Russo, a friend of Gina Whitmore. She got to know Gina when they were working as early childhood teachers at the same school.

"Had been?" asked Joe.

"Yeah," replied Sam. "I didn't ask her for details since she's coming in for an interview at three o'clock."

"That was quick."

"Seemed eager to help."

Joe was impressed that Sam could schedule an interview with Gina's friend so quickly. Eager, indeed.

Ten minutes before three o'clock, Sam got a call saying a woman named "Bianca Russo" was asking to see him. Sam brought her to the interrogation room and introduced her to Joe. She was a full-figured woman in her mid-thirties with large, expressive eyes, someone who reminded him of a professor he had in college.

"Thank you for coming in," said Sam.

"Glad I could help," Russo replied.

"Can we get you anything? Coffee? Soda?" asked Joe.

"No, thank you. I'm fine."

They sat at the table and began the interview with Sam asking, "How is it you knew Gina Whitmore?"

"I'm an early childhood teacher at Winterset Elementary School, and she was a colleague. Worked as my assistant."

"For how long?"

"Three years."

"What can you tell us about her," asked Joe.

"She was very sweet. Soft-spoken, a little shy and introverted, but she was smart and capable. Wonderful with the children. I liked her a lot."

"But you said you also dated her brother, David. Is that right?" asked Sam.

"That's correct."

"Was it before or after she was employed as your assistant?" asked Joe.

"After. She talked about him, and I eventually met him through her. David was an attractive guy and had a good-paying job. Seemed nice, and we hit it off...at first."

"At first?"

"Uh-huh."

"How long did your relationship last?"

"About a year. Not quite."

"So, what ended it?" asked Sam.

"I couldn't put up with his controlling behavior any longer."

"Was he abusive?"

"No, but I think it could have progressed in that direction if I hadn't dumped him."

"Was this fairly recent?"

"A few months ago."

"How did he take it."

"Not very well."

"What else can you tell us about him?" asked Joe.

"David has one of those flash tempers. He would blow up at something, and then half an hour later, it would be all over. It was like he vented, and then he was fine. Like it never happened."

"What about Gina? Did you see her after she moved in with her cousin? Perry Gardiner?" asked Sam.

"Once. She lost her job due to budget cuts and decided to give up her apartment. I felt bad about that. She moved into her uncle's house with her cousin to save money since she didn't have a contract for fall."

"When was this?"

"After the school year ended, I lost contact with her. I couldn't reach her by phone, so I went to the house where she was living. She'd changed during the last weeks of the semester. Became closed off and didn't want to interact with anybody. Very strange. I asked her if anything was wrong, and she said there wasn't. I got worried about her."

"So, what happened when you went to the house?" asked Joe.

"Nobody answered the door, but I heard voices, so I went around the side of the house. They were doing some repairs on a window. Her cousin, Perry, he was hostile. Claimed they were busy and said in no uncertain terms she didn't have time to see me. She stood there and looked at the ground the whole time. Wouldn't look at me. Wouldn't say a thing. So, I walked away and left."

"How long ago was this?"

"Several days before she died."

"What do you think about this? Any ideas?" asked Sam.

"My opinion…Something weird was going on. She acted drugged or something. She was like…spaced out. I mean, she was always shy around people she didn't know. But I was her friend. I was expecting a big smile, but she wouldn't even acknowledge me. Not like her at all."

"Do you think her brother knew about her change?" asked Joe.

"I don't know. He hated Perry. I mean, he *hated* him."

"How so?"

"After he heard Gina moved in with him, he told me if Perry did anything to Gina while she was living there, he'd kill him."

Joe's eyebrows went up. "Oh? His own cousin?"

"You think he was serious?" asked Sam.

"I don't know. I never saw him get violent with people, but I did see him throw a glass across the room that shattered against a wall when he got angry once. I don't know what he would do if he thought Perry abused his sister."

"Was he prone to exaggerating, saying things like that? When he got angry?" asked Joe.

"Hyperbole, you mean? No, not really."

After a few more questions, the interview concluded. They thanked Russo for her cooperation, and she went on her way.

Joe thought about what he had learned from Harley McManus earlier. If Whitmore knew Gardiner was abusing his sister, that they were in some master-slave relationship, it would give him motive for murder.

"I think we need to bring David Whitmore in, don't you?" asked Sam.

"Oh, yeah," agreed Joe.

"It's the first solid lead we've got. He's a hothead. Loses his cool pretty easily."

"I can understand David Whitmore killing Perry Gardiner, but what about Gina? He wouldn't strangle his own sister."

"Maybe Gardiner would," suggested Sam. "What if Gardiner killed Gina, and Whitmore found out and killed Gardiner? Then, to cover it up, he staged the fire?"

"Possibly. He works at a dealership. He'd have access to gasoline at one of those places. Wouldn't have to buy it at a service station and be caught on security camera filling a container."

"Let's go pick him up."

"Maybe it would be better to call and have him come in. If he's in the middle of a sale with a client, picking him up and interrupting a sale could be a problem," countered Joe.

"You think he'll come in?"

"If he balks, we pick him up."

"Sounds good."

Joe called the dealership and asked to speak with David Whitmore. The receptionist transferred the call to Whitmore's desk.

"Dave Whitmore," answered Whitmore.

"Detective Joe Erickson," replied Joe.

"Yes, Detective."

"We have some additional questions for you, and we'd like you to come into our Area 3 office where we can speak with you."

"I'm swamped right now. I don't know what questions I haven't already answered."

"Well, Mr. Whitmore. You can either come in, or we can pick you up at the dealership and bring you in. Your choice."

"Christ! This is harassment."

"No, Mr. Whitmore. This is a murder investigation. We'll expect to see you tomorrow. You pick the time."

There was a pause. "All right. How's nine o'clock? Let's get this over with so I can get back to work. I have appointments."

"Nine o'clock it is. You know the address?"

"I do."

Click! Whitmore hung up. *What a dick*, thought Joe. *This interview ought to be fun.*

Chapter Twelve

At nine o'clock, Joe received a message that David Whitmore had arrived. He alerted Sam and met Whitmore in the public access area. Joe greeted Whitmore and thanked him for coming in. Whitmore was in no mood for casual conversation and refused to speak as they walked to the interrogation room.

Upon entering the interrogation room, Sam asked, "Can I get you anything? Coffee, soda—"

Interrupting him, Whitmore said, "Nothing. I only want to answer your questions so I can leave."

Joe glanced at Sam, who raised his eyebrows. "Fine," said Joe. "Take a chair."

Sam placed his cup of coffee on the table and pulled a notebook from his pocket before sitting.

"So, what's your question?" asked Whitmore.

Joe didn't like his hostile attitude, so he didn't hold back. "We have a witness who told us you said if Perry Gardiner abused your sister, you would kill him. Is that right?"

"Oh, come on," protested Whitmore.

"Did you say that?"

"That was just..."

"Just what?" pressed Sam.

"You know how people talk sometimes? They say things they don't mean literally. It's...exaggeration."

"Why should we believe you?"

"You're kind of a hothead, aren't you, David?" asked Joe, leaning on him harder. "You told us you wanted to belt him the last time we spoke. You sound like you have a violent streak."

"Look, I—"

"Did you find out Perry was abusing your sister?"

"No."

"Well, he was. Sexually, too."

"What?" asked Whitmore.

"Oh, yeah," added Sam. "She was his slave. He had her under his spell. She'd do anything he wanted. And she did."

"She was his cousin, for chrissakes!" exploded Whitmore.

"Pretty sick, huh?"

"Is that why you killed him?" asked Joe.

"I didn't kill him, god dammit!"

"Did you find out he strangled your sister, and you killed him for it?"

"No. I told you. I didn't kill him or anybody else!" yelled Whitmore, slamming his fist on the table.

Whitmore stood and said, "I don't have to put up with this shit. I'm leaving."

Joe and Sam both stood to block him from the door. "You're not going anywhere," said Sam.

"Sit down, David," ordered Joe. "I mean it. Sit down. We're not through."

"I want an attorney."

"What do you want an attorney for, David? You're not under arrest."

Whitmore looked back and forth at Joe and Sam, and after a moment, he complied. His hostility was now replaced by anxiousness.

"Now, when's the last time you spoke to Gina?" asked Joe.

"Like I told you before. When I went to their house. I haven't seen them since."

"Where were you on the night of June 10th?"

"June 10th?"

"Yeah."

"Let me check." Whitmore pulled out his cell phone and began pushing buttons. After a moment, he found what he was looking for. "I was downstate

58

with my girlfriend. Visiting her parents in Table Grove."

"We'll need phone numbers to verify that," said Sam.

"All right," replied Whitmore. And he pressed some additional buttons on his phone and gave them his girlfriend's name, phone number, and her parents' names and phone numbers.

"We'll check this out and go from here," said Joe. "You know, Mr. Whitmore, this could have gone a lot better if you had simply controlled your temper."

"Are we done?" asked Whitmore, giving Joe the stink eye.

"Yeah, as a matter of fact. We are done...for the time being."

Whitmore rose and left the interrogation room. Sam finished the little bit of coffee left in his cup and looked at Joe. "You think his alibi lets him off the hook?"

Joe pulled out his cell phone and began dialing. "If he wasn't in town, he couldn't have been the offender. I'm calling the parents' number right now before he has a chance to call them. In case he's making it up."

"Where's Table Grove? Never heard of it."

"Small town in the west-central part of the state. I was there once." Looking at Sam's inquisitive expression, he said, "Don't ask."

During the call, Joe discovered that David Whitmore and his girlfriend, Jennifer Engdahl, had indeed visited her parents in Table Grove on June 10. He looked over at Sam and said, "The girlfriend's mother just confirmed Whitmore was where he said he was on June 10th."

"Looks like we need to press restart, huh?"

"Not necessarily," said Joe. "I think we need to speak with Tyrell Williams in Narcotics. See if his informants knew Perry Gardiner as a buyer or small-time seller."

"Thinking he could have gotten into trouble with someone who saw him as a threat?"

"He hasn't had a job we know of since he came back from San Francisco. He could've been sponging off Gina's school teacher salary, but...What was he doing before that? He had to have some kind of income to be able to fix the house and live day to day."

"Maybe he brought some cash with him when he left San Francisco," said Sam.

"I don't know. Sounds like he was strapped. That's why he came back."

"So, you think he was dealing?"

"It would explain a lot, don't you think?"

"It would."

"The killing appears to be a hit. Retribution for something," said Joe.

"And Gina could simply have been in the wrong place at the wrong time," added Sam.

"Right. That's what I'm thinking."

Joe and Sam walked over to speak with Detective Tyrell Williams, who worked Narcotics. Joe's and Williams' paths had crossed occasionally on homicide investigations that had narcotics connections.

"Hey, Tyrell," said Joe.

"What's happenin', you guys," replied Williams, looking up from his computer screen.

"We need a favor," said Joe.

"Gonna cost ya," quipped Williams.

"Yeah. Always does with you," chuckled Sam.

Williams laughed and sat back in his chair. "What can I do for homicide?"

"We have a murder victim, Perry Gardiner. We think his death may have something to do with him buying or dealing drugs. We were wondering if you could check with your informants and see if someone may recognize him as either a dealer or a customer. Maybe know something else about him."

"Perry Gardiner…Okay, I can look into it for you. Got a picture of your vic?"

"Yeah. I can send it to you. It's an older one. He was sporting long hair and a beard at the time of his death."

"Got it. I'll let my people know that when I circulate his picture."

"What makes you think there's a drug connection?"

"He and his girlfriend were killed, and then their pickup truck was set on fire with them in it. Wasn't much left of them to identify."

"Damn. Sounds like they pissed somebody off."

"That's what we were thinking," said Sam. "Drug dealer sending a message?"

"Could be. Think he could've been working as a snitch?"

"No idea. But that hasn't come to our attention."

"Normally, we should have been notified of that if he was," said Joe.

"Normally," scoffed Williams. "He wasn't for us, or I would have known about it."

"Thanks for looking into this, Tyrell. We owe you one."

As Joe and Sam returned to their desks, Sam asked, "You don't suppose Gardiner turned snitch, do you?"

"Given what we know about him, I don't think he was snitch material. Too unstable. But it's worth checking. Let's wait and see if any of Tyrell's informants turn up anything."

When Joe returned to his desk, he emailed Williams with Perry Gardiner's photo. Moments later, he and Sam were called to the scene of a body found north of the Loyola University campus. It had been doused with gasoline and set on fire. The hair on the back of Joe's neck stood up. Could this provide a link to the Gardiner-Whitmore case?

Their investigation would take them well into the evening and add a fifth investigation to their caseload. Joe called Destiny and explained why he would be late getting home.

"That's fine," she said. "But I need a favor. Liz called and wants to know if we can babysit Autumn for a few days."

"Her Lhasa Apso puppy?"

"Well, she's not a puppy anymore. She's an adult now. Anyway, Liz and Jared are flying to North Carolina to visit his brother, and the person who was going to take Autumn has a family emergency. She's in a tight spot."

"I guess it's all right," said Joe.

"Thanks. Liz is going to be so relieved."

The body was found in a fenced-off area under a roof extension of an abandoned building. Joe looked past the fence's gate and the yellow crime scene tape and saw the body near the building. The victim had been burned so severely as to make visual identification difficult. But the fire was not intense, and the body was not charred like those of Gardiner and Whitmore.

Medical Examiner Felix Alvarez was already on the scene. Joe had worked with him previously and chose to avoid contacting him while he was working, knowing he could become irritable if interrupted. He would wait and speak with him later when he concluded his work.

While interviewing witnesses, a woman identified an individual she had seen occasionally wandering aimlessly in the area. Leseda Baylor, who worked at a print shop, described the man as a thin, white man in his fifties with graying hair wearing a long tan coat. She said she saw the man carrying what could have been a fuel can earlier in the day.

"He looked like he was poor or homeless, maybe," said Baylor.

"What makes you say that?" asked Sam.

"Because his coat was dirty, and he needed a shave. You know how homeless people look?"

"I do. Did you notice any facial features?"

"Medium-colored skin, kinda wrinkled face. Oh! And he wore glasses. Old style metal-kinda-rims, you know what I mean?"

"Uh-huh. You said you've seen him around here before?" asked Joe.

"Yeah. I don't know what he does, but I've seen him around here a few times."

"Ever said anything to you?"

"Oh, no. I steer clear of creepy guys like him."

"Understandable." Joe handed her his card. "If you see him again, give me a call. We need to question him."

"I will."

When Joe and Sam finished their interview with Leseda Baylor, they noticed Alvarez and his assistant pushing a gurney holding the victim toward their van. They walked over to get a word. Alvarez saw them coming and stopped, telling his assistant to go ahead and load the body.

"Good evening, gentlemen," he said.

"Doctor," greeted Sam.

"What can you tell me?" asked Joe.

"Male victim severely burned. Appears to have been doused with an accelerant after death," said Alvarez as he removed his Tyvek suit.

"After death, huh?" asked Sam.

"Yes. The body wasn't burned so badly I couldn't see that his throat had been cut."

"Throat cut?"

"Uh-huh. I can give you more after the autopsy."

"I'm interested, given the other burned victims' case we're investigating," said Joe.

"Got another one?"

"Yeah."

"Any ID on him?" asked Sam.

"There's a wallet, but I won't be able to get at it until I get him on the table. Stuck to him like glue. I can text you the victim's name and address if I get any information from it."

They thanked him and told uniformed officers to canvas the area for witnesses. Joe returned to Area 3 and put out an APB on their suspect, hoping uniformed officers cruising the area would spot him and pick him up.

As he drove to his house, he spotted Liz's car parked out front. He was tired and hungry and hoped she would not be staying long. Maybe she was there to simply drop off their dog. He pulled into the garage, and as he entered the house, he heard bubbling voices.

Surprise! It wasn't just Liz sitting at the kitchen island; Jared was also sitting there. Great. They were drinking wine and laughing as he entered. When Jared saw Joe, he stood up and greeted him.

"We've been waiting for you," said Jared as he walked over and shook Joe's hand.

"Good to see you," said Joe, even though it wasn't. "Unfortunately, homicide doesn't happen from nine to five."

"You want a glass of wine?" asked Destiny.

"Please. I could use one."

As she poured him a glass, Liz turned on her stool. "We brought Autumn over."

Joe looked around. "Where is she?"

"Oh, she's in her carrier. She needs to get used to her new surroundings gradually."

"How's the new car working out?" asked Jared. "Destiny said you popped for a new ride."

"Great. It's everything my other car was. The previous owner made most of the modifications I did."

Destiny handed Joe his wine. "Why don't you show it to him?"

"I was just going to ask if I could see it," said Jared.

"Sure. Let's go," replied Joe, and he turned and walked to the door leading to the garage. He hit the light switch, and the black Camaro appeared, parked next to Destiny's black Mercedes.

Upon seeing it, Jared's reaction was, "Nice." He walked around it, giving the car a close inspection while Joe opened the hood to show him the engine.

After looking over the engine bay, Jared asked, "How's it run?"

"Scary fast," Joe replied. "Six-hundred-fifty horsepower from the factory, and it's been tweaked some beyond that."

"Same engine I have for my Camaro project. Just got it and the transmission bolted into the Roadster Shop chassis. Powder-coated black. Looks great. You should stop over and see it sometime."

"I should. You have the body set on the frame."

"Uh-huh. Here, I'll show you." Jared pulled out his phone and began showing Joe multiple pictures of his project. Joe pretended he was interested.

"I have all the parts to finish it sitting around in boxes. It's just a matter of putting everything together and then having it painted and getting the interior done."

Jared went on and on about his pro-touring Camaro project. Money appeared to be no object as he spoke about the costs of components and labor, and the conversation became all about him, as usual. When Joe finished his wine, it gave him an excuse to return to the house and leave the garage. He hoped Liz would be ready to go home.

When they entered the house, Liz said, "Jared, honey. We should go."

Thank god," Joe thought.

"I suppose." Jared looked at Joe. "We came by to drop off Autumn, and we wound up staying over an hour. We're flying out early in the morning, so we'd better get home."

"It's always good to see you," said Destiny. She hugged Liz. "Have a nice visit."

"We will."

"Stop over when we get back. You have to see my Camaro," said Jared.

"I will," said Joe. "Have a good flight."

When Liz and Jared left, Joe asked, "Have you eaten?"

"No, I was waiting for you. You want to cook or have something delivered?"

"I don't feel like cooking this late. I'm beat. Let's get something delivered. I'll let you decide."

"Chinese?"

"Sounds great."

Joe kneeled down to Autumn's carrier and peered through the door. "What do you say, Autumn?" She looked out at him with her expressive brown eyes, seemingly sizing him up. He held his hand up to the door and let her sniff it.

"What did she say?" asked Destiny.

Joe got up from the floor. "She thinks Mongolian Beef would be a good choice."

Chapter Thirteen

It was drizzling the next morning, not a pleasant day to jog. Joe had never let a light rain stop him in the past, but he decided to cut a mile from his usual three-mile run. When he got home, he hung his wet jogging clothes in the garage and hit the shower. As he was eating breakfast, Destiny was amused watching Autumn eyeing Joe.

Autumn walked over to Joe's stool and looked up at him. When he didn't acknowledge her, she gave a snort. Joe looked down and said, "Are you begging?" She continued looking at him with her soft brown eyes. "I don't think toast with hummus is good for dogs. Sorry."

"Aw," said Destiny. "I think she wants you to pet her."

Joe looked down at Autumn. "Is that what you want?" Then Autumn jumped up and put her front paws on his leg. He petted her, and after a moment, she got down and walked back to her bed.

"See. I told you," said Destiny. "She only wanted some attention from you."

"So, if I come and stare at you and snort, will you give me some attention?"

"Not the kind you want."

Later that morning, the rain stopped as Joe and Sam began canvasing homeless shelters in the area of the incident. At the second one, they checked out, the attendant, a large man with the name 'Warren' embroidered on an old green work shirt, greeted them.

"Hello there."

"I take it you're Warren?" asked Joe.

"Yup, that's me."

"Warren, what?"

"Warren Davenport."

When Joe and Sam displayed their IDs, Davenport became visibly nervous. "What can I do for you?" he asked.

Joe described who they were seeking. Davenport listened attentively, nodding his head and annoyingly repeating "uh-huh, uh-huh" as he described the man. When they finished, he responded, "That sounds like Virgil."

"Virgil. You got a last name," asked Sam.

"Sorry. I don't."

"Is he here?" asked Joe.

"No. If he stays here, he leaves pretty early. What do you want him for?"

"He's a person of interest in an incident yesterday."

"Really?" exclaimed Davenport, pulling a handkerchief from his back pocket and wiping perspiration from his bald head. "I never thought Virgil would be any kinda problem. Always quiet. Never gives nobody trouble."

"Well, we need to speak with him," said Joe, handing Davenport his card. "You need to call us if you see him, okay?"

"Yeah. I'll let the night attendant know about this when he comes in. But I'd be surprised if he did anything. He seems harmless enough."

"You could be right about that," said Sam. "But he might know something that could aid us in our investigation. Thanks for your help."

"No problem."

When they stepped outside, Joe said, "What would make someone like Virgil set this dead guy on fire? Even if he was the one who cut his throat. It doesn't make sense."

"It might make perfect sense to Virgil."

"Nutcase, you mean?"

"Uh-huh, uh-huh," said Sam, mimicking Davenport. Joe ignored him.

"Could be a connection between this murder and the Gardiner-Whitmore case. The throat cut bothers me, though. Gardiner was clubbed, and Whitmore strangled. The MOs are all over the place."

"I know. Maybe his identity will provide a link of some kind."

"Maybe."

Joe's phone rang. "Detective Erickson."

"Tyrell Williams here."

"Tyrell. I didn't expect to hear from you so soon."

"Well, I didn't expect to get an answer for you so soon. But one of my people recognized the guy in your picture. Called him a crazy bastard."

"Well, if he bought drugs, it goes with the territory, doesn't it?"

"He remembered him, so evidently, he made an impression. Anyway, it turns out he was an occasional buyer of pills."

"So, why did they deal with him?"

"He always had money. Money talks."

"Sure does. Did he buy in quantity? Enough to deal to others?"

"No. From what I was told, it was in small amounts. Sounded more like personal use."

"Okay. Thanks, Tyrell."

Joe turned to Sam. "Gardiner's buys were small. For personal use, not for resale. So, where did he get his income?"

"Maybe he was leeching off his cousin," said Sam. "She had a good job with the Chicago Public Schools. Probably had savings."

"Yeah. Let's get a court order for her bank records. He may have been bleeding her bank account. Gaining financial control over a person is a common objective for Svengali types."

Later, Sam sent through a warrant for Gina Whitmore's bank records while Joe entered information into his computer about their newest case. Shortly after lunch, he received a call from the 20th District informing him their person of interest had been detained. Joe and Sam drove to 20th Police District headquarters to question the subject.

When they arrived, they met with Officer Bryan Peterson, who spotted the individual and brought him in for questioning. "The guy had an old military ID on him that says his name is Virgil Simerdla. He gave me his address as 'North America.' But his ID says Chicago. It's pretty clear he's homeless."

"Anything else?" asked Sam.

"He smells like gasoline."

"Yeah?"

"It's preferable to his body odor. Jesus. I had to deodorize my squad car."

"Where is he?" asked Joe.

"Interrogation room one."

Joe and Sam, along with Sergeant Diane Albritton, entered the area behind the window of the interrogation room to get a look at Simerdla. As they looked through the window at the man cuffed to the table, they realized how accurate Leseda Baylor's description was. Simerdla's reddened, unshaven face was dirty, and his features suggested Slavic ancestry. His graying hair was covered by an old navy blue stocking cap. The tan trench coat was worn over a gray sweatshirt covering a red flannel shirt, each equally filthy. His hands were darkened by dirt that had been worn in over a long period of time. As they observed his behavior, his eyes darted around the room through old-style aviator wire-rimmed glasses.

"Well, shall we?" asked Joe.

Sam only chuckled incredulously in agreement as they moved to question Simerdla.

"Good luck," said Albritton.

When Sam opened the door, Simerdla lurched in surprise. Simerdla's odor had already permeated the room. Joe and Sam introduced themselves and advised him of his rights. After a few angry utterances, they decided to leave Simerdla's cuffs on.

"Mr. Simerdla," said Joe. "Mind if we call you Virgil?"

Simerdla shook his head "no."

"We just have a few questions for you, and after we're done, maybe we can let you go, okay?"

Simerdla nodded. "yes."

"I see you're a veteran," said Sam.

Simerdla looked up. "Uh-huh."

"So am I. Army?"

"Mm."

"Desert Storm?"

Simerdla nodded.

"I served in the Middle East myself. Afghanistan." Going out on a limb,

Sam said, "I was in some firefights, just like you. What unit were you with?"

That got Simerdla's attention, and he looked up at Sam and said, "Rangers."

"You were a Ranger? You're one helluva soldier, Virgil."

Simerdla's shrug was the only reaction to Sam's compliment.

"Thank you for your service, Virgil," said Joe. After a moment, Joe breached the subject by asking, "Do you know why you're here today?"

Simerdla looked back down at the table. Silence.

"You smell like gasoline, Virgil. What were you doing with gasoline?" asked Sam. There was a pause, and then Sam continued. "It's all right, soldier. You can tell us. We're here to help you."

During a long pause, Simerdla's hands formed fists, his eyes narrowed, and his features tightened. Still looking at the table, he mumbled, "It was the devil."

Joe nodded to Sam in an effort to keep him questioning Simerdla since they had established a common bond. "You said 'the devil'?" asked Sam.

"Uh-huh."

"You saw the devil?"

"Uh-huh."

"Can you tell me what happened, Virgil?"

"Came to me. When I was sleeping. Wanted to take me."

"Take you where?"

"To hell." Simerdla began to shake, and tears welled up in his eyes. "I wasn't going to let him take me to hell!"

"What did you do? To the devil?"

"I fought him. I fought him with everything I had. I cut him...And then I burned him up!" Simerdla began pulling against the table with his cuffs. Yelling, he blurted, "I set him on fire and sent him back to hell!"

Sam reached across and put his hand on Simerdla's arm. "It's okay, Virgil. It's okay, soldier. Your war with the devil is over...It's over, man. The devil is dead."

"He's not dead. You can't kill the devil. He's in hell. And he'll come again. But I'll be ready for him."

Once Simerdla calmed down, they found he kept a gasoline can to light a fire in a homemade firepit by the abandoned building. After fighting the "devil" using techniques he learned as an Army Ranger, he doused him with gasoline to send him back to hell. A deluded homeless veteran needing mental health hospitalization was the offender who killed the unidentified victim. Case solved. And it had nothing to do with the Gardiner-Whitmore investigation.

Joe and Sam left the interrogation room and met Sergeant Albritton in the hall.

"You have all that recorded for the DA?" asked Joe. "Simerdla will never be able to write it down or sign a confession."

"Yeah, we got it. Well done, detectives."

"Well done, Sam," said Joe. "Gaining his confidence like that did the trick. I knew you were in the army, but I had no idea you saw combat in the Middle East."

"I didn't."

"What?"

"Sometimes you have to lie."

Chapter Fourteen

Two days later, a judge signed a search warrant for Gina Whitmore's bank records. Joe traveled to her bank and obtained her records, which revealed regular debits for things like groceries, insurance and credit card payments, occasional small ATM withdrawals, and purchases that did not suggest any suspicious activity. Her savings account remained static with no deposits or withdrawals. Nothing suggested Perry Gardiner was bleeding her account.

So, where was Gardiner getting his money? He had no bank account, yet he was remodeling his residence. Where was the money for sheetrock and supplies coming from? He must have been dealing in cash. Did he bring money back from San Francisco even though he claimed he was broke? Was he getting money from his father? Stealing from someone? It didn't make sense.

Then, a call came in from Julianne Hendricks. The urgency in her voice got Joe's attention.

"Detective Erickson. I'm at my father's house—the one my brother and cousin were living in?"

"Yes. We unsealed it so you could enter. Is there a problem?"

"That's why I'm calling. I was looking around. Snooping, you might say, and I was poking around in the attic. And under some insulation, I saw a leather strap, so I lifted the insulation and found a leather duffel bag. I brought it down, and when I opened it…it was stuffed with cash."

"Well, leave it alone. Don't touch it anymore. My partner and I will be right over."

Hendricks met them at the door. They followed her into the dining room, where they saw a leather duffel bag sitting on a chair beside the table. Putting on gloves, Joe and Sam began examining the contents. The cash was in denominations of twenties and fifties. The bills were banded together, but the serial numbers were not in sequence.

"I guess we know where Perry's income came from," said Joe. He looked at Hendricks. "Any ideas?"

"I'm totally in the dark about this."

"Looks like the proceeds of a payoff or something."

"Blackmail? Drug buy?" speculated Sam.

"Oh, Jesus. I can't believe he'd be mixed up in something like that. There's no way I can tell my mother about this," insisted Hendricks.

"I wouldn't. We don't know anything yet."

"Whatever it is, it can't be good. It's got to be illegal."

Joe called in Evidence Techs. Half an hour later, Big John Gustafson and his assistant, Lenny Andrews, arrived on the scene and began processing the bag and the attic. No more cash was found in the attic area. They took possession of the duffel bag full of cash, sealing it in a large plastic bag. The lab would be fingerprinting the bag as well as the cash and attempting to pull DNA from any surface that could have been touched. In addition, they would check the serial numbers on the bills to see if they had been recorded in the event of a ransom or undercover operation.

Outside, Hendricks asked, "Are you going to seal the house again?"

"No," replied Sam. "We don't need to seal it. But if you find anything else that may be out of the ordinary, we'd appreciate you letting us know."

"Dad moved a lot of the furniture to Florida with him. I don't want anything Perry might've had. But now I have the joyful task of cleaning out the refrigerator and tossing all the spoiled food in there."

"I'm sorry about that," said Joe. "Hopefully, there isn't much you have to toss. I'd suggest rubbing Vicks inside a medical mask to avoid the odor of spoiled food."

"Thanks," mumbled Hendricks, and she turned around and went back inside.

On their way back to their office, Sam asked, "What was Gardiner doing with all that money?"

"And what did he do to get it?" asked Joe. "If those serial numbers were recorded, and he was spending any of the money, which he probably was, red flags should have been going up all over the place."

"They would've traced those bills to where they were spent, and he would've been arrested by now."

"Has to be something that's flown under the radar."

"Drugs come to mind, but it doesn't appear he was involved with any traffickers. At least that we know of. And if he was, would he be brazen enough to have double-crossed one of them?"

"I doubt it." Joe paused for a moment. "Not unless he did it in San Francisco and then took off for Chicago."

"I thought he came back because he was strapped for cash."

"I did, too. Maybe it was a clever deception. An excuse he used to escape the San Francisco area."

"If he stole a huge amount of cash from a drug trafficker or a mobster, he'd be signing his death warrant if they found out."

"Maybe they did, and they finally tracked him down. And he and Whitmore paid the price."

"But you would've thought they'd found the money and taken it back."

"Yeah. Well, it may be worth a call to San Francisco PD to see if they know anything about Perry Gardiner."

When Joe returned to his desk, he called the San Francisco Police Department and spoke with Detective Daniel Weston, who agreed to run a check on Perry Gardiner. From here on out, it was hurry up and wait. Wait on the San Francisco police, the lab results, and the Evidence Technicians' findings.

Then, Joe received a phone call from Destiny.

"Joe," she said, her voice filled with emotion. "I received some frightening news."

"What? What is it?" Immediately, Destiny's mother came to mind.

"Liz and Jared's plane is missing."

"What? Where did you hear that?"

"Liz's sister called. She told me she received word their plane never arrived back here from the Charlotte airport. Jared filed a flight plan that stated they were scheduled to arrive back in Chicago at Midway eight hours ago, but they never did. Midway Airport authorities contacted the Charlotte airport, and it was confirmed they took off as scheduled. But neither Midway nor Charlotte has had contact with the plane."

"Look," said Joe, "They could've developed a problem and landed at a small airport or made an emergency landing somewhere. Have you tried calling Liz's cell phone?"

"I have, and there's no answer. I tried Jared's, same thing. Everything goes to their voicemails. I'm scared, Joe."

"I'm coming home."

Joe explained the situation to Sam and the desk sergeant, then drove home as quickly as possible.

Chapter Fifteen

When Joe entered the house, Destiny threw her arms around him. He held her tight as she shed tears of despair. He said nothing for the moment as he could think of nothing to say that could remedy what she was feeling. Autumn came running and remained at their feet, looking up at them as if she sensed their feelings.

"I'm so frightened for them," said Destiny.

"I know," replied Joe. Normally, Destiny was a pretty tough cookie, capable of controlling her emotions in the field and able to physically defend herself against an aggressor twice her size. But it was deeply personal when it came to Liz, and she could not suppress her feelings.

"Can I get you something, a glass of water or—"

"Wine would be good."

Joe poured them both a glass of Cabernet from an opened bottle on the counter. Destiny picked Autumn up and placed her in her lap, stroking her as she sat at the island. When handing Destiny the glass, Joe asked, "How long has it been since you spoke to Liz's sister? What's her name?"

"Jacquie. Jacquie Lambert. An hour ago. When she first called me."

He pulled out a stool and sat next to her. "Is she going to keep you informed?"

"She added me to the contacts list for authorities to call or text with updated information. It would save her forwarding the news to me."

"Did she give you any information other than their plane didn't arrive?"

"They're launching an investigation. It's all she said. Maybe it's all she knew."

"If they're launching an investigation, it's still early, and they're just beginning to trace their flight. There won't be any news for a while."

"This waiting is...."

"Hopefully, it will turn out to be nothing to worry about." Joe was trying to put a positive spin on it but feared the worst. Destiny looked at him, but she didn't believe him. Maybe his face betrayed his true feelings. If the plane did not arrive and they could not reach them on either the plane's radio or their cell phones, the outlook was bleak. If the plane went down over the Blue Ridge Mountains, which would have been on their flight path, locating the wreckage in that heavily forested region could be problematic. And if Liz and Jared did survive a crash and sustained injuries, finding help would be a struggle, especially if cell phone reception is non-existent.

As Destiny drank her wine, Joe noticed Autumn snuggling in her lap, something she usually did not choose to do. Could she sense Destiny's despair?

Joe wondered. "Was Jared an experienced pilot?"

"I don't know. I think he bought the plane a couple of years ago. He's been a pilot for a while, but I don't know how long."

The memory of JFK, Jr.'s plane crash entered Joe's mind—an inexperienced pilot encountering a problematic weather situation. "I see...Well, I guess all we can do is wait while the authorities conduct their search and hope they were able to land somewhere."

"I'm going to be a wreck until we find out."

Joe needed to refocus Destiny's thoughts from the bad news, so he made a suggestion. "I'll tell you what. Let's do something to take our minds off all this. You up for that?"

"What did you have in mind?"

"Let's cook something. By the time we get done, it'll be time to eat dinner."

Joe's phone rang. Destiny looked at him. Looking up from his phone, he said, "It's okay. It's Sam."

"Yeah, Sam."

"A minute ago, I got a call from forensics. They got a hit on the description and photograph of the duffel bag."

"Already?"

"The thing is hot!"

"Hot?"

"You remember the case of the kidnapped girl who was found dead after her parents paid the ransom about a year ago? Cardona and Murphy caught the case when the girl was found dead."

"Yeah, vaguely."

"After they made the arrest, the two kidnappers claimed they never received the ransom money. And the ransom money was never found."

"You're telling me they didn't receive it because Perry Gardiner did?"

"Something to think about. Everything all right at home?"

"Don't know yet. Friends aboard a missing plane. We're waiting to hear."

"Sorry to hear that," said Sam. "I hope everything turns out all right. Talk to you tomorrow."

Now Joe had something else to occupy his mind. How did Perry Gardiner get his hands on the ransom money? Was he part of the kidnapping plot? Or did he somehow steal the duffel bag? It sounds bizarre.

"Joe?" asked Destiny. "What was that about?

"The case Sam and I are working on. He discovered an answer we were looking for, and it opens a new set of questions we have to explore. Our crime now ties into another crime."

"Getting complicated, huh?"

"It just did." But he had to put thinking about the case aside for the time being and concentrate on the present. So…What do you want to cook?"

"We have all the ingredients for broccoli-stuffed manicotti with burrata cheese."

"Sounds good to me. We have the ingredients for that Italian chopped salad we like."

"Okay. You make the salad, and I'll make the manicotti," said Destiny.

"Deal. After we finish our wine. Right, Autumn?" Autumn opened her eyes and looked at Joe. "I think that was passive yes."

"What are we going to do with Autumn if…"

"Don't think about it. It's more emotional clutter you don't need to have in your head right now." Joe drank the remainder of his wine. Rising from his seat, he walked to the sink and began washing his hands. "I'm going to start making the vinaigrette."

Ninety minutes later, the manicotti came out of the oven, and they were eating their dinner. The conversation was subdued, and Joe tried to distract Destiny by getting her input on the Gardiner-Whitmore case.

"We speculated Perry Gardiner stole money from organized crime or a drug deal in San Francisco and then escaped to Chicago in an effort to disappear. That's what made sense to us at the time. But now this news has tied him to a kidnapping here."

"You said the kidnappers claimed they never received the ransom?"

"Yeah. That's what Sam told me, but I don't have details yet."

"It doesn't sound to me like he was part of the plot to kidnap the victim, does it? You would've thought he'd been arrested with the other offenders at some point."

"You'd think they would have given him up to get lighter sentences. But apparently, that didn't happen."

Destiny put down her fork. "You'll need to interview the kidnappers. See what they have to say."

"And the parents. We'll have to revisit the kidnapping and find out about the ransom money."

"You said the kidnapping victim was found dead?"

"She was, but I don't know what happened. Cardona and Murphy caught the case and made the arrests. We'll need to work with them to begin with."

"I guess my question would be, if Perry Gardiner wasn't part of the kidnapping plot, how did he get his hands on the ransom money?"

"That's the first question. The second question would be, were he and his cousin killed for it?"

"And the third question, who killed them?

They finished their dinner and cleared the kitchen. Afterward, they moved to the living room, where they watched back-to-back programs on Masterpiece Mystery. Masterpiece, one of Destiny's favorites, successfully distracted her for two hours. By the time ten o'clock rolled around, they decided to go to bed, where they found a further distraction.

Chapter Sixteen

The following day, when Joe returned from his three-mile jog, he asked Destiny if she preferred him to call in sick so he could spend the day with her. She told him to go to work.

"I'll contact you if I hear anything."

"Are you sure you want to be alone?" Joe asked.

"Autumn will keep me company, and I'm working on a project with the police department in Denver. They suspect four deaths may have been committed by a single offender. They contacted me, and I may eventually be creating a profile based on the information they've collected. It'll keep my mind off Liz and Jared."

Feeling assured Destiny would be okay, Joe drove to the office, where he met with Sam to map out their agenda for the day. First, Sam and Joe met with Detectives Michelle Cardona and Rick Murphy, investigators on the kidnapping case, so they could fill them in on the events leading up to the loss of the ransom money.

"Thirteen months ago," began Cardona, "Paul and Jamie Franklin's fourteen-year-old daughter, Penelope, was kidnapped. Franklin owns a number of office supply stores around the city. Wealthy guy. He did what the kidnappers asked. He didn't call the police. He put together fifty grand in unmarked bills, placed the cash into a leather duffel bag as instructed, and left it behind a dumpster in an alley."

The amount struck Joe as an odd amount. "Fifty thousand wasn't that much of a ransom demand. You would have thought the offenders would've asked for at least double that or more."

"I know. Evidently, these amateurs weren't greedy."

"That part went as planned," said Murphy. "The deal was, they were supposed to get a phone call telling them where Penelope could be found once the kidnappers had the money. But the kidnappers never got the money. They claimed it wasn't there."

"While they were threatening each other in back-and-forth phone calls, Penny, as she was called, was getting sicker and sicker, and the kidnappers were getting scared and finally decided to abandon the whole thing. The female kidnapper used a burner phone to tell them where the girl could be found."

"But when we got there, she was dead. The medical examiner concluded she choked on her own vomit."

"When we found her, she was bound and with tape over her mouth. Evidently, she vomited, aspirated it, and choked to death."

"Oh, god," lamented Joe. "The kidnappers couldn't have foreseen that happening."

"They said she complained about not feeling well, but they had no idea she was going to throw up," said Cardona.

"Out of curiosity," Sam asked, "how did you catch the offenders?"

"They had no criminal backgrounds and made mistakes seasoned criminals wouldn't have made. After several calls, we got a location on their apartment during a phone call when Penny's father was arguing with the male offender about the ransom. He should never have used the burner phone from his apartment."

"Yeah, that was pretty dumb."

"Amateurs after a quick score," said Murphy.

"Who were these two brain children?" asked Joe.

"Bryce McKendrick and his girlfriend, Iris Schumer. Maybe they can rekindle their relationship in twenty years when they get out of prison," quipped Cardona.

"Well, you know what they say," said Sam. "Love will find a way."

Cardona snorted a chuckle. "Right."

"You think your victim was part of this kidnapping scheme?" asked

Murphy.

"We need to interview the kidnappers to see if they know anything about either one of our victims. See if there's any kind of connection," said Joe. "Right now, we don't know of any, and you'd think it would've come out during your investigation."

"One thing we do know, McKendrick and Schumer never got the ransom. Apparently, your guy got the duffel bag before they could pick it up. God only knows how he got it before they did," said Cardona.

"Did Penny's father have the money marked?"

"Not that I know of. He got strict instructions to get bills with random serial numbers."

"But he still could've had the serial numbers recorded, random or not."

"I don't know. It's possible, I suppose. He never said he did."

Joe looked at Sam. "We need to interview the Franklins, too."

"Motive?" asked Sam.

"If they found out Gardiner nicked the money. Yeah."

Cardona tapped Joe's arm. "One thing about Franklin you need to know. He inserted himself into our investigation. He talked to the owners of stores to see if they had surveillance video of the alley. We had to threaten him with obstruction to get him to knock it off."

"And did he?"

"So far as we know."

Joe looked at Sam. "Ten to one, he had the bills marked."

That afternoon, Joe and Sam drove the ninety minutes to Dixon, Illinois, the location of the Dixon Correctional Center, a medium security adult male prison of the Illinois Department of Corrections. It housed Bryce McKendrick, one-half of the team that kidnapped Penelope Franklin.

They met with McKendrick in the visitors' area. McKendrick was a slight, thirty-year-old with curly blonde hair, someone who looked like he belonged on a college campus, not in a prison. After introductions were made, McKendrick's attitude was guarded but not hostile.

"We're here to ask you some questions about the Penelope Franklin kidnapping," Joe began.

"Well, I'd rather not talk about that. You probably read all about it."

"We're investigating another crime, and we've found something linked to the kidnapping. Thought you might be interested."

"Oh?" said McKendrick, showing a degree of curiosity. "What's that?"

"We found the ransom money."

Immediately, McKendrick sat up in his chair. "You did?"

"It was found in the home of a homicide victim. Perry Gardiner."

"Perry! Perry's dead?"

Joe and Sam glanced at each other. "You know Perry Gardiner?" asked Sam.

"He's my cousin!"

"Your cousin?"

"Yeah. How the hell did he get hold of the money?"

"That's what we'd like to know," said Joe. "Was he part of your kidnapping scheme?"

"Hell, no. He didn't have anything to do with it. He didn't know anything about it. It was Iris and me. The two of us. Swear to god."

"Then how did Perry wind up with the ransom money?" asked Sam.

"Beats the hell out of me. What happened to him, anyway?"

"He and his cousin, Gina Whitmore, were murdered," said Joe.

"Aww, fuck! Gina, too."

"So, nobody told you?"

"Nobody tells me shit in here. Oh, man. That really sucks."

Clearly, McKendrick was taken aback by his cousins' deaths. Joe thought he might be able to use his emotional pain to gain some empathy and get him talking about the kidnapping.

"We're sorry to deliver bad news like this, Bryce. I'm sure you'd like to get justice for Perry and Gina. It's why we've come to you, hoping you can provide some information that could help our investigation."

"Yeah…Yeah, I guess. Oh, man…" Then, there was a long pause followed by McKendrick taking a deep breath and letting it out. He looked at Joe and Sam, saying, "Okay. Ask away."

It was the answer Joe was hoping for. "I want to ask about the ransom.

Tell us what you told Franklin to do."

I told him to get fifty grand—nothin' bigger than fifties—in unmarked bills with random serial numbers. Put the cash in a black leather duffel bag and put it behind a dumpster in an alley behind Papa Gino's Pizzeria. I got a call from him saying he had left the duffel bag. I got there a minute later and saw him walking down the street. I waited until he was out of sight and then walked to the dumpster. When I looked behind it, the bag wasn't there!"

"What did you do?"

"I ducked into the Pizzeria and ordered a pizza, thinking it was a setup."

"Did you see anyone in the alley?"

"No. Not a soul."

"The amount of time you waited before you entered the alley—would it have been enough time for someone to grab the duffel bag and hightail it out of the alley?" asked Sam.

"Well, yeah. I suppose. If they were already in the alley and watching Franklin planting the bag."

Again, Joe looked at Sam, thinking Gardiner might have been in the right place at the right time. Joe thought maybe Gardiner was in the alley scoring pills from one of his connections and happened to duck behind something when he saw Franklin enter the alley with the duffel bag. After Franklin left, Gardiner must have grabbed the duffel bag and run down the alley, walking out onto the street a block away from where McKendrick was waiting to enter.

"When was the last time you spoke with Perry Gardiner?" asked Joe.

"Oh, god. It's been a couple of years or more. He was home on leave from the Coast Guard when I saw him last."

"So, you weren't close."

"Well, we were closer when we were kids. But as we grew older, well, you know how it is…"

Joe and Sam ended their interview with McKendrick and drove back to Chicago. On the ninety-minute drive, they discussed where they needed to proceed. Joe explained his theory of serendipitous acquisition by Perry Gardiner, and Sam agreed it was the best theory they had to go on at the moment.

"I think now more than ever we have to interview the Franklins, don't you?" asked Joe.

Sam nodded. "That's what I'm thinking, too. If, by one way or another, they found out Gardiner grabbed the money, it could have driven Franklin to kill him. I mean, it's the best we have so far, right?

"Uh-huh. He could have marked those bills and traced them back to where they were spent. He could have figured out Gardiner was spending his ransom money and made him pay for screwing up getting his daughter back alive.

When Joe returned to his desk, there was a message saying Detective Weston called from San Francisco PD. Joe returned the call, and Weston answered.

"I found one reference to Perry Gardiner, Detective Erickson. A police report was filed about two years ago. Perry Gardiner filed a report stating he was assaulted outside a bar on First Street, not far from the Waterfront. A patron found him lying on the curb and called the police. Gardiner reported he was jumped when he left the bar but claimed he couldn't identify his two assailants. That's the only reference we have for Perry Gardiner. According to his address, he was living in a seedy area of the city at the time. He stated he was unemployed, having been recently discharged from the Coast Guard."

"Did he say what may have caused the assault?"

"He stated he was attacked from behind when he left the bar. He didn't say what may have motivated his assailants."

"Thank you for checking, Detective. I appreciate your time."

Joe thought: *That wasn't much help.*

Chapter Seventeen

When Joe was driving home from work, he saw the white Lexus belonging to Destiny's mother parked in front of the house. Joe's heart jumped into his throat. He didn't know if this meant the worst had happened to Liz and Jared or if Vivien had simply driven in from Winnetka to keep her daughter company. Surely, Destiny would have contacted him if she had received tragic news. Wouldn't she?

Destiny heard Joe enter from the garage and called, "We're in the living room." Joe felt relieved knowing he was not coming home to a house in mourning.

"I hear you." After locking up his Glock, Joe walked into the living room and saw Destiny and Vivien snacking on cheese and vegetables while holding glasses of wine. Autumn was curled up on the floor between them.

"Hi, Vivien. Nice to see you."

"Destiny called and told me about Liz. So, I thought I would drive down here and keep her company while she waited to hear something."

"Well, you know you're welcome to stay as long as you like."

"Thank you, Joe."

"Join us," said Destiny.

"Let me get a glass, and I will." Joe got a wine glass from the kitchen, and Destiny poured him a glass of Merlot from the bottle sitting on the coffee table. Sitting next to Destiny, he asked, "Have you received any updates today?"

"One. They've narrowed the search to the Blue Ridge Mountains."

Joe glanced at Vivien. Her expression had turned glum.

"I guess it's good they've been able to narrow the search area, huh?" said Joe, trying to put his best spin on it. Joe needed to change the subject. "So, Vivian. What have you been doing to keep busy these days?"

"Staying out of politics, for starters. Things have become so ugly it makes me sick. Now, I concentrate on donating to charities for children: St. Jude's, Shriner's, Special Olympics. I traveled to Louisville and toured St. Jude's facility earlier this year. I was amazed. You wouldn't believe what they're doing for kids with cancer."

"That's an honorable thing to do," said Joe. "People don't know how lucky they are to have children who don't need those services."

"I do," said Vivien, looking at Destiny.

"Thanks, Mom. I consider myself fortunate."

For a woman of wealth and privilege who knows governors and senators, Joe appreciated the fact Vivien never looked down on him for who and what he was, given he was her only child's life partner. If she had expectations for Destiny to marry someone from her own station in life, someone from society, she never revealed any disappointment. On the contrary, all things pointed to her liking and respecting him. Maybe her daughter's happiness was of utmost importance to her and overrode other considerations.

Vivien decided to stay the night and suggested a trip to Burnham Harbor to see Loretta Affannato on her yacht the next day. Destiny agreed to an afternoon visit as long as she could work on her profile during the morning. Vivien asked Joe if he would like to accompany them, but he declined, thankful he had to work. Funny how investigating grisly deaths could be preferable to spending time with three women for several hours.

The next morning, Joe and Sam decided their next move was to question Paul Franklin regarding the ransom he paid to release his daughter. Joe checked the file and found Franklin had an office on North Clark Street in the Andersonville neighborhood. He called his office and found Franklin was in and available between 11:00 a.m. and noon. Joe told his receptionist to expect them at eleven.

"Before we interview Paul Franklin, I want to see the alley where the ransom money was placed," said Joe.

"Your theory?" asked Sam.

"Yeah."

They drove to the alley's address and walked inside. They spotted a dumpster still in the approximate area, as depicted in photographs from the investigation. As Sam looked behind the dumpster, Joe walked farther into the alley.

"Hey, Sam. Come here."

Sam rose from his kneeling position and walked toward Joe. The building jutted in about six feet and continued back another thirty feet before it jutted out again.

"Someone, as in Perry Gardiner, could have concealed himself behind this wall while making a drug deal. After his connection left, he could have looked around the corner and seen Franklin placing the ransom money behind the dumpster. Once Franklin left, Gardiner would've had a perfect opportunity to snatch the duffel bag and leave the alley in the same direction as his dealer."

"This is a shady area that's concealed from view. A drug deal taking place in here wouldn't be a stretch."

"There's no way to prove it," said Joe, "unless we can find the dealer who sold him dope in here on that particular day."

"Yeah, and good luck with that."

Before leaving the alley, Joe took pictures with his phone. When he was finished, they drove to meet Paul Franklin.

Franklin's office was on the ground floor of the one-hundred-year-old three-story brick structure. Joe and Sam entered the outer office and announced themselves to the middle-aged receptionist a few minutes before eleven. The name sign on top of her desk read "Carolyn Wilkins."

They introduced themselves, and she looked at her computer screen and said, "I'll let him know you're here."

Seeing no wedding ring, Sam smiled at her. "Thank you, Ms. Wilkins."

She returned his smile, picked up her phone, and pressed a button. A moment later, she said, "Your eleven o'clock is here...very well." Then she rose from her chair, saying, "If you'll follow me, please." She led them down a short hallway and knocked on a door. A voice from inside said, "Come in."

The man behind the desk began walking toward them, straightening his tie. He was tall, in his mid-forties, with thinning brown hair, which he wore cut short. He was courteous, but his attitude was frosty. After introductions were made, they sat to begin their interview.

Joe began by saying, "We're investigating a case that has a direct link to your daughter's kidnapping. We're sorry to open up an old wound, but information has come to light, and we'd like to ask you some questions."

"What information would that be?" asked a skeptical Franklin.

"We found the ransom you paid in the home of a murder victim."

Franklin's expression suddenly changed, and he leaned forward in his chair. "You found the ransom money?"

"We did."

"Who had it?"

"A cousin of one of the kidnappers."

"So, there was another person involved in my daughter's death?"

"At this point, we aren't sure," said Sam. "We interviewed Bryce McKendrick, and he appeared honestly surprised to hear his murdered cousin had the ransom money. He swore he and Iris Schumer were the only ones who kidnapped your daughter."

"Criminals lie all the time," countered Franklin.

"They do. But since his cousin was dead, he could've given him up as an accomplice. What would it hurt? But he didn't. I think he was telling the truth."

"If he wasn't in on it, how did the money come into his possession?"

"According to the report, you placed the ransom money behind the dumpster, correct?" asked Joe.

"I did."

"Did you see anyone in the alley when you walked to the dumpster?"

"Well...I saw a person—a man—walking away toward the end of the alley. I made sure he didn't look back when I squatted to place the duffel bag behind the dumpster. And I made sure no one saw me go into the alley or walk out."

"So, the man walking at the end of the alley never looked back?"

"No, I'm certain of it. So, how did he get the money?"

"We have a theory but no proof. And given the amount of time that's passed, we may not be able to prove it. What's important to us right now is who killed him?"

"The money—fifty thousand in fifties and twenties, right?" asked Sam.

"Right. Random serial numbers."

"Did you mark the bills in any way? Note the serial numbers. Use UV marking?"

Franklin hesitated.

"You marked the bills, didn't you?" pressed Joe.

"I had the serial numbers written down. I've been trying to track them. See if they've been spent."

"And have they?"

"Yes, but not many. They turn up once in a while, which makes the person spending them hard to track."

"Did you tell the police about this?"

"No."

"And what were you going to do when you figured out who was spending your ransom money, Mr. Franklin?" asked Sam.

"Get it back."

"Uh-huh."

"And did you try to get it back from Perry Gardiner after you figured out he was spending your ransom money?" asked Joe.

Franklin became defensive and said, "I've never heard of anyone named Perry Gardiner."

"Because he was spending a lot of your money on home repairs," said Sam.

"And he had your ransom money cleverly hidden in his house, and he and his cousin were found murdered," added Joe.

"Did you kill him, Mr. Franklin?"

"Hell, no!" With that, Franklin stood and yelled, "Get out of my office."

"I don't think so," said Joe. "Now sit down." After a moment, Franklin complied. "Where were you on the night of June 10th?"

"I…don't know. But I can check." Franklin removed his cell phone and pulled up its calendar. Suddenly, his face dropped. "Uh…looks like I was home."

"With your wife?"

"She was…out of town. Visiting her sister in Sacramento."

"Can anyone verify you were there?"

"I don't know. Probably not."

"You have another child, do you not?"

"She was with her mother."

"This does not bode well for you, Mr. Franklin," said Sam.

Franklin was getting angrier with each additional question, and Sam's comment was the last straw.

"I'm not saying another word until I speak with my attorney."

"You're not under arrest, Mr. Franklin."

"I don't care. I'm not saying another word."

"If you think you need an attorney, so be it." Joe looked at Sam. "I guess we're done here, huh?"

Sam eyed Franklin. "I guess we are. I'm sure we'll be seeing each other again."

Rising, Joe and Sam left Franklin's office. As they passed the receptionist's desk, Sam stopped and turned. "Your assistance was most appreciated, Ms. Wilkins."

"You're welcome," she smiled. Joe's eyes rolled.

Once outside, Joe nudged Sam. "Were you flirting with her?"

"I call it 'creating a positive impression' in case we need her help at some point."

"So, what you're saying is, you were cultivating a potential source."

"You can't say you haven't done it."

Joe laughed. "I think you're becoming suave and debonaire, Sam."

"Swave and deboner, that's me!"

Chapter Eighteen

Arriving back at their office, Joe and Sam discussed what they had learned from their interview with Paul Franklin.

"He's hiding something," said Sam.

"Joe concurred and paused to collect his thoughts. "Franklin had motive, but did he have opportunity? We need to find out if he was actually home at the time of Gardiner's death."

"That might be tough. Even if he wasn't, he could afford to pay somebody else to do it."

"That's what I've been thinking. Let's get a warrant for his financials. See if he has any suspicious withdrawals around the time Gardiner was killed."

Sam stood up. "Okay. You know, it's too bad there was no security footage from inside that alley."

Joe began picking up his notes from the table. "Too bad there wasn't security footage from inside the park where Gardiner's truck was set on fire. That tells me the offender was familiar with the park." Joe rose from his chair. "I'm going to check with Franklin's bank and see if he had the ransom money marked and, if so, whether they've been letting him know where it's been spent."

While Sam was filling out a warrant, Joe called Big John Gustafson, the Evidence Technician who took possession of the ransom money at the Gardiner house.

"Gustafson."

"Good morning, John. Joe Erickson calling. I have a quick question about the cash in the leather duffel bag you took possession of a couple of days ago."

"What cash?"

Silence. Then Gustafson began chuckling.

"Don't mess with me like that, John."

"Couldn't resist. We haven't finished processing it yet."

"I figured that. But I was wondering if you could tell me if the bills had been UV marked."

"That, I can tell you. We tested for that, and I assure you they were not."

"Did you observe any other kind of marking on them?"

"No."

"Okay. That's what I needed to know. Thanks."

Joe wanted to clarify that before he spoke to Franklin's bank. The only other way the bank notes could be marked would be to list serial numbers. He drove to the Lakeview Bank & Trust building on Wacker Drive in the Loop.

Stepping out of the elevator on the tenth floor where the legal department was located, Joe was greeted by a man in his late twenties sitting behind a large mahogany desk.

"Good morning. Do you have an appointment?" he asked.

Joe showed his ID and identified himself. "I need to speak with one of your legal representatives. Martin Andrews, if he's here."

"He is. Let me see if he's available." Jeremy, according to his ID tag, picked up the phone and made a call. "There's a Police Detective named Joe Erickson asking to speak with you, Mr. Andrews. Are you available?… Okay…okay… I'll bring him down." Jeremy rose from his chair. "If you'll come with me, please."

Joe followed Jeremy down the hall to an office with double doors. "This is Mr. Andrews' office. You can go in."

Joe opened the door and saw a white-haired man walking toward him. Dressed in a black pinstriped suit, Andrews had the polished look of wealth. His expression was one of concern.

Joe identified himself, and after shaking hands, Andrews asked, "Has something happened regarding the bank?"

"Not directly. This has to do with a case we're investigating. We've found it intersects with another case you may know something about. The kidnapping, ransom, and subsequent death of Penelope Franklin."

Andrews took an immediate interest and directed Joe to take a seat in the wingback chair in front of his desk.

"You may be interested to know that during a homicide investigation, we found the ransom money."

"Indeed. Well…that's certainly good news. It's been missing for quite some time."

"It has. Because of that, we have some questions since Paul Franklin worked with you to put the ransom money together."

"That's correct."

"Did the bank record the serial numbers of the bills used for the ransom?"

"We did. Paul said the kidnappers specified bills with random numbers, but we were able to put several of our staff members on it, and they recorded all the serial numbers of the bills used for the ransom."

"Thank you. My other question involves the report of those bills showing up if they were spent. We know that some of the bills were spent by one of the victims in our investigation. Were those bills flagged?"

"They were."

"Was it possible to trace where those notes were spent?"

"For the most part, no. Most of the bills were used for small purchases. We found a source in only one case where a large amount of cash was used to make a purchase."

"And was Paul Franklin notified of that location?"

Andrews paused and considered his answer. "He was."

"And where was this purchase made?"

"If you'll excuse me, I'll have to check my file. I don't recall." Rising from his chair, he pulled a manilla folder from a filing cabinet and returned to his chair. Opening the file, he looked through several papers, finally focusing on one. "It was a Home Depot."

"And Paul Franklin knew this?"

"He did."

Andrews looked suspiciously at Joe as he closed the file. "It sounds like you're looking at Paul as a suspect in your victim's death."

"We have to look at all possibilities, Mr. Andrews, and we have to ask Paul some questions about his involvement in his daughter's kidnapping. The investigating detectives told us he got so involved in investigating the case on his own, they had to lean on him pretty hard to let them do their jobs. We always have to look at the revenge angle in every homicide case."

"I can't imagine Paul taking the law into his own hands. He doesn't strike me as the type who would do something like that."

"That could very well be. But as investigators, we have to look at everything. No stone unturned, so to speak." Joe rose from his chair. "Thank you for your time, Mr. Andrews. I appreciate your assistance."

"I hope you solve your case, Detective Erickson. It's just too bad it's been linked to the Franklins. They've been through so much."

On the drive back to Area 3, Joe thought about Franklin's knowledge about the money spent at Home Depot and how he may have been able to trace it back to Perry Gardiner. Maybe his bank records would turn up a clue to his involvement in the Gardiner-Whitmore homicide.

As Joe was walking from the parking lot into the building, his phone rang. Destiny's mother was calling.

"Hello, Vivien."

"Joe, I'm afraid we've received bad news."

Chapter Nineteen

Joe came through the door and saw Destiny and Vivien sitting at the kitchen island. Destiny had been crying, but she seemed to have pulled herself together.

Joe hugged her. "I'm so sorry."

"Thank you. They found the plane. They didn't survive the crash."

Joe noticed even Autumn seemed to sense the sadness as she lay curled up in her bed in the corner and didn't come running to greet him. Destiny noticed Joe looking at her.

"What are we going to do about Autumn?"

"Don't worry about her. We'll figure something out when we talk to Liz's sister."

"I guess I knew the odds weren't in their favor. Part of me was expecting it. But it's still hard when you hear the news."

"I know. Have you spoken to Jacquie?"

"I have. I finally worked up the courage to call her. She didn't know any more details than I did."

Facts about the crash would be slow to come out. Joe knew Destiny wanted to know more than the fact Liz and Jared had died. He could use his police connections to learn more details about the crash from authorities in North Carolina. But his inquiry would not be official police business, and he felt uncomfortable using his badge to gain information for personal reasons. He thought if he was upfront about his reasons for knowing and if he spoke to a sympathetic official open to professional courtesy, then he could obtain additional facts about the crash.

"Do you know if they gave her a phone number to call if she wanted more information?"

"They did. I have it, too."

"Maybe, as a police detective, I can make a call in the morning. It's my day off, so I'll be home."

Vivien finally spoke up. "Is their home secure? If thieves know they've been killed, their home could be vulnerable to a robbery."

"They have a sophisticated home security system, Mom. If someone tries to break in, the police will be notified."

"That's good. People can be so deplorable, stooping so low as to rob the deceased. I had a home security system installed in my home years ago. It doesn't make any difference if you live in a good neighborhood anymore. They'll seek you out and break in anyway. God knows what they'd do if they found you at home."

"Do you have something for protection?" asked Joe.

"A gun, you mean? Good heavens, no. I hate guns."

Destiny looked at Joe. "She has Otto." Joe looked at Vivien.

"Otto's a Doberman Pinscher. He's all the deterrent I need. I've always had a Doberman as a companion."

"Where is he now that you're here?"

"I board him at a facility I've used for years. They're very good. I wouldn't trust my boy to just anyone."

"I had an offender tell me once he would rather face a man with a gun than a big dog. He said he could predict what a man might do, but not a dog. I think you're adequately protected. One look at a Doberman would make an offender think twice."

That night, following the dinner of smoked salmon bruschetta Joe prepared, Destiny and Vivien moved to the living room, where they reminisced about Destiny and Liz growing up together. Destiny cuddled Autumn, a tangible link to her friend. Joe, who felt like a fifth wheel, remained in the kitchen, working his laptop, trying to find additional phone numbers to call to get information about the crash. By eleven o'clock, they were talked out, and everyone went to bed.

The next morning, Joe waited until 9:00 a.m. to begin making phone calls. He used the number Destiny was given but was referred to the Buncombe County Sheriff's Office in Asheville, North Carolina, which was conducting the investigation along with the National Transportation Safety Board. He was transferred to the desk of Deputy Darren McCain.

"Deputy McCain."

"Good morning. This is Detective Joe Erickson calling from Chicago. I'm inquiring about the light plane crash that killed two Chicago residents, Jared and Elizabeth Harlow. What can you tell me about the crash?"

"Are you investigating up there?"

"No, actually. It's personal. I was hoping you would be willing to share what you know. Professional courtesy, let's say."

"I understand. Well, I can tell you that both victims were killed on impact. The Asheville airport received a faint transmission from the pilot saying he was having engine problems and was turning around in an attempt to land at their airport. That's the last they heard from him. Given the terrain, it took some time for us to locate the wreckage."

"Thank you, Deputy."

"Do you know by chance if Mr. Harlow's under investigation up there?"

"Not that I know of. Why do you ask?"

"Well, you may want to see that somebody initiates one."

"I don't understand."

"When we were looking through the wreckage, we found a briefcase intact. When we opened it, we found five kilos of uncut cocaine."

"Holy shit," mumbled Joe.

"Surprised?"

"Uh, yeah. Jared Harlow's an attorney. My partner and his wife were good friends. That's why I'm calling. Where was the case found?"

"In the cabin."

"My god. Well...I'll let our people know so you can coordinate with authorities up here. Would you be the contact person?"

"I'm handling the communications for the Sheriff's Office, so you can give them my number. Thank you, Detective."

Joe's stomach was churning. As soon as Joe ended his call, he turned and saw Destiny standing there with a concerned look.

"What did you find out?"

Joe was torn. He did not want to mention the cocaine, but she would be furious and disappointed in him if he wasn't truthful. There was no keeping it from her. He had to tell her.

"Apparently, Jared radioed the Asheville airport saying he had engine trouble. He was trying to make it to the airport when their plane went down. They were both killed by the impact."

"Oh, god…Thanks for checking for me, Joe."

"Uh…That's not all, I'm afraid."

Destiny looked at him, not understanding what he was alluding to.

"The plane didn't burn, so they could sift through what was left of the cabin. They removed a briefcase that contained five kilos of cocaine."

Destiny's jaw literally dropped. "Omigod…Liz would never…."

"I know. I believe you. I'm sure she didn't know." After a moment, Joe asked, "What about Jared? At least a hundred-fifty grand worth of uncut coke was aboard that plane. How much do you really know about him?"

"Not a great deal. They'd been married for three years. Liz was crazy about him. You know what a charming guy he was. Successful attorney, working with his father's real estate companies. Seemed the epitome of a guy on his way up. His involvement in drug trafficking doesn't make any sense."

"Doesn't make sense given what we knew about him. But it could explain all the money he spent on his cars, his airplane, the vacations they took. It's possible he could've been laundering drug money through his father's real estate companies and been an occasional courier for drugs and drug money when he flew from Chicago to Florida and back to check on his father's business. He may have been a master at concealing his illegal activities."

"That's hard to believe."

Vivien came into the room and helped herself to a cup of coffee. "Most men have secrets."

Joe looked at her with astonishment. "We do?"

"I didn't say 'all.' I said 'most.' That's been my experience."

"And women don't?"

She paused from taking a sip of her coffee. "Of course we do. All people do. Some people's secrets are bigger and darker than others."

With a wry smile, Joe found himself nodding. "I think I'd have to agree with you, given my experience."

"And mine as well," added Destiny. "So, maybe Jared did have a dark, corrupt side he kept hidden from everyone."

After taking a sip from her coffee, Vivien looked at Destiny. "Or maybe he was pressured or blackmailed into doing it. He may have found himself involved in something and gotten in over his head. It doesn't mean he wasn't a nice guy."

Joe was struck by Vivien's insight. She was right. Maybe Jared was being blackmailed over something. His financials could provide a clue if he needed money. It could be that he was in debt and desperate for cash. Or maybe not. Maybe it was something else entirely. But this was all speculation. It was not in his purview to investigate any of this. He would need to alert the Narcotics Unit this morning about the crash and drugs found aboard the plane since Jared and Liz's residence was within a police district covered by Area 3. No doubt the FBI would become involved since crime was an interstate matter. What a mess this will be. As intriguing as it was, Joe could not let this tragedy interfere with his own investigations.

Joe only interacted with Jared on rare occasions, mostly when Destiny and Liz wanted them to go out to dinner together. Jared was always charming and personable, and he connected with Joe because they both liked working on their high-performance cars. He didn't mind talking with Jared about the subject, even though the conversation eventually became about him. Jared struck Joe as one of those guys who had more money than sense. Those things put Joe off just enough that he preferred to keep Jared at arm's length, so he remained an acquaintance rather than a friend. Liz must have seen something in him that Joe didn't. Maybe he acted one way around her and another way when he was around guys he knew.

Chapter Twenty

Back at work after two days off, Joe met with Sam. They decided to follow up on how much Paul Franklin knew about Perry Gardiner, and they would start with Home Depot.

Joe called the Home Depot office closest to Gardiner's residence and found they delivered one large supply of building materials to his location. According to their records, the sale was paid for in cash. That accounted for the new drywall installed in the dining room area and possibly the supplies for stripping the finish from the stair railing.

Joe and Sam decided to drop by the Home Depot location, hoping to find a person who recalled if Paul Franklin paid them a visit inquiring about who made a cash payment for a large purchase. Joe printed a photo of Paul Franklin from his internet business page to help identify him as one who may have been seeking such information from a Home Depot employee.

When Joe and Sam arrived, they asked to speak with the general manager. A balding, middle-aged man wearing a Home Depot shirt met them near the customer service desk.

He introduced himself as Roger Hall. "You wanted to speak with me?"

They produced their IDs and asked if they could talk to him in private. Looking back and forth between Joe and Sam, he seemed hesitant but agreed. "Follow me."

Hall pointed to plastic chairs near his desk and told them to have a seat.

Before sitting down, Hall asked, "What is it you need? I don't understand what you could want from me."

Joe began, "We're investigating a case where an offender used stolen money to make a purchase at your store. We're not interested in the fact he used stolen money. We're interested in a person who may have asked one of your employees if a delivery was made to his address."

Hall bristled at the question. "That violates our privacy policy. We don't give out that kind of information."

"We understand that," said Sam. "As my partner said, we only want to know if someone in particular asked about it."

Joe produced the photo of Paul Franklin and showed it to Hall. "This is a picture of the person in question. We want to ask your employees if they remember this person as someone who may have made such an inquiry."

Hall thought for a moment. "All right, but keep it discreet. Don't go flashing your badges around in front of customers, all right?"

Joe and Sam thanked him and went first to the customer service department. No one there recognized the photo of Franklin. Moving on to the building supplies department, they spoke with Darlene Moore, who was staffing the desk. She did not recall anyone inquiring about such a purchase, nor did she recognize Franklin's photo.

Moore thought for a moment. "Tell you what. Let me get Byron for you. He's my assistant. He might be able to remember something." She picked up the phone and paged Byron Nicholson.

A few moments later, a slender young man in his twenties appeared, and Moore introduced him. Joe explained what they were looking for.

Showing Nicholson the photo of Franklin, Joe saw his eyes light up. "You remember this man?"

Nicholson ran his fingers through his red curly hair and looked at Joe. "Uh-huh. I kinda remember him. Vaguely. He asked about a delivery and wanted the address." Looking at Moore, he continued, "I said we couldn't divulge that information." Moore nodded her approval.

"Thanks," said Sam. "That's what we needed to know." Joe and Sam began walking out of the store. When they rounded a corner, they heard Nicholson's voice. "Excuse me. Detectives?"

They turned and saw Nicholson, who asked them to follow him into a nearby aisle where hand tools were on display. "I didn't dare tell you in front of my supervisor, but I screwed up."

"What do you mean?" asked Joe.

"I was a rookie when the guy in the picture asked me about the address for the delivery. I'd only been working here a month, and I wasn't that familiar with store policy about privacy. I'm afraid I confirmed it for him. The address, I mean."

"You did?"

"Yeah. I'm sorry. Please don't tell my supervisor. I could lose my job."

"It's okay. But we might need you to sign a deposition stating Paul Franklin asked you about a delivery address, and you confirmed it for him."

"Oh, shit. That's just great."

Sam stepped in to ease his concerns. "Look, nobody here will know anything about you signing a deposition. So, don't worry about it."

"That's good. Cuz, I like working here."

Outside the store, Joe and Sam agreed they had enough information to bring Paul Franklin in for questioning. They drove to his office and were told by his receptionist, Carolyn Wilkins, that he was home. Figuring she would have called informing him of their visit, Joe and Sam were prepared for Franklin knowing about their arrival.

When they got to Franklin's residence, they were met by not only Paul Franklin and his wife but also their attorney, J. William Gilmore. Gilmore was a portly, fifty-something man with a gray beard that gave him the look of 19th-century European royalty. He must have arrived at the Franklins shortly before Joe and Sam.

"The reason we're here," Joe began, "is we've come across some information, and we'd like to ask Mr. Franklin some questions."

Gilmore stepped in before Franklin could respond. "I have advised Mr. Franklin not to respond to your questions. We consider your questioning and inferences harassment, and if you do not cease this line of inquiry, we are prepared to file suit against the Chicago Police Department for harassment and mental cruelty."

Joe looked at Sam and then responded, "If that's the way you want it, so be it. Good day."

On their way back to Area 3, Sam was annoyed the Franklins had lawyered up. "We need to get more evidence on him so we can make an arrest."

Joe agreed. "I know. But I don't think Franklin is the kind of guy who would get his hands dirty, you know what I mean? Can you picture him killing Gardiner, strangling Whitmore, and then driving them to that park and torching their truck?"

"No. He's the type who would hire it done."

"Then, if he did, there has to be a money trail."

"We need a court order for his financial records."

"Yeah. Can you get going on that?" asked Joe.

"No problem."

Back at Area 3, Joe walked over to talk with Detective Tyrell Williams in Narcotics. Williams saw him coming and swung out his chair.

"You're back again. What's goin' on, Joe?"

"I spoke with a deputy sheriff from Asheville, North Carolina, yesterday about a plane crash that involves our acquaintances from here in the city. They were flying back from Charlotte when their plane went down and—

Williams interrupted. "Say no more, Joe. I already know about it. Lieutenant North called me this morning and told me he got a call from Asheville about it. Looks like I'm assigned to investigate on this end."

Joe was surprised at how quickly the crash and drugs had been filtered down to a detective in Narcotics. North Carolina authorities didn't waste any time contacting the Chicago Police Department.

"The wife was my life partner's best friend, but her husband was only an acquaintance. I only met him a handful of times, so I didn't know him all that well. But if we can be of any assistance, let us know."

"Thanks for the offer, man."

"And I'd appreciate it if you could keep me in the loop on this since Destiny has an emotional stake in this investigation."

"Yeah, sure."

Returning to his desk, Joe continued working on the final report for a homicide he and Sam closed when Virgil Simerdla confessed to killing and burning a man the deranged Simerdla thought was the devil. The Medical

Examiner's Office identified the victim as Charles Duane Costello, 61, a homeless veteran whose last known address was in Northbrook, Illinois. Simerdla is now undergoing a psychiatric evaluation to determine if he is fit to stand trial.

Shortly before noon, Sam walked over to Joe with a completed application for a search warrant seeking Paul Franklin's financial records. "You want me to run this application down to Judge Warner's office for a signature or hold on to it for a day or two?"

"No reason not to send it through. I'm finishing up the Simerdla report, so go ahead."

"Will do."

"Out of curiosity, where does Franklin do his banking?"

"Federal Bank and Trust. Same place I do. Main office is downtown."

"Gonna lay a search warrant on your own bank, huh?"

Sam smiled. "Nothing like shakin' up one of your own."

After lunch, Joe finished the Simerdla report and began a background check on Paul Franklin. He was born forty-five years ago in Chicago, the third son of Douglas Vernon Franklin and Isabella Sophia Ferlito. He graduated with honors from high school and summa cum laude from Loyola University with a bachelor's degree in business. Partnering with his father, he expanded his office supply business to multiple outlets and incorporated an online store, which became successful. Upon his father's death, he bought out his brothers' shares of the business and became the sole owner. When he was twenty-eight, he married Jamie Suzanne Steiner. They had two children: Penelope and Laura. Penelope was the victim of a kidnapping gone wrong last year. Their other daughter, twelve-year-old Laura, attends a private school. Franklin is a political conservative, and his net worth is around fifty million dollars. The family is affiliated with the Presbyterian church. Their residence is a multi-million-dollar townhouse on North State Parkway, the Gold Coast area of the city. A Jaguar F-type, a Mercedes-Benz sedan, and a Lincoln Navigator are registered in his name.

At forty-five years of age, Franklin appears to have the world by the tail. But Joe's gut tells him something about Franklin is not right. He needed to find out what it is. Perhaps Franklin's financial records will provide some insight. And if that does not pan out, observing his movements may tell them something. Hopefully, Judge Warner will not delay or object to signing the warrant.

While Sam was downtown, Joe got a call from Lieutenant Bellamy. Robert Bellamy was the permanent replacement for the head of the Homicide Unit, formerly held by the disgraced and imprisoned Lieutenant Yvonne Briggs. Bellamy came in from Area 2 and had extensive experience with their Homicide Unit. From Joe's limited experience with him, Bellamy seemed fair and open-minded.

Joe walked past the sergeants' desks and knocked on Bellamy's partially open door.

"Come in, Joe," said Bellamy, rising from his chair. "Have a seat. Where's Sam?"

"He's getting a search warrant signed downtown."

"I need to know what's going on with Paul Franklin. I got a complaint from his attorney stating you and Sam harassed his client when questioning him about a homicide."

"He was never harassed. We simply questioned him about his role in the death of Perry Gardiner, who was murdered along with his cousin, Gina Whitmore. When Franklin's daughter was kidnapped, he paid fifty thousand in ransom, which went missing. When the kidnappers were apprehended, they claimed they never received it. We found the ransom money hidden in the home of Perry Gardiner, who apparently had nothing to do with the kidnapping. Franklin had been tracing the marked money and had followed it to a cash purchase made at Home Depot by Perry Gardiner. Franklin's now our main suspect in the Gardiner/Whitmore murders."

"Got it. So, this complaint is just so much bullshit on his attorney's part."

"Yeah. Franklin wants us off his back, so he sicced his attorney on us."

"You have enough for an arrest?"

"Not yet. Sam's getting a search warrant for Franklin's financial records, email, and phone records because we believe he may have paid someone to dispose of Gardiner. Whitmore may have been an unwitting victim."

"Okay, I'll deal with the complaint. Just make sure you don't stir the pot any more than you have to. He's one of those rich guys with a powerful attorney on retainer who does what he asks. You know what assholes those guys can be."

"Oh, yeah."

Bellamy rose from his chair. "Good work, Erickson. Keep at it."

Joe interpreted that as Bellamy's way of ending the meeting. A lot different than Lieutenant Vincenzo's brusque, "All right. Get outta here."

As Joe was walking back to his desk, he met Sam, who was returning from downtown.

"The judge's clerk told me I should be able to pick up the warrant tomorrow morning around eleven."

"Was he sure he'd sign it?" asked Joe.

"He read it over and seemed confident he would."

Joe told Sam about the complaint that was filed, but before Sam lost his temper, Joe explained Bellamy would handle it. Sam was not fond of rich people jerking around the police just because they could, and it was one of the few things that would set him off.

"Well, good. Bellamy's okay if he agreed to handle it," said Sam. "I assume you explained things with your usual 'aptly chosen' words."

"Trippingly on the tongue."

Chapter Twenty-One

As Joe neared his house that evening, he noticed Vivien's white Lexus was gone. Either Destiny's mom decided it was time to return home or they decided to go somewhere. He entered from the garage and was greeted by Destiny, who had a stranger in tow, a petite woman pushing forty with sun-streaked blonde hair.

"Joe. Hi. This is Liz's sister, Jacquie Lambert. She flew in from Honolulu yesterday, and she called me this morning. I told her to come over to the house."

Joe shook her hand. "My condolences. This business comes as quite a shock to Destiny and me."

"Thank you."

"Your mom go home?"

"She decided to head back so she could pick up Otto before the kennel closed."

Joe looked at Jacquie. "Destiny told me you were in touch with the investigators in North Carolina. Have you learned anything new?"

Joe didn't know if Jacquie knew about the drugs or not and didn't know if he should mention that fact. He glanced at Destiny, who acknowledged, "She knows about the cocaine found on the plane."

"I've asked the detective in our department working as the liaison to keep me updated about their investigation up here. They've undoubtedly sealed their home by now. But I work homicide, so it's outside my responsibilities. There's not a lot I can do."

"Destiny and I were talking, and I can't imagine my sister would ever be a part of some drug smuggling operation. The thought of it just blows my mind."

Destiny added, "I don't think she could have been, either."

"It may turn out that she had no knowledge of any drugs aboard the plane," said Joe. "We'll have to wait for the investigation to play out."

"How long will that take?" asked Jacquie.

"It's hard to say."

Jacquie looked at Destiny, looking for clarification.

Destiny picked up on it immediately. "It could take some time. They'll want to be thorough."

She looked back at Joe, and he nodded in agreement and decided to alleviate her frustration by changing the subject. "Do you know anything about a funeral or memorial service yet?"

"My dad's gone, but my mom's still living. She took the news pretty hard. She wants me to take care of all the communication with the Harlows. Since I'm Liz's only sibling, it falls on me. I haven't been in touch with them yet, so I don't know what their intentions are. Maybe after the autopsies are done, and they're prepared to release the bodies, I'll hear something. If not, I'll contact them."

"Unfortunately, waiting is the way it works in a situation like this. Part of the problem is that we're dealing with multiple agencies when a plane crashes. You've got the state and local law enforcement, and then there's the feds— FBI, FAA, and NTSB. Each one has people on the ground conducting their own investigation, and each one is generating mountains of paperwork."

"Maybe the time factor is what's frustrating to me. I've already decided to have her cremated. Given the crash and the autopsy, there isn't much use returning her body and expecting an open casket. Mom's okay with it. A memorial service can be scheduled at any time. I just want it over with."

After an uncomfortable pause, Joe broke the silence by saying, "I think I'm going to pour myself a glass of wine. Would either one of you care to join me?"

"I don't drink anymore. But feel free. It won't bother me if you do," said Jacquie.

"Destiny?"

"No, thanks. I have water left in the living room."

"As do I, but don't let me stop you. I wish I could join you, but I take a medication that doesn't react well with alcohol. So, I can't have fun anymore."

Destiny smiled. "Oh, I have a feeling you have plenty of fun back home in Hawaii."

"Well, Hawaii is paradise for some and hell for others. It's all relative. For most people, it lies somewhere in between. That's me."

Destiny sensed her need to talk. "Come on. Let's go sit down."

Joe took Autumn for a walk. When he returned, he poured himself a glass of Pinot Noir from an opened bottle on the counter. While Destiny and Jacquie continued to chat, Joe knelt down and began petting and talking quietly to Autumn. He gave her a treat and she took it to her bed and began eating it. She still seemed unnerved by all the commotion. When he was done, he sat down at the kitchen island with his wine, opened his laptop, and pulled up a new page in a Word document.

He prepared to write questions, a technique he learned from a critical thinking course he took in college. At the heart of critical thinking is the ability to formulate effective questions. In theory, one question segues into another question, which leads to yet another question, and on and on it goes, producing more penetrating questions. And hopefully, these deeper questions lead to more critical thinking about a crime and its offenders. Having served Joe well over the years, he considers the technique a valuable tool in helping him solve homicides.

Joe began typing questions onto the blank page regarding Paul Franklin's participation in the deaths of Perry Gardiner and Gina Whitmore. As he began the process, questions flowed so quickly that he could barely keep up typing them. One page went by, and soon a second as his stream-of-consciousness questioning generated more and more questions. By the time he finished, there were five pages of questions about how Paul Franklin could be involved in the killing of Perry Gardiner. As he reviewed the questions, his thoughts logically led him to the theory that Franklin paid someone to punish Gardiner for stealing the ransom money and indirectly causing his daughter's death. Payback.

But what still didn't make sense was that Franklin never got his ransom money back. Could it be that, given how much wealth he had accumulated, the fifty thousand dollar ransom was a drop in the bucket, and vengeance was the motive? One would have to get inside Franklin's head to figure that out. Something he and Sam would pursue the next day.

Joe looked at his full glass of wine and realized he had yet to take a drink since he began his critical thinking exercise over an hour ago. When he began concentrating on a focused exercise like this one, time often flew by, and he became oblivious to his surroundings.

Destiny entered from the living room. She put her hand on his shoulder, jolting him out of his thoughts. "Are you getting hungry?"

"I don't know. I hadn't thought about it. I got lost in this work thing."

"Well, Jacquie and I were talking about going out to dinner. Would you like to go with us?"

"You sure I wouldn't be excess baggage?"

"Of course not. Why don't you come with us? You'll enjoy it. It's the Serbian restaurant we like so much."

Joe smiled. "I'm not going to pass that up. We need a reservation?"

"I already called it in. I assumed you'd go."

"You know what they say about 'assume?'"

Destiny kissed him. "Yes, I do."

Chapter Twenty-Two

Midway into his morning jog, an idea struck Joe about Paul Franklin. He was their primary suspect at this point, but if he killed Gardiner or even paid to have someone do it, why didn't he create a fool-proof alibi for himself? His wife certainly had one. According to Franklin, she was in California on the night of the Gardiner-Whitmore murders. Why didn't he go with her? It didn't make sense for him to be home alone with no one to give him an alibi. He couldn't be that dumb, could he?

If Franklin paid someone to kill Gardiner, there had to be some communication between him and the killer, as well as a financial trail for the payment. They needed to scrutinize Franklin's email messages and his financial records. Chances are he didn't use his regular email to communicate with the killer, so he must have a separate, personal email or made use of a burner phone. If he was a smart criminal, that phone and any such email messages would be long gone. But one cannot presume he was smart.

When Joe returned home and was making his breakfast, he asked Destiny about how long Jacquie planned to stay in Chicago.

"She's hoping to be allowed access to Liz and Jared's residence, but you know how that goes. It could take weeks for the police to release it. She's meeting with their attorney today to look into some legal matters and to see about their will."

"Staying in a hotel here will eat up a lot of cash. It might be better for her to go back to Hawaii and wait it out from there."

"Well, she can't stay here. I just got an offer for a consulting job from the police department in Seattle. I need this since the job in Denver fell through."

"It did?"

"They arrested a suspect."

"What's going on in Seattle?"

"They have a series of deaths linked to one person and want me to work up a profile."

"Another Green River Killer?"

"I hope not. It's bad enough they went through that once. That's why they're calling me in early on."

"When do you leave?"

"The day after tomorrow. Sorry it's on such short notice, but they want this done as soon as possible. I didn't get a chance to tell you yesterday when they contacted me."

Joe poured himself a second cup of coffee. "Hey, it's what you do. You have to go where the work is. Don't worry, I'll hold down the fort."

"As you always do."

"You sure you can handle it? Given everything…" He was concerned about her emotional state and whether it would hinder her from working effectively.

"I can. Don't worry."

Later that morning, Joe and Sam decided to wait until they got the search warrant before moving on Paul Franklin. They would examine his bank and credit card records first and then check his email messages. The search warrant would require Franklin to reveal any personal email accounts he may have in addition to his business email account.

Sam left and traveled downtown to pick up the search warrant shortly before eleven o'clock. Joe did not bring his lunch, so he left at noon, grabbed a salad at a Wendy's drive-through, and brought it back to work.

That afternoon, Joe and Sam took the search warrant to Paul Franklin's office. Carolyn Wilkins, his receptionist, confirmed he was in his office. Walking past her, they went directly to his office, opened the door, and entered. A surprised and annoyed Franklin looked up from his desk and rose from his chair.

"What the hell's going on here?" he yelled.

"Mr. Franklin," Wilkins started to say, "They just—"

"Shut up, Carolyn!"

That riled Sam, and he walked up to Franklin and shoved the search warrant in his face. "We have a search warrant for your phone, email, and all financial records. We'll need all your email accounts, phone numbers, and passwords."

"This is outrageous. I'm calling my attorney."

"Mr. Franklin?" asked Wilkins.

"Get back to work, Carolyn!"

Wilkins complied and returned to her desk. Franklin picked up his phone and called his attorney, who must have told him to keep quiet because when he hung up, he told Joe and Sam he wasn't saying another word, and they would have to speak with his attorney, who would be arriving shortly.

Shortly was half an hour, and his attorney, J. William Gilmore, walked in carrying his briefcase.

"I guess you don't take my threats seriously, detectives. When I said I was prepared to sue the police department, I wasn't kidding."

Joe responded matter-of-factly to Gilmore's bluster. "Your client is a suspect in the death of a man who stole the ransom money meant to free his daughter from her kidnappers, Mr. Gilmore. We don't kid around, either. I suggest you read the search warrant and have your client comply with it. Otherwise, we are prepared to place him under arrest."

Gilmore read through the search warrant and requested privacy to consult with Franklin. Joe and Sam left the room. Joe waited outside the door while Sam went to console Wilkins. After about five minutes, Franklin's office door opened, and Gilmore let Joe inside.

Franklin let his attorney do all the talking. "Mr. Franklin has nothing to hide and will comply with the stipulations stated in the search warrant. He will provide you with this information by ten o'clock tomorrow morning. You may retrieve this information from his receptionist at that time. Is that acceptable to you?"

"That would be acceptable, Mr. Gilmore. We will be here promptly at ten o'clock."

As Joe turned to leave, Gilmore said, "You haven't heard the last from me, detective."

Joe ignored him and walked to the lobby, where Sam was still conversing with Wilkins.

"Ready?" he asked Sam.

"Sure." Sam turned to Wilkins. "Sometimes our jobs can be unpleasant. Things will look up tomorrow. Have a good night."

"Thank you, Detective. I hope so."

When Joe and Sam reached the parking lot, Joe had a comment. "I noticed you're still cultivating."

"Hey," Sam replied, "We may need her cooperation in the future."

"Ah."

"That's all."

"Okay."

"Why? Do you have a problem with me trying to establish a source with Franklin's receptionist?"

"Oh, so that's what you were doing."

"Yeah."

"No, I don't have a problem with that."

"Oh. I thought maybe you did."

"No. Not at all."

"Okay."

"As sources go, she's pretty attractive," remarked Joe.

"Let's get back to the office."

Sam was flirting, pure and simple. Joe knew it, and Sam knew that Joe knew it, but he had a strange way of denying it. Truth be told, Joe did it, too, if he thought he could benefit by establishing a cordial relationship with a member of the opposite sex during an investigation. But he liked to good-naturedly needle Sam when he caught him doing it.

Back at their office, Joe and Sam discussed splitting up the research on Paul Franklin. They decided Joe would dive into his financial records while Sam would examine his email and phone records. But they could only begin once they received the contact information tomorrow morning.

In the meantime, they had other homicide investigations on their caseload, and they worked the rest of the day on those cases. Joe had his mind on Destiny leaving the next day. She would be gone for about ten days, the time it took for her to research the situation and develop a profile. He would need to make the most out of tonight.

When Joe got home, Destiny was in the bedroom, closing up her suitcase. "All done packing," she said as she placed it on the floor and wheeled it out of the way.

"What time does your flight leave?"

"I got a straight-through flight on United. It leaves at nine. I'll need to be at O'Hare by seven-thirty to check in and get through security, so I'll be leaving early."

"Want me to take you?"

"No, I'll use an Uber ride."

Joe followed her out into the kitchen and looked at the wine selection. "What are you thirsty for? Pinot Noir, Cabernet, Merlot?"

"How about Pinot?"

Joe opened a bottle of Pinot Noir and got two glasses from the cupboard. Putting one in front of Destiny, who had seated herself at the island, he filled her glass and then his own.

Lifting his glass, Joe clinked her glass and said, "To your Seattle assignment."

"Thank you."

"What would you like to do tonight?"

"I thought we could send out for food and spend a quiet evening at home. How does that suit you?"

Joe smiled. "That suits me just fine. You pick the restaurant."

"Thank you. I'll have to think about it."

They finished their wine, and Destiny said, "Come back into the bedroom. I have something to show you."

As soon as Joe entered the bedroom, Destiny turned, put her arms around his neck, and put him in a lip lock.

When he came up for air, Joe asked, "Is this what you wanted to show me?"

"For starters."

An hour later, they were drying each other off after a warm shower.

Chapter Twenty-Three

The next morning, the alarm rang at five-thirty, and both Destiny and Joe got up and readied themselves for her early morning trip to the airport. Joe skipped his daily jog to see her off when the Uber driver arrived.

Once Destiny was on her way and Joe had fed and walked Autumn, he left for work. Destiny always called or texted him when she arrived at her destination, and they made it a habit of talking each night. Whenever she was away, he threw himself into his work and cooked up a storm each evening so he would not think so much about her absence.

As Joe walked toward his desk, he spotted Sam at his computer already. He walked over and placed a cup of Starbucks coffee beside Sam's keyboard. Sam looked up. "Thanks, partner. You're getting in later than usual today."

Joe explained Destiny was flying out this morning for a job in Seattle, and he saw her off before coming to work.

"Batchin' it for a week, huh?"

"Ten days, yeah. But I have a little golden girl to keep me company."

Sam did a double-take, and Joe laughed. "The little golden girl is Autumn, and she's a dog. We're in charge of her until we can find her a home."

"I didn't figure you as a dog type."

Joe just shrugged. "I have to say she's growing on me."

"I'll get a squad car for our trip to Franklin's office this morning. They better have that stuff ready at ten, like his lawyer said."

Joe agreed. He was anxious to get started looking through Franklin's financials to see if there was any questionable spending.

At 9:30, they were on their way to Franklin's office. With morning traffic, it would take them about half an hour to get there. A few minutes after ten, they entered Franklin's office suite and found Carolyn Wilkins seated at her receptionist's desk. She looked up when they entered and smiled.

"Good morning, detectives," she said.

"Good morning, Carolyn," replied Sam. "Do you have something for us?"

Wilkins glanced toward the hallway leading to Franklin's office and looked back at Joe and Sam. Then she reached into her desk drawer and removed a sealed nine-by-twelve envelope with "Detectives Erickson & Renaldo" written on it.

"Mr. Franklin told me to give this to you."

"Is he in?" asked Joe.

Lowering her volume, she said, "He is, but he's not in a very good mood this morning. He just slammed that down on my desk as he passed by my desk on his way to his office."

"Thank you for this," said Sam.

"You're welcome."

Sam opened the envelope and slid out several sheets of paper. Looking it over, he glanced at Joe and nodded, sliding them back into the envelope.

"Looks like we have what we need. Have a good day, Carolyn," said Sam.

"You, too, detectives."

Outside, Joe nudged Sam. "So, you're on a first-name basis with her now, huh?"

"We got what we wanted, didn't we?"

Back at Area 3, Sam made photocopies of the documents in the envelope for Joe. They contained bank account numbers, credit card numbers, cell phone numbers, email accounts, and passwords to all the accounts mentioned in the search warrant.

Joe began by researching his bank accounts. Once he was finished, he planned to investigate Franklin's credit card expenditures. Franklin has multiple bank accounts, and it took Joe considerable time to sift through each account, looking for unusual expenditures.

At 11:30, Joe's phone rang. It was Destiny.

"I just got in and am waiting to pick up my luggage."

"You have a good flight?"

"Some turbulence over the Rockies, but not bad."

"Glad to know you got there all right. Call me tonight."

"I will. Love you."

"Love you more."

That afternoon, Joe was combing through one of Franklin's private savings accounts when he came across a large withdrawal–$10,000–three weeks prior to the deaths of Gardiner and Whitmore. That sent up a red flag. What would that have been for? That account was used primarily as a savings account with occasional deposits but virtually no withdrawals. He noted the account number and date and moved on to another account.

The next account had a considerable sum in it, more than Joe ever had in any of his bank accounts. What was unusual about this account was the automatic monthly withdrawals of $2400 to Deluxe Apartments Properties. Was this an apartment rented by his company for out-of-town guests or what? He looked up the address and phone number of Deluxe Apartment Properties. He found they specialized in luxury apartments, and the $2400 per month rental was on the lower end of properties they represented.

Half an hour before they were due to end their day, Joe and Sam met to discuss what they had found. Joe mentioned the mysterious ten-thousand-dollar withdrawal from one of Franklin's accounts three weeks before the Gardiner-Whitmore murders.

"We need to find out what that was for," said Sam. "I found a lot of calls to a particular phone number I couldn't identify. Probably a burner phone. But after the date of the murders, the calls tapered off and eventually ceased entirely."

"Those were on his personal phone?" asked Joe.

"Uh-huh. His business phone didn't show any unusual repetitive calls being made around that time. The most common calls were to his wife's number."

"Did you call that suspicious phone number?"

"I did, but it went to an automated voicemail."

"What do you think?" asked Joe.

"That ten grand is pretty suspicious if you ask me. More so than the apartment rental."

"And all those phone calls to that unidentifiable number. We need to know what that's all about.

Sam nodded in agreement. "Have you gone through any of his business records yet?"

"No. Just his personal banking records today. His business records could take me some time. He could easily bury money inside his business dealings. I don't know how long it will take me to get to his credit card records."

"I haven't started on his emails yet, either," said Sam. "I can take his credit card records if you get bogged down."

"You may have to."

Before going home, Joe stopped at the grocery store and bought the groceries he had on a list for meals he had planned for the next several days. Since Destiny is a vegetarian, he brought home salmon, tilapia, steak, and chicken breasts for his main courses.

That evening, he made grilled salmon on a bed of wilted spinach topped with asparagus spears and bearnaise sauce. Autumn watched the entire time, sniffing the air occasionally, curious about the unusual aromas. Accompanied by a glass of oak-aged Chardonnay, the result was exquisite.

After dinner, he walked Autumn several blocks, and when they returned home, he adjourned to the living room with Autumn by his side on the couch. Joe pulled up a Norwegian crime series he had been watching on Netflix, and toward the end of the episode, his phone rang. A call from Destiny."

"Did you get squared away?" he asked.

"I did. They put me up in a nice hotel downtown. I met with the head of the investigation team this afternoon and got the files I need. I'm meeting with the entire team tomorrow."

"Sounds like you're going to be busy."

"It always is the first two days. Then, I work by myself with occasional meetings as I need them. How are things at home?"

"Autumn had her nose working hard while I made my dinner."

CHAPTER TWENTY-THREE

"What did you have?"

"Salmon with bearnaise sauce."

"Seems she has a nose for good food. How are things going with your investigation?"

Joe went into what he and Sam were doing and what they were focusing on for the next few days. Then the phone went silent.

"You still there?"

"Just thinking. Given what you know about Paul Franklin, does he strike you as someone who has the personality or the connections to hire a hitman?"

Joe thought for a moment. "Not really. But you never know about people who have an axe to grind. And he certainly did. He had motive and the money to get even."

"You're right, of course. It's hard to tell how far tragedy and anger can push people. You need to keep probing. First-time criminals are prone to making mistakes."

"Yeah."

"If he's your guy, you'll find something."

"We have a lot to look through. I doubt he was all that good at covering his tracks."

They talked a while longer and then said good night. Joe returned to watching his brooding murder mystery and caught himself nodding off around ten o'clock. Deciding it was time to hit the hay, he gave Autumn a treat and went to bed.

Chapter Twenty-Four

J oe spent the next morning sifting through Paul Franklin's company's financial records. His income was considerable, but Joe was not concerned about that. He was most interested in the payments for the period before and after the Gardiner-Whitmore murders. The records revealed repeated payments to the same suppliers, building rentals, utilities, and employee salaries and wages. There were payments to heating and air conditioning contractors, advertising agencies, attorneys, and accounting firms. Nothing stuck out as suspicious or out of the ordinary.

At noon, Joe checked with Sam, who had concluded examining Franklin's emails on both his business and personal accounts. They decided to grab lunch at the nearest fast-food place where Joe could order a salad.

Sitting in a booth, Sam asked, "You find anything interesting this morning?"

Joe looked up from squeezing Italian dressing on his salad. "Nothing suspicious in his business accounts so far. Everything is pretty much repetitive from month to month. I didn't see anything he's tried to hide."

"Well, his personal email account wasn't helpful. A lot of emails to his wife and daughter. But there was one deleted email to someone named Stacey."

"What was that about?"

"A lunch date."

"How far back does that go?"

"About three months after his daughter's death."

"I wonder who she is."

"Business related?"

"Then why wasn't it on his business email account? There weren't any others?"

"Just a confirmation return email from her."

"It may be nothing. Or...it could be he's seeking comfort in the arms of another woman. Wouldn't be the first time a guy responded like that. A way of distracting himself from the pain of his daughter's death."

"Could be. But it's only one message."

"If he was having an affair, he'd probably use a burner phone. Anything else curious?"

"I didn't find any emails to anybody who could be a source for a contract on Perry Gardiner."

"He's too smart for that. He either used a burner phone or contacted him face-to-face." Joe remembered something Destiny said and then asked, "I've been thinking. How would a businessman like Franklin know how to contact a criminal capable of murder for hire? And do it for only ten grand?"

Sam thought for a moment. "Good question. Maybe the ten grand was a down payment. It could be somebody from his past who has a criminal background. A former colleague, someone he knew from school, a former employee..."

"Maybe. That apartment. I wonder where it is and if anyone's living in it."

"There's one way to find out."

"Bring him in?"

"No. Let me call Carolyn and see if she knows the address of the apartment."

After finishing their lunch at a little past one o'clock, Sam figured Franklin's receptionist was back at her desk. He called the number she gave him, which was her cell phone. After two rings, she picked up. He said he needed a favor and asked her for the address of the company apartment.

"As far as I know, the company has no such apartment," she stated.

"Oh," replied Sam. "I was under the impression the company maintained an apartment for out-of-town clients."

"That's news to me if we do. I can ask Mr. Franklin if you like."

"No, no, no. Don't do that. I must have made a mistake. If he's not in a good mood, he might not appreciate you asking about something like that."

"That's true."

Sam thanked her and clicked off. "She doesn't know anything about a company apartment for out-of-town clients."

"Good to know. Well, the real estate company isn't going to give us the address. Not without a warrant."

Sam paused. "Sounds to me like he could be using it as a place to rendezvous."

"Uh-huh. Maybe we should find out if this Stacey person is someone we should check out."

"If he's having an affair, when do you suppose he meets her? During the day?"

"That would be my guess. His wife would get suspicious if he was gone a lot at night. Maybe your friend, Carolyn, can tell us which afternoons he's not in the office."

"My friend," scoffed Sam. "Yeah."

"If we can use his mistress against him, maybe we can pressure him into giving up what he used that ten grand for."

After finishing their lunches, they returned to their office. Joe continued reviewing Franklin's business records while Sam began work reviewing Franklin's credit card charges for the months before and after the murder. By the end of the afternoon, they had finished with disappointing results. Nothing suspicious. But the ten-thousand-dollar withdrawal was sticking out like a canary among sparrows.

"Either he's brilliant at hiding money, or he amassed a lot of cash over the years and dipped into it for this," concluded Joe.

"That wouldn't surprise me. I'll call Carolyn tonight and see if she'll cooperate with us. She'd have access to the names of all of Franklin's employees and when Franklin took time off from work."

"Great. See you tomorrow."

When Joe got home, he took Autumn for a ten-minute walk, which he found as invigorating as she did. Once back inside the house, he began to think about the case as he prepared his dinner of grilled tilapia with mango salsa.

If Paul Franklin had a mistress during the Gardiner-Whitmore murders, did he actually have an alibi and simply did not want it known? Was he with her when the murders were committed? When his wife and daughter were in Sacramento? That would let him off the hook for committing the act himself, but that didn't excuse him from paying someone else to carry out his revenge. They needed a lead to connect him to a felon capable of murder. Without that, their investigation was at a dead end.

After an hour, when his dinner was ready, he poured himself a glass of Sauvignon Blanc, which paired well with the tilapia. He sat at the island and savored his dinner. Following the kitchen cleanup, he gave Autumn a treat and moved to the living room with his laptop. It wasn't long until his cell phone rang. Destiny was calling.

"How are you?"

"I had an exciting day looking through financial records."

Destiny chuckled. "Any progress?"

"We found out Franklin may have a mistress. And the ten thousand he withdrew from an account is still hanging out there suspiciously. We'll keep digging tomorrow."

"Well, I got some news from North Carolina."

"Oh?"

"The police reviewed video footage of Jared and Liz's plane sitting on the tarmac, and it shows someone placing the case of cocaine inside the cabin of their plane."

"That doesn't necessarily let them off the hook."

"I know, but it does create another theory about the drugs."

"Could they get a description based on the video?"

"They told me the quality wasn't good enough to get facial details. But they're operating

on the theory that Jared and Liz may not have been aware the case was on board."

"So, when they landed back here, someone would have been waiting to remove the case once Jared and Liz had disembarked."

"How did they come to that theory?"

"Neither Jared nor Liz's fingerprints were anywhere on the case or anything near it. And given the unlikelihood of their involvement in drug trafficking, they began viewing other footage of small private planes looking for a person placing similar cases aboard. They discovered one other instance with another plane."

"Have you spoken to Jacquie?"

"I did. She's flying back to Hawaii tomorrow. I told her I would try to handle some of the things in Chicago so she wouldn't have to make so many trips back. One other thing I found out from her—apparently, Liz had a will, but Jared didn't, so legally..."

"That could get messy with Jared's family."

"Uh-huh."

It got Joe thinking. "Do you have a will?"

"I do. How about you?"

"I don't."

"We need to have a talk about that."

Chapter Twenty-Five

When Sam spoke with Carolyn Wilkins the previous evening, she hinted that if he would take her out to dinner, she might be more inclined to check if anyone named Stacey was employed by A-1 Office Supplies. Sam didn't mind complying with her little quid pro quo, and they enjoyed a late dinner that night at a bistro not far from where she lived.

He found out that Franklin owned twelve stores around the city, which meant he had many managers, assistant managers, and employees. Carolyn stated since his daughter's death, his personality has changed, and he has become more insulated, seldom coming out of his office and rarely chatting with his office employees the way he used to. He relinquished many of his previous responsibilities when he hired a business manager to oversee the personnel and direct the day-to-day running of the business.

"Has he been leaving the office at various times on certain days?" asked Joe.

"She told me he takes Tuesday and Friday afternoons off. Claims he plays golf."

"Right. The game he's playing, you don't count strokes."

Sam laughed. "Yeah. I think we need to tail him. See where he goes."

"Carolyn's going to contact you about anyone named 'Stacey' today, right?" asked Joe.

"Right. I should have an email message from her sometime this morning."

"So, was your dinner date pleasant?"

"Yeah, it was. I told her I'd like to see her again, but I couldn't, given our investigation. She looked a little disappointed. So, I told her I would let her know when the investigation was over. Then we could go out to dinner again."

"Well, it's good she's agreed to help us."

At ten o'clock, Sam received an email message from Carolyn stating there is one person named Stacey employed by A-1 Office Supplies. "Stacey Berg" is an assistant manager of a store on West Fullerton Street in the Logan Square neighborhood. Joe and Sam began researching Stacey Berg on social media and other databases.

After viewing her photo on the A-1 Office Supply store website, Joe checked the Illinois Driver's License database and found she was Stacey Louise Berg, age 28. She is five-foot-eight inches tall, one-hundred-twenty pounds, has blue eyes, blonde hair, and lives in the Lincoln Park neighborhood. He followed that up by checking the Secretary of State's vehicle registration database and found she has a two-year-old red Hyundai Sonata registered in her name. After that, he checked her Facebook page and looked through photos and posts. She is a very attractive young woman with Nordic features. After some digging, he found her email address and matched it to the one message on Franklin's personal email.

Joe thought about the connection. That lunch with Franklin could be totally innocent, a meeting between the boss and one of his assistant managers. They had her home address and her workplace address. It would be easy to surveil her to determine if she also took Tuesday and Friday afternoons off. If she did, they could follow her and Franklin to see if they wound up at the same location. If they didn't, then maybe by following Franklin, they could find the rendezvous address and get a glimpse of someone else.

Joe met with Sam just before eleven o'clock to compare notes. They agreed that Stacey Berg was a good lead. Since today was Friday, they decided if they hurried, they could split up and set up surveillance on Franklin and Berg. Sam chose to observe Franklin's office while Joe drove to the A-1 Office Supply store on West Fullerton. Berg's Hyundai was parked behind the store. He found a parking place half a block away where he could keep watch on the storefront.

Joe called Sam. "Berg's car is at the store. What about you?"

"Franklin hasn't left yet. His Mercedes is still here."

"Call when he leaves. I'll do the same."

Joe waited and waited. He got there a few minutes before 12:30, and it was now 1:15. He was beginning to wonder if Berg was going to leave. Then, at 1:30, a black Honda Civic pulled up in front of the store. Berg walked out the front door and got into the Honda's back seat.

She's taking an Uber somewhere, thought Joe. He called Sam and let him know Berg had left the store, and he was tailing her. He followed the Honda to a tower on North Des Plaines Street, where she got out and went inside. Nice place.

Shortly thereafter, Joe saw a silver Mercedes pull into the tower's parking garage.

Joe called Sam. "You follow Franklin's Mercedes to a tower on North Des Plaines Street?"

"Yeah. Do I assume you're here, too?"

"Uh-huh. Stacey Berg got out of her Uber ride and walked inside. What do you want to do?"

"I've got my camera. I think I'll stick around and try to get photos of her coming out and him leaving. Maybe I'll get lucky and snap one of them together."

"Good luck. I'll go back to the office and get things together so we can bring him in for questioning tomorrow."

"I'll call you when I'm done here. Let you know what I got."

Shortly after 4:15, Sam called Joe from his position at the tower. "I got some photos. One of them together in the lobby. It's behind glass, so it's not Diane Arbus, but you can make out who they are. Kissy-kissy stuff. And I have shots of her walking to her ride and him leaving in his car. He happened to have his driver's side window down, so I got a good shot of him."

"Nice going. He can't deny this."

"Nope. Sure can't. See you in a few. I'm coming in to print these."

When Sam returned to Area 3, he printed half a dozen 8X10 photos on white card stock. The quality was quite good, and the images behind the glass in the lobby were better than Sam had initially let on. They were clear enough to identify the lovers as Stacey Berg and Paul Franklin. The one of them kissing was crucial in defining their relationship.

Sam handed the prints to Joe. "What do you think?"

Joe shuffled through them and smiled. "Nicely done, Sam. Let's go home."

Chapter Twenty-Six

Before they went to pick up Paul Franklin the next morning, Sam called to see if Franklin was in his office. The time was shortly after ten o'clock, and Sam figured most people would be at work by ten. Sam recognized Carolyn's voice when she answered the phone.

"Carolyn, this is Sam. Is Mr. Franklin in today?"

"He is."

"Good. We need to ask him some questions."

Quietly, she stated, "He won't be pleased."

"You're right. He won't be pleased. Keep this to yourself."

"No problem."

Joe and Sam arrived at Franklin's office at 10:35 and asked Carolyn to let Franklin know that they were there to see him. She rang his office.

"Detectives Renaldo and Erickson are here to see you, sir."

Joe could hear his response through her headset. Carolyn's expression turned fearful as she looked at Joe and Sam.

"He…He said he was…too busy to see you."

"But not in those words, though," said Sam.

"Not in those words."

"We'll see about that," said Joe, and he and Sam barged past Carolyn's desk and walked to Franklin's door. Sam opened it, and they walked in. Carolyn was right behind them.

"I'm sorry, Mr. Franklin, they just walked past—"

"GET THE HELL OUT, CAROLYN!" yelled Franklin as he came around his desk. Carolyn made a quick exit and closed the door. His rude response infuriated Sam, and Joe feared Sam would deck him.

"I don't care how busy you are, Franklin," said Joe, stepping in before Sam said something he would regret. "We need to ask you some questions, and you're coming with us. Now you can come willingly or in handcuffs, your choice."

Franklin paused, looking back and forth from Joe to Sam. "I want to call my attorney."

"You can do that on the way. Let's go."

Franklin was steaming. He reached for his suit coat and followed them out the door. As he passed Carolyn's desk, he said, "Call my attorney. I'll be at Area 3."

"Let's go!" said Sam as he grabbed hold of Franklin's upper arm to begin escorting him out. He turned and gave Carolyn a wink, and she tried her best to stifle a smile.

After arriving at Area 3, Franklin was placed in an interrogation room by himself. Fifteen minutes later, his attorney, J. William Gilmore, showed up and asked why his client was brought in. Joe explained they wanted to ask him questions based on the search warrant for his financial records. Gilmore asked to speak with Franklin and emerged from the interview room a few minutes later.

"I have advised my client to answer any questions you may have as long as I am present during questioning. Is that satisfactory?"

"That's satisfactory, Mr. Gilmore. Let's get to it."

They entered the interrogation room and sat down.

Joe began. "When we were perusing your financial records, Mr. Franklin, we came across a withdrawal of ten thousand dollars on May 11th. What was that ten grand used for, Mr. Franklin?"

"None of your business."

"It is our business, Mr. Franklin. It would be in your best interest to tell us. You see, we believe it could have been used as a down payment on a contract to kill Perry Gardiner."

"That's preposterous!" piped up Gilmore.

"Not preposterous at all," said Sam.

"Logical as a matter of fact," added Joe. "Your client traced ransom money spent by Perry Gardiner to a Home Depot. And as a result, he found out his identity. He blamed Gardiner, who stole the ransom money, for his daughter's death. We believe he wanted vengeance and, as a result, had him killed."

"That's not what happened," stated an angry Franklin.

"Then tell us what you used the money for."

Franklin sat silent rather than answer. After a minute of staring at each other, Joe broke the silence.

"During our investigation, we also found something you may find interesting." Joe looked at Sam, who slid the 8X10 photos out of their envelope and laid them between Franklin and Gilmore.

"What are these?" asked Gilmore.

Franklin looked at each one and then dropped them on the table. "You bastards!"

"It appears you've been paying $2400 monthly for a love nest on North Des Plaines Street."

"I must admit Stacey Berg is a very attractive woman," said Sam. "Does your wife know about her?"

"Go to hell!" replied Franklin.

After looking over the photos, Gilmore said, "I'd like to consult with my client."

"Certainly."

Joe and Sam left the interrogation room and went to get coffee. They returned and waited outside the door for Gilmore to come out. It wasn't long until Gilmore invited them back in.

"Mr. Franklin admits to an affair with Ms. Berg. It may be immoral, but it's not illegal. And his wife does not know at the moment, but he's planning to ask her for a divorce in the near future." He looked at Franklin and said, "Go ahead and tell them."

Joe and Sam resumed their seats. Franklin sighed deeply. "I...withdrew the money and...gave it to Stacey so she could pay for her breast augmentation. Those things aren't covered by insurance."

"Ten thousand for a boob job?" reacted Sam.

"Well, when you figure it all up…pretty much."

"We'll need to interview Stacey Berg to corroborate that," said Joe.

Franklin glared at him. "What do you want her to do? Show you her incisions?"

Gilmore quickly interjected, "I can arrange to show you the hospital bill if that will suffice."

"Yeah, I want to see the hospital bill."

"All right. I'll get a copy of that for you. Now, will you leave my client alone from now on?"

Before Joe could answer, Franklin spoke. "You know, I didn't want that shitbag dead. I just wanted my god damned money back."

"Maybe if you would have cooperated, we wouldn't be sitting here right now," said Sam.

Glaring at Franklin, Joe said, "I would have respected you more if you said you wanted him dead. Get your client out of here, Mr. Gilmore. He nauseates me."

Joe and Sam were both angry. They had spent an inordinate amount of time investigating Paul Franklin as a suspect in Perry Gardiner's and Gina Whitmore's deaths, and now they were back to the drawing board. They just sat there staring at their coffee. Then Joe thought of something and looked at Sam.

"Well, there's one good thing to come out of this."

"What could that be?"

"You're free to ask Carolyn out to dinner."

Chapter Twenty-Seven

That evening, after walking Autumn, Joe treated himself to a grilled, extra-thick ribeye steak with a smoked paprika rub accompanied by grilled potatoes and a sour cream and onion sauce. The preparation took his mind off his disappointment and annoyance about their case falling apart. And he compensated by eating delicious food. What would his shrink say about that?

After cleaning the kitchen, giving Autumn a treat, and pouring himself a second glass of Cabernet Sauvignon, Joe sat on the couch with his laptop and began reviewing his notes before Paul Franklin became a suspect. He still liked David Whitmore as a suspect, but Whitmore had what appeared to be an ironclad alibi for the night of the murders. Maybe part of his suspicion came from his dislike of the man. Whitmore was a prick, and Joe would like nothing better than to arrest him and hear handcuffs ratcheting around his wrists. But there is nothing illegal about being a prick. If there was, a considerable number of Chicago's citizenry would be looking out from behind bars.

After an hour, he closed his laptop, knowing it was not good to bring his work home. He was about to turn on the television and continue watching the Netflix mystery he had been following when Destiny called.

"How are things going?" asked Joe.

"I'm working on the profile right now. I should have it done tomorrow and ready for presentation the next day. It won't be long until I'm done and flying back."

"Great."

"How about you?"

"Well…our case against Paul Franklin fell apart today."

"Oh, no…"

Joe went on to tell her about the case they had been making against Franklin, the suspicious ten-thousand-dollar withdrawal, and the breast augmentation for his mistress.

"So, now you have to pick up the trail before he became your suspect."

"Yeah. Back to the beginning."

Destiny could hear the melancholy in his voice. "Sounds like you need a hug."

"I could use one about now."

"I'll make it up to you when I get back."

"Yeah."

She knew she had to say something to get him out of his present funk. She could have brought him out of it if she was there, but since she was out of town, she felt she needed to talk him through it.

"Look at it as a positive, Joe. You can reset your investigation and focus on evidence that could lead you in the right direction. That's a good thing."

"I guess it is."

"Of course, it is. When you're driving and you come to a dead end, you don't just sit there and brood, do you? No, you put it in reverse, turn onto another street, and try to find the address you're looking for. It's just a temporary detour."

Joe considered what she was saying and agreed. "Yeah…Well, that's what Sam and I will start doing tomorrow. Taking a detour."

"I know I'm mixing metaphors here, but it's like the old cliché, 'when one door closes, another one opens.' You'll see."

They talked for another half-hour, and by the time their conversation ended, Joe's attitude about his investigation had improved. Destiny often had that effect on him. She seemed to sense his needs and succeed in diverting his negative feelings. He sometimes wished he was as good at doing the same for her.

Rather than continue watching the dark Norwegian mystery on Netflix, he decided it would be better to watch something that would lighten his mood. *Young Frankenstein* was just the ticket, and he slid the DVD into the player. The Mel Brooks film was one of his favorites, and despite seeing it innumerable times, he still found it funny.

Joe was taking a drink of his wine when the film got to the part when Dr. Frankenstein and Igor were digging up a corpse in the cemetery. At that point, an idea flashed in his mind about the case and the area in Gardiner's backyard where the soil was disturbed. Then he thought to himself, *Not tonight, Joe. Tomorrow. You can take that detour tomorrow.*

Joe planned to meet with Sam the following day, but Sam called in sick. Bummer. He wondered if Sam had bottle flu or whether he had a hot night with Carolyn Wilkins. Getting drunk was not like Sam, so maybe he was sick. Or he was snuggling with Carolyn. Oh, well. He decided to go to the Gardiner house and check out the backyard's soil disturbance.

After Joe finished entering his notes into the computer, he checked out a squad car and drove to the Gardiner house. Opening the gate of the dilapidated wooden fence surrounding the backyard, he walked to where the soil had been dug up and smoothed over. Leaning down, he tested the area with his hand. It had been dug up, but clearly, it had been packed down. He examined the area closely. Because it had rained since the Gardiner-Whitmore murders, any marks made across the area had been obliterated. But as he looked around the edge where the soil met the grass, he saw remnants of marks left by what looked like a rake. Given how compacted it was, Joe doubted someone was attempting to put in a garden.

Residents are responsible for water and sewer lines on their own property, so there was no easy way to check if a licensed plumber had done work. But if it was a sewer or waterline repair, the ground would typically have been dug up all the way to the house. Given what he saw, Joe concluded that was not the case. The area was suspicious and needed to be investigated. They already had a search warrant for the house. Still, they would need another warrant for the grounds. So, when he returned to Area 3, Joe began filling out another application, citing evidence from a kidnapping ransom found in the house and something of value possibly buried in a recently excavated area in the backyard. He specified they are seeking a forensics team to check the area in question. Usually, Sam filled out their search warrants. He liked doing it, but since he was not in today, the responsibility fell on Joe. He was anxious and did not want to wait until Sam returned to work.

He worked through lunch and completed the application shortly after two-thirty. He ran it downtown to Judge Warner's office and left it with his judicial assistant. Hopefully, Judge Warner would have time to read it and choose to sign it by tomorrow afternoon so Joe could request a forensics team. He had a gut feeling Evidence Techs would find something there.

Maybe Destiny was right when she said, "When one door closes, another one opens." He left work upbeat and grabbed Autumn's leash when he returned home. She was ready for a walk and trotted beside him at a good clip. By the time they had walked around three-quarters of the block, Autumn had slowed her pace, and her tongue was hanging out. But when they rounded the final corner, she recognized the house and picked up her pace as they grew closer.

"Good to be back home, Autumn?" Joe asked her.

When they reached the front of the house, Autumn trotted up the steps and stopped at the door. Looking up at Joe, it seemed like she was saying, "Come on. Open the door!" Joe pulled out his keys and said, "Give me a minute, okay?" She woofed a response as he put his key in the lock and opened the door. Autumn trotted in, and Joe followed. They were in for the evening.

After disposing of the doggie waste bag, Joe looked at Autumn and realized he had become attached to this little Lhasa Apso. It would be hard if he had to give her up if Jacquie or her mother wanted her. And he wasn't keen on finding a home for her, either.

Chapter Twenty-Eight

Two days later, as he finished his morning jog, Joe contemplated two things he was looking forward to. First of all, Destiny was flying home today from Seattle. And secondly, since Judge Warner signed his application for a search warrant yesterday, and Lieutenant Bellamy helped push through a request to have a team of Evidence Technicians excavate the area in the Gardiner house's backyard. It was imperative the work should start today as rain was forecast for three days from now.

When Joe arrived at his desk, he received a message from Sam. "Still sick. Got tested for COVID, but the results were negative. Just have a nasty cold virus." *Thank goodness for that*, thought Joe. COVID is all I need right now. Joe emailed him a get-well image that had a picture of a dog drinking out of a toilet with the phrase, "Drink plenty of fluids."

At 10:30, he received a message saying the Evidence Technicians had begun excavating the Gardiner house's backyard. Taking a late lunch, he used the time to check out the Evidence Techs' progress. When he got there, he saw technician Art Casey standing beside the area where soil had been dug up. His partner, technician Jerry Bristow, was standing several yards away, speaking on the phone.

Joe walked up to Art, who was removing his nitrile gloves.

"You finished already?" Joe asked.

Art turned, apparently surprised to see him. "For now. We had to stop and call in a forensic archaeologist."

"Oh?"

"We discovered human remains."

Joe was a little surprised. He suspected something dubious about that patch of soil after he examined it. But he wasn't expecting a body.

"Really."

"Have a look."

Art led Joe over to the excavation. Peering down into the hole, Joe saw several rib bones attached to a sternum. Within the excavation, there was a white material.

"What's that white stuff?" asked Joe.

"It's lime."

"Lime?"

"Somebody probably thought it would help make the body decompose faster." Art chuckled. "People believe all the nonsense they read about or hear on television. That's a misconception. Lime doesn't do that. It actually retards decomposition. All lime does is cut down on the odor."

That was something Joe didn't know. "Learn something every day. It should come in handy if I ever turn to a life of crime." Art snorted a laugh.

After looking at the bones, Joe turned to Art. "This body wasn't buried very deep, was it?"

"No. Only about two and a half feet down. Whoever dug the hole only went down about three feet. Our ground scan found the anomaly right away."

Jerry Bristow finished his phone call and joined Joe and Art. "I take it this is your case, Joe?"

"It's related to it. I don't suppose you can tell how long the body has been here?"

"That's going to be hard to tell," said Art. "Even with the remains out of the ground. But if I had to guess, it's not hundreds of years old."

"Do you know when the archaeologist will get here?"

"Tomorrow," said Jerry. He looked at Art. "Guess we'd better get the tent set up, huh?"

"Will both of you be here?"

"Yeah, we'll be here to assist."

"Could you call me when he has the remains uncovered? I'd like to see if there's any identifying evidence."

Jerry smiled. "Curious, aren't you?"

"It could have a bearing on my current case."

"Yeah, we'll call you," said Art. "Or you could just stop over."

As soon as he was back in the office, he emailed Sam and alerted him to the body found in the Gardiner's backyard. In less than five minutes, he received an email saying he would probably be back in the office tomorrow full of Mucinex and a cough suppressant. Sam wasn't the kind of cop to miss out on a major revelation in a case.

Joe started making notes. Depending on how long the bones had been in the ground and whether an identification could be made, they would have to re-interview Perry Gardiner's mother and his father if they could. Perry had not lived alone in the house very long, but his parents and great-uncle's family had lived there for many years. The body could date back to the time of Perry's great-uncle and have nothing to do with the present murder case.

But if it did date back to when Perry's great-uncle's family was living in the house, why was it being dug up now? And by whom? Perry? Someone else? But who would that be? Why not leave it buried if it had been in the ground for a long time? It didn't make sense. But a lot of things about this case did not make sense.

Joe walked to Lieutenant Bellamy's office to update him on what the Evidence Techs found. He stopped at Sergeant Joel Pierce's desk, which sat closest to the lieutenant's door.

"Is the lieutenant in?"

"He is."

Joe knocked and stepped inside. "Got a minute, Lieutenant?"

"Yeah. Come in."

"Thanks for expediting the forensics on the backyard. It paid off."

"How's that?"

"Evidence Techs located human remains in that suspicious area in the backyard. A forensic archaeologist will excavate the remains starting tomorrow."

"Well...So, your suspicions were right. You think this has something to do with your murder case?"

"Hard to tell. Three generations of Gardiners have lived in the house, so the remains may have nothing to do with it. It all depends on how long the body's been in the ground and if the remains can be identified."

"But you're thinking it's recent, aren't you?"

"I do. Why would someone try to dig it up if it was really old? I think the body is fairly recent. And it has something to do with our case. That's my gut feeling."

"Then, keep following your gut. And continue to keep me updated."

"Thanks, Lieutenant."

Joe left Lieutenant Bellamy's office knowing he had Bellamy's blessing to follow where the trail on this investigation may lead.

At 4:15, Destiny called to say she had arrived home. She had not been gone that many days, but Joe missed her. He would see her in an hour, but it seemed like that last hour of work took hours to pass.

Once he arrived home, he was greeted by the aroma of something in the oven and a smiling Destiny holding a glass of wine.

"Welcome home," she said, putting her arms around him and kissing him.

"Mm. I should be saying that to you," replied Joe, kissing her back. "I missed you."

"You did?"

"Uh-huh."

"I was only gone nine days."

"I know. I missed you all nine."

"I missed you, too. I wish you could have come with me. Seattle is a nice place. But I probably wouldn't have completed my work on time."

Joe felt Autumn pawing at his leg. Looking down at her, he said, "Yes, Autumn. I missed you today, too." Leaning down, he petted her and pulled a treat from his jacket pocket. "Speak!"

Autumn gave a short bark, and then Joe gave her the treat.

Smiling, Destiny walked around the island and filled a glass with wine. "Here you go," she said, handing Joe the glass.

He thanked her and sat down on a stool at the island. "I assume the police were pleased with your profile?"

"Oh, yeah. I think it should help them narrow their search. Hopefully, they'll make an arrest before there's another victim." She sat beside Joe and asked, "How's your double homicide case progressing?"

Joe explained about the discovery of the remains in the Gardiner's backyard and the forensic archaeologist being called in to excavate the skeleton tomorrow.

"That complicates your investigation, doesn't it?"

"It may, if the remains are recent. But it opened another door."

"You think the remains are recent?"

"My gut's telling me they are, and they have some link to our case. I don't know what that link might be, but I'm determined to find out." After taking another sip of his wine, he held up his glass. "This is really good. What is it?"

"It's a Pinot Noir from a winery I found in Seattle. I had a glass while I was out for dinner and thought you'd like it. I checked with the Bottle Shop, and they had a few bottles in stock, so I picked them up when I got home."

"Nice. What's that wonderful aroma?"

"It's a surprise."

"Ooh! Another mystery for me to solve?"

"If you like."

"From the aroma, I'm sure it's worth waiting for."

"I hope so," she said. Then she tipped up her glass and finished the last swallow. "You'll just have to wait another twenty minutes." She reached over and poured herself more wine from the bottle on the island.

Joe clinked her glass.

"I hope you're hungry," said Destiny.

"You have no idea."

Chapter Twenty-Nine

Sam didn't live up to his message about coming in to work. Joe received an email stating he was still coughing and didn't want to infect others with his cold virus. Joe was on his own for another day.

At eleven o'clock, Joe left for the Gardiner house to view the work of the forensic archaeologist. Arriving at the residence, he walked to the backyard gate, lifted the yellow crime scene tape, and made his way toward the tent set up over the excavation. Art Casey and Jerry Bristow were working alongside a woman he had never seen before. The sun was shining with temperatures in the upper eighties, and the white Tyvek suits they were wearing had to intensify the heat because they were sweating profusely as they worked.

All three were busy using their picks and brushes, methodically removing small bits of soil. The entire skeleton was now in view, and they were concentrating their efforts on removing soil to expose more of the bones. They didn't notice Joe standing there observing until Jerry sat up and spotted him. He put down his brush and pick and stood.

"You here to help?" he asked as he reached into his pocket for a bandana and used it to wipe drips of sweat from his face.

"I'll leave this business to you professionals," replied Joe.

At this point, Art and the gray-haired woman also stopped working and rose to their feet, stretching and then joining Joe and Jerry. Handing them each a bottle of water, Jerry made the introduction.

"Joe, this is Dr. Maryanne Gillespie, our forensic archaeologist. Maryanne, this is Detective Joe Erickson. He's the lead detective on this case."

"Nice to meet you," said Gillespie. "I'd shake hands, but..." She held up her soiled hands. Rivulets of sweat ran down her weathered face, and she unzipped her suit to get some ventilation. Her white t-shirt looked soaking wet and clung to her as if she had gone swimming in it.

"Another time," replied Joe. "You found anything interesting?"

"Actually, we have." Gillespie took a long drink from the water bottle and then wiped her face with a handkerchief.

She gave Joe an engaging smile. "Sorry about that. Hot day. What I was going to say was, you may get a break identifying the remains."

"Oh?"

"Yes. Since the body was buried with no clothing, I assume whoever buried him didn't want him identified if the remains were ever found. But at some point, this male individual had a serious break in his right tibia. So serious, in fact, that a surgeon attached a metal plate to the bone to help it heal. Come here, I'll show you."

Gillespie walked Joe over to the excavation and knelt down. Joe knelt next to her. She pointed to the thigh bone with a pen, and Joe could see the metal plate with screws attaching it to the bone.

"These implants have serial numbers from the manufacturer that can be traced to the hospital where it was sold. And the hospital should be able to identify the patient who received the implant."

"That's good news."

"Without it, it could take months to go through missing person records and compare dental records."

Joe hoped Gillespie could pin down the time period so he would know if it was recent enough to impact his case. "So, can you tell how long this guy's been in the ground?"

"Given the soil and the condition of the bones, I'd say within the last twenty years, give or take. But that's only my educated opinion. The exact time is hard to pin down."

Joe looked at the sternum, which had a hole through it. He pointed and asked, "Is that what I think it is? In the sternum?"

"That, Detective, is a bullet hole. If the slug stayed in the body, we should be able to locate it."

"Let's hope it wasn't a through and through. So, how much longer do you think it'll take for the removal?"

"We'll have the remains extracted sometime tomorrow. Then your ME can take possession, track the implant, and hopefully send a slug to ballistics."

That was the kind of news Joe wanted to hear. The sooner they could identify the victim, the sooner he could set up an interview with Phyllis Gardiner and press her about what she knew about the person buried in her backyard. And Joe was not about to stop there. He would not be satisfied until he questioned her ex-husband, Bill Gardiner, about what he knew as well. But the fact he lived in Florida could be an impediment. Maybe he could get all the information he needed from his ex-wife.

Back at Area 3, Joe told Lieutenant Bellamy about the discovery of the metal implant on the leg bone of the skeleton. Bellamy said he would press to have the ME identify the recipient of the implant if things backed up. Joe was hoping the ME would be Kendra Solitsky since he had a good working relationship with her. She might be willing to do him a favor and expedite the implant's identification. He decided to call her.

"Joe. To what do I owe the pleasure?" asked Kendra.

"I have a job for you."

"A job, huh? As if I didn't have one already."

"We have a skeleton being excavated in a backyard, and it has a metal implant that a surgeon used to fix a badly broken tibia. I need the ID number on the implant sent through ASAP so we can get an ID on the remains."

"Who's doing the excavation work?"

"A forensic archaeologist named Maryanne Gillespie, along with Art Casey and Jerry Bristow."

"Oh. I know Maryanne. I worked with her a couple of times. Let me give her a call. I can make sure she notifies me when she needs an ME to pick up the remains."

"And you can expedite the serial number business?"

"Of course. I'll make it a priority."

Joe was glad to hear that Kendra agreed to assist him. She had done him the occasional favor in the past, and he always did his best to maintain a good relationship with her. Today, it was paying off. He would send her a bottle of her favorite single malt scotch as a way of saying thank you.

Good news came through on an unrelated front. A homicide Joe and Sam had been working on for several months closed—a domestic incident where they arrested a woman for killing her husband. His DNA was found on a kitchen butcher knife, and minute blood spatter was collected from the sleeve of her blouse. Given the history of domestic abuse, the murder charge had been pled down to voluntary manslaughter. On the advice of her attorney, the wife accepted the DA's plea deal. The woman admitted that one night, after giving her a beating, her drunken husband had fallen asleep on the couch. She snuck into the kitchen, got a butcher knife, and plunged it into his chest several times. Joe hoped she would receive a minimum sentence given the circumstances. He had no use for men who abused women.

Chapter Thirty

Two days later, Sam was back at work. He was still coughing occasionally, so he chose to wear a mask. But he said he was feeling much better. A lot had happened since he had been out sick, and it took Joe an hour to bring him up to speed on all the developments. They met in the interrogation room, which was not in use.

"Damn, Joe! You've been busy since I've been out sick. Maybe I should take time off more often."

"This stuff kinda fell in my lap. Now, it's hurry up and wait until Kendra gets back to me with the ID from the metal implant. It's key to identifying the remains."

"You think this has anything to do with the murders of Gardiner and Whitmore?"

"I don't know. What bothers me about it is why Perry was digging it up? It almost had to be him. He and Whitmore were the only ones living there. And why was it covered and packed down again?"

"Something of value buried with the remains?"

"The remains were undisturbed. The disturbed soil didn't go that deep, and the actual hole was off—the remains were about eighteen inches away."

"The question is," said Sam, "Who would want to make sure the body was never found? This guy was buried, partially uncovered, and covered again. Someone's got a lot to lose if this was ever found out."

"My suspicion would be either Perry Gardiner or his father."

"Or the great-uncle, depending on how old the remains are."

"The forensic archaeologist guessed within the last twenty years."

Sam began calculating. "Twenty years. Let's see. That would put Perry in his teens. Not likely, given what we know about him growing up. More than likely, it was his father."

"The great-uncle lived with them, didn't he?" asked Joe.

"Uh-huh. I'll have to check the file, but I think he passed when Perry was about twelve years old. He lived to be about seventy-five, if I remember correctly. If the remains are only twenty years old, we can't rule out the great-uncle. Could be the old man shot somebody he thought was an intruder or something, and his son buried the guy to cover it up."

"This is getting complicated, and at the moment, it's not getting us any closer to finding out who killed Gardiner and Whitmore. We need to find out more about this. Once we have an ID on the remains, we can question Phyllis Gardiner. She would have to know something about it."

"What about her husband?"

"Ex-husband. Undoubtedly. But he's living in Florida, so let's start with her, and we'll deal with him if we need to."

"Sounds good."

They left the interrogation room and headed for their desks. Joe began working on another homicide they had on their caseload. An elderly woman had been bludgeoned to death in her apartment two weeks ago. They suspected she came home and interrupted a burglary. There were signs of a struggle, and the jewelry box in her bedroom was open, the contents strewn on the floor. The dresser drawers also showed signs of being tossed.

Joe and Sam were waiting for fingerprints and DNA evidence to come back from forensics before they could move forward. They had a suspect in mind, a neighbor with a rap sheet for theft and assault, but they did not have enough evidence for an arrest. Hopefully, the forensics would implicate the person and lead to an arrest.

Shortly before noon, Joe received a phone call from Kendra.

"Are you ready for some good news?" Kendra asked.

"I could use some," replied Joe.

"I was able to trace the titanium implant's identification number from the manufacturer to Northwestern Memorial Hospital. It was implanted in the leg of Dennis R. Patton twenty-one years ago to repair a broken bone."

"Dennis R. Patton," repeated Joe, and he spelled out the last name to make sure he had it correct. Kendra confirmed his spelling was accurate.

"Did they provide you with any other information?"

"No. They weren't going to provide me with the identity, but when I explained the situation, they complied."

"Well, you do have a way with people."

"Mostly dead ones."

"Thank you. I owe you, Kendra."

"Yes, you do."

Joe began a search for Dennis R. Patton. He found a missing person report filed for a Dennis Reese Patton from July fourteen years ago. His wife, Renee, filed the report after he failed to come home for forty-eight hours. After an investigation, he was never located. The case remains open.

Joe began a search for Renee Patton and found that she filed for divorce from Dennis Patton five years ago. He also found a marriage license for Renee Williams Patton and James Stephen Calhoun dated four years ago. Further checking showed they live in Evanston. Joe noted the address and phone number. He also conducted a search for James Stephen Calhoun and found he is a chiropractor practicing at a clinic in Evanston.

After updating Sam, they decided to pay a call on Dennis Patton's ex-wife in order to learn as much about him as possible. After lunch, Joe called the chiropractic clinic to speak with James Calhoun since he could not find a link to where his wife worked. The receptionist told him Dr. Calhoun was with a patient and could not come to the phone. Joe explained the call regarded important police business, and that Dr. Calhoun should return his call as soon as he had time.

Dr. Calhoun proved to be prompt because, at 1:20, Joe received a callback.

"I received a message that a Detective Erickson called about important police business," said Dr. Calhoun. "Maybe you could clarify this for me." His baritone voice was very professional and without emotion."

"Thank you for returning my call," replied Joe. "I'm Detective Joe Erickson. Actually, we wish to speak to your wife. She's not in any kind of trouble.

But as you may know, her ex-husband went missing fourteen years ago, and we'd like to speak with her about it."

"I don't understand. Has he turned up or something?"

"In a manner of speaking. His skeletal remains were found buried in a backyard several days ago."

Silence.

Dr. Calhoun finally whispered, "Oh my."

"My partner and I would like to arrange a time to speak with her. To answer a few questions that could help in our investigation."

"Should I assume this was foul play or something?"

"You can assume that."

"Dear god."

"Where does your wife work?"

"She's the secretary at the First Methodist Church."

"So, would you rather break this to her, or would you prefer us to do it?"

"No, I'll tell her when I get home. It would be better if she heard it from me."

Joe was fine with that, but he wanted to emphasize the importance of a face-to-face meeting. "Would you have her call me to set up an interview? It's very important we get as much information about Mr. Patton as possible so we can find out who's responsible for his death."

"Of course. I'll have her call you first thing in the morning. Uh, look...I'm sorry, but I have to go. I have a patient waiting. Thank you for letting me know."

Joe walked over to Sam's desk and updated him about what he had discovered. Sam had been researching Dennis Patton and had found a photograph. He pulled it up on his computer to show Joe. Patton was a man with Hollywood good looks: medium brown hair, a winning smile, and handsome features.

"Kinda reminds you of George Clooney a little, doesn't he?" observed Joe.

"Yeah. Kind of," agreed Sam.

"Where did you find that picture?"

"He was an assistant principal of a school. His Facebook page was never deleted, and he posted photos of school activities, himself, his wife…"

"Interesting. I guess we'll find out more when we talk to his ex-wife."

When Joe heard Patton was a teacher, gears began turning in his mind. Phyllis Gardiner was a teacher, too. And he winds up buried in her backyard? That is a development worth pursuing.

Chapter Thirty-One

The next morning, Renee Calhoun called Joe and made a 1:30 appointment to meet with Joe and Sam at Area 3. She said she needed to find out any details she could regarding what happened to her late husband.

Right at 1:30, Joe got a call saying Renee Calhoun was waiting for a scheduled appointment with him. When Joe met her and introduced himself, he could tell she was a little uncomfortable about being there. Calhoun was a tall, full-figured woman dressed in a dark blue silk suit and silvery blouse. A petite silver pendant with a singular black pearl hung from her neck and matching pearl earrings adorned her ears.

"Thank you for coming in," said Joe. "I'm sure this news wasn't something you were expecting to hear."

"It certainly wasn't," she replied. "I found it quite distressing, if you want to know the truth."

"If you'll follow me, we have a room waiting where we can sit down. My partner is waiting there."

Calhoun followed Joe to an available interrogation room and was introduced to Sam, who offered her something to drink.

"Water would be fine, thank you," she said as she took her seat.

After Sam placed a bottle of water in front of her, they began their interview.

"Before we get into the details about your husband, could you tell us where he worked at the time of his disappearance?" asked Joe.

"He was an assistant principal at Warren G. Harding Elementary School."

"And had he been employed there long?"

"About five years."

"I see."

"Where was he found? All I know is what Steve told me. He was buried in someone's backyard?"

"That's correct. We were investigating a homicide, and when we were inspecting the backyard of the victim's home, we found an area where the soil had been disturbed. It looked suspicious, so Evidence Technicians were called in to investigate, and when they excavated that area, they found human remains. Your husband was identified by the serial number on a titanium plate in his leg."

Calhoun didn't speak for a moment, her eyes looking off into space. Once back in the moment, she acknowledged, "His motorcycle accident. A car ran through an intersection and hit him. Broke his leg rather badly. He wanted me to go with him, you know. And I would have, but my mother called, so I told him to go on by himself...Fate." She shook her head as she recalled how fortunate she was that day.

"Did he still ride a motorcycle after his accident?"

"Oh, yes. Him and his damned crotch rocket."

"Did his motorcycle disappear at the same time he did?"

"It did. He was riding it when he went missing."

"It was that unfortunate injury that made his identification possible. Otherwise, it could have taken months, maybe even years, to make an identification," said Sam.

"What kind of man was Dennis, Mrs. Calhoun?" asked Joe.

"Well...He was handsome and outgoing. He liked to have fun—riding his motorcycle, going Cubs and Bears games with friends, just enjoying himself. I can still see that smile of his and hear his laugh." She paused for a moment and then continued. "We liked to go out to restaurants, see plays, movies. He was popular with all the teachers in his school, and he was good with the kids and the parents. He could handle even the difficult ones."

"You have children?"

"No. We couldn't have children, and he didn't want to adopt, so we were agreeable to live in a child-free marriage."

"Understood," said Sam. "Kids aren't for everyone. From what I've seen in law enforcement, some people should never have had them."

"Do you happen to know Bill or Phyllis Gardiner?" asked Joe.

"No, those names aren't familiar. Why are you asking if I know those people?"

"Some time ago, Perry Gardiner and his cousin were found murdered. It was in the papers a few weeks ago. Maybe you read about it."

Calhoun shook her head slightly.

Without missing a beat, Joe moved on. "Anyway, they were living in the house on the property where your husband's remains were found. Several generations of his family lived in that house before he did, and we're trying to sort through how your husband came to be buried in their backyard. It's also possible the family had nothing to with it since the house remained vacant at various times."

"Obviously, this was foul play of some kind, right?" asked Calhoun.

"Uh-huh. It was determined he'd been shot in the chest."

"Omigod…I don't know what could have led to something like that. Dennis was never the type to get mixed up with criminals or get into altercations with anyone. He was such a jovial guy. I can't see him ever getting into a confrontation with anyone."

"A bullet was recovered from the excavation, and it's being run through ballistics to see if a match can be found to any weapons that may have been used in other crimes."

"Have you notified his brother about this?"

"No. Since you're his next of kin, we notified you. It's up to you to notify any other family members."

"I understand. Do you know when his body will be released? So we can hold a memorial service?"

"Right now, it's evidence in a crime, and further tests may need to be conducted by the Medical Examiner's Office," said Sam. "But we'll give the ME's office your contact information, and they'll call you as soon as arrangements can be made."

After a few more questions, the interview had drawn to a close.

"Thank you, Detectives. Not knowing what happened to Dennis has been a strain on me for years. After a while, I assumed he was dead because he would never have deserted me. I thought maybe some accident occurred, his bike collided with a car, and he fell in the river...all sorts of horrible things to provide some kind of an answer. But I never imagined he'd been murdered. This is just...." Tears rolled down her cheeks, and she dabbed at them with a handkerchief.

Joe looked at Sam who nodded that he had no other questions.

"Thank you for coming in, Mrs. Calhoun," said Sam. "We're done here unless you have some questions for us."

"I don't think so. Thank you for being so nice. I've never been in a police station before. I didn't know what to expect."

"We don't put a person in a dark room, shine a bright light in their face, and sweat answers out of them," smiled Joe.

Calhoun snorted a laugh, which caused a little snot to shoot out her nose. She quickly wiped it away and managed to smile. "That's good to know."

Joe walked her back to her Cadillac, and he asked if he could call her if he had any more questions.

"Of course," she replied. "I loved Dennis. He was a wonderful man. Anything that will help."

Back inside, Joe and Sam put their heads together and began discussing their next move.

The revelation that Dennis Patton was employed by Warren G. Harding Elementary School threw up a red flag since Phyllis Gardiner was employed as a teacher there, too. They needed to interview her, and they needed to do it today without an appointment.

Normally, Joe would have phoned Phyllis Gardiner's daughter, Julianne Hendricks, who asked that they go through her to set up any interviews with her mother. But he didn't want Hendricks warning her mother about their impending visit. Or worse yet, being there and interfering. If she did have something to do with his death, they didn't want to give her time to flee or do something rash, given her so-called "emotional nature."

In addition, he figured since this had the potential to involve personally sensitive information, Gardiner may not want to discuss it with her daughter present.

Joe looked at Sam and said, "Let's pay Phyllis Gardiner a visit."

Chapter Thirty-Two

J oe buzzed Phyllis Gardiner's apartment number, and after a few
moments, she answered.

"Ms. Gardiner, this is Detective Joe Erickson, Chicago PD. There
have been some developments in our case, and we need to speak with you."

"Can we set up a time when my daughter can be here?"

"This has to do with your previous home on West Victoria Street. We
found a person in your backyard. More precisely, buried in your backyard.
Are you sure you want your daughter present?"

Silence.

Over the intercom came a shaking voice that was barely audible. "No...not
this time." She buzzed them in.

Sam knocked on Gardiner's door, and it immediately opened wide for
them to come in.

"I knew this would come back to haunt me sooner or later," said Gardiner
as she closed the door behind them. "Let's go into the living room and sit
down."

Before Joe or Sam could begin, Gardiner began the interview with a
question. "How did you find Denny?"

Joe decided to answer her before they began their questioning. "There was
a disturbed area in the backyard, an area that looked as though it had been
dug up and then filled in and packed down. Because it looked suspicious,
Evidence Technicians were called in. They excavated and found the remains."

"Ah."

"Maybe we should start at the beginning. You knew Dennis Patton?"

"I did. He was the assistant principal in the grade school where I was a special education teacher."

"Warren G. Harding School?"

"Yes."

"And how long were you teaching there at the time of his death?"

"Seven years."

"Could you tell us how Mr. Patton came to be buried in your backyard?" asked Sam.

Gardiner stopped wringing her hands and placed them on her knees. Looking up, she got straight to the point. "Denny and I were having an affair. He was a good-looking guy with a lot of charm, and I was attracted to him. I wasn't the type to go looking for that sort of thing, but I could tell he was attracted to me as well. And my husband and I had grown apart in the last several years. I was feeling unloved and unappreciated. And his wife...well...it happened, what can I say?" She paused and began turning the ring on her finger.

"Okay. The affair happened. It doesn't explain why he ended up buried in your backyard," said Joe.

Gardiner looked at Joe, a little annoyed with his persistence. "I'm getting to that. This isn't easy for me. We tried to be discreet and plan our rendezvous with great care. On this particular summer afternoon, Bill had gone out of town with one of his Air Force buddies, Julianne was away at camp, and Perry's baseball team had an away game, so we thought it safe for Denny to come over to the house." She paused and took in a breath before she continued. "What we didn't know was Perry's game got canceled, and he came home and caught us. He...He didn't say anything. He just left the bedroom. We got up and started to get dressed, and then..." Tears began flowing as she tried to continue. "Perry flung the door open. He held up Bill's gun, and...he shot Denny."

"Perry shot Dennis Patton?" asked Sam.

"Uh-huh. It was horrible. Denny...he...he slumped to the floor. I–I went to him, and I could see he'd been shot in the heart. I tried doing CPR, but...it was no use. He was dead."

161

"What did you do?" asked Joe.

"Well...I hurried and got myself cleaned up and dressed. Then I tried to find Perry, but he'd taken off. He left the gun on the dining room table, so I wiped it off and put it back where Bill kept it. I didn't want to call the police because I didn't want Perry going to prison, and I didn't want the publicity—the scandal coming out would be horrible. I'd probably lose my job. So, I worked up the courage to call Bill and asked him what I should do."

"That took guts," said Sam.

"It didn't matter. At that point, I was planning to move out and divorce Bill anyway."

"What did he say?"

"He said, 'Don't do anything until I get home.' That's what he told me."

Joe looked at Sam after he finished writing in his notebook, making sure Sam had also written everything down. Then he moved on. "What happened to Perry?"

"Bill found him at the baseball field watching a game. He talked to him and then brought him home. He said he would make sure this incident would go away and everybody would forget it ever happened. And he emphasized to Perry that he should never ever speak about this to anyone, or he could go to prison for a long time. For all I know, he never breathed a word about it."

"And the burial?" asked Sam.

"Oh, god," Gardiner began. "Bill said we were going to bury Denny in the backyard, and nobody would be the wiser. Once it got dark, we started digging. He forced me to help. He said, 'This is all your fault, so you're gonna help dig.' So, we dug a hole, and then Bill carried Denny's body out, stripped off his jockey shorts—that's all he had on when he was shot—and laid him in the hole. Then he threw in some lime from a bag he'd used on the lawn, and then we covered him up. I found an apartment the next day and left. I never stepped into that backyard ever again."

"That's quite a secret to keep all these years," said Joe.

"I had to seek therapy to help me deal with it. God. I loved Denny. I really did. We'd talked about divorcing our spouses so we could be together. Maybe it was a pipe dream. But I loved him, and he said he loved me. I believed him. We were great together. I met his wife a few times at school functions. It's no wonder he was looking for love."

Gardiner dried her eyes with her handkerchief and blew her nose. "I can't tell you what it's like to be looking into the lifeless face of the man you love just before your husband pours lime all over him. It was horrible." Tears ran down her face, and she sobbed into her handkerchief.

Joe and Sam looked at each other, feeling helpless. "Can I get you a glass of water?" asked Sam.

Looking up from her handkerchief, she said, "No, I think I need something stronger if you don't mind." She rose and walked to a small cabinet. After removing a glass, she picked up a bottle of scotch and poured herself three fingers. She returned to her chair. "I'd offer you a drink, but I know you're on duty."

"Thanks, but feel free if it helps," said Joe. "It sounds like this is something you've needed to get off your chest for a long time."

With a shaking hand, she took a drink from the scotch, savoring it before swallowing. "It's been a cancer on my soul. I've lived with this nightmare for fourteen years. Telling you is like an exorcism." She looked down at her perfectly manicured nails. Then, looking up, she said, "Denny used to say he loved my hands. I've always kept my nails manicured. He said I...had...beautiful hands." To avoid breaking down again, she took another drink and then apologized. "Sorry."

"What did you do with Patton's car?" asked Sam, knowing that Patton rode his motorcycle. He was testing her story. "I assume he drove to your house."

"He rode his motorcycle. Bill rode it to an area in the city where he knew it would get stolen if he left it there. He wore gloves so he wouldn't leave any fingerprints on the bike. I followed and picked him up after he parked it. Then we drove back to the house."

"Does your daughter know about any of this?"

"No. No, she knew her dad and I weren't getting along, so my moving out and filing for divorce came as no surprise. She came to live with me, and Perry stayed with his dad. Ever since, he's held a grudge and hasn't wanted much to do with me."

"Do you have any idea why someone would try to dig up Patton's remains? That's what led us to the area in the backyard in the first place."

"I don't know. If I had to guess, I'd say Perry had something to do with it. He's been mentally unstable, and I wouldn't put it past him to do something outrageous like that."

Sam had been listening, holding back on his own questioning, but he had one crucial question he wanted to ask Gardiner. "Is it possible someone found out that Perry was responsible for Patton's death and killed him for it?"

Gardiner was taken somewhat aback by his question and paused before answering. "No, I don't think that's possible. I know my ex-husband would never have spoken of it to anyone. I certainly didn't. Julianne never knew about it, and I don't think Perry would've said anything, given he could've gone to prison."

Joe closed his notebook. He felt the interview was over. He looked over at Sam. "Any more questions for Ms. Gardiner?"

"No, I think we have what we came for."

"Before you go...I have a question for you," said Gardiner. "Does Denny's wife have to know about this? I mean, I'd hate to see his memory tarnished with her knowledge of our...indiscretion."

"That may be difficult," replied Sam. "It all goes to the motive behind his murder."

"If she wants to know the full story, it's going to come out," added Joe. "And you never know about the press. It makes a compelling story for some intrepid reporter looking for a scandal to expose."

"Dammit. I was hoping that wouldn't happen. She deserves to remember him fondly."

"One good thing, though. You and your ex-husband won't be charged with the illegal disposition of a body since the statute of limitations has passed."

"Thank goodness for small miracles, huh?" Gardiner took another drink from her scotch. "Are we done here?"

Joe and Sam rose. "We are," said Joe.

As they opened the door to go, Sam turned to Gardiner. "Thank you for your time."

"We appreciate how candid you were about everything," added Joe. "I hope this gives you some peace."

As they were walking to the car, Sam asked, "How would you like to carry that around with you for over a decade?"

"That would be tough. No wonder she sought therapy in order to deal with it."

"Maybe all this had something to do with Perry's mental problems. Suppose?"

Chapter Thirty-Three

When Joe arrived home that evening, Destiny wasn't there. A note on the kitchen island said she had gone to the grocery store to pick up a couple of items and she would be back shortly.

Joe took Autumn for a walk around the block. Once back in the house, he opened a bottle of Pinot Noir and poured himself a glass. After giving Autumn a treat, he sat down at the island, pulled out his notebook, and began reviewing his notes from the interview with Phyllis Gardiner. He read over the part where she said she believed Perry was the one who may have been digging up the backyard.

He began writing questions. Why was the hole covered up again? Neatly filled in and packed down? If Perry was looking for the remains, why didn't he keep digging until he found them? Did someone else fill in the hole to cover up his digging? Could that have anything to do with his death?

Joe was well into his questions when the door to the garage opened, and Destiny entered. She was carrying two large bags of groceries, which she placed on the counter.

"Hi, sweetheart," said Destiny.

"You talking to me or the dog?"

"Both."

"Your note said you were going to pick up 'a couple' of things," kidded Joe. "That doesn't look like a couple to me."

"Once I got there, I saw more and more items we needed. I got carried away." She looked over at his full wine glass. "You just get home?"

"No, I've been home for forty-five minutes or so."

"Just wondering. Your wine glass is full."

"Oh. Well, I was reviewing my notes from an interview today. I got lost in thought and was writing questions about something she said."

"Mm. You want to help me put this stuff away or go back to your questions?"

"I'll help. My concentration's broken now. I'll get back to thinking about the interview tomorrow."

"Care to talk about it later?"

"Sure."

Once they put away the groceries, Destiny poured herself a glass of wine and sat next to Joe at the island.

"I got news about Liz and Jared today."

"Oh, yeah?"

"Jacquie called and said the authorities in North Carolina released the bodies. They called her and asked what she wanted to do, so she contacted Jared's family. They agreed with her that they should both be cremated. I guess Jared's brother is going to bring back the cremains so they can organize a memorial service."

"Will Jared's family be taking care of the arrangements?"

"Apparently, since Jacquie doesn't live here, her mother has decided to talk with the Harlows."

"That makes sense. Is she okay with that?"

"She is. But an issue may create a fissure between her and Jared's parents. Liz had a will, but Jared didn't. Jacquie told me that Liz named her and her mother as the beneficiaries."

"So, does that mean their entire estate will go to Jacquie and her mother since Jared didn't have a will?"

"She checked with an attorney, and he said that's the case. Jared's family won't be inheriting anything."

Joe shook his head, incredulous about Jared's gross negligence about a will. "I know this sounds hypocritical coming from me, but how could someone like Jared, who had so many assets, fail to have a will?"

"Same reason you don't have one, I suppose. He never got around to it.

It didn't seem like a priority, given his age and good health. I'm going to make an appointment for you to speak with my attorney so you can have one drawn up. Given your line of work, you need one."

"I'll leave everything to you."

"That's up to you."

"You're all I've got. Who else would I leave it to?"

"Some charity."

"I'd rather leave everything to the one I love."

That was worth a kiss. "You're sweet." Destiny had enough of this dreadful discussion and decided to change the subject.

"Jacquie's going to be flying in next week. I think she's assuming there'll be some sort of memorial service soon. She'll need to be here for the reading of Liz's will and deal with the legal wrangling that she thinks will happen."

"If she needs someone to put Jared's cars on the market so she can get the best price out of them, I can help her with that."

"I'll let her know."

After a dinner of Mushroom Bolognese, Joe and Destiny settled into the living room. Destiny wanted to learn more about what Joe discovered during his interview with Phyllis Gardiner.

Joe related Gardiner's narrative about her affair with Dennis Patton, Perry Gardiner's discovery of them in bed together, and the subsequent shooting and burial. Destiny was all ears.

"That poor woman," she said. "Seeing her lover murdered by her son and then forced to help bury him in the backyard. And living with it for years. How awful."

"Yeah, and it doesn't get us any closer to who killed Gardiner and Whitmore."

"It sounds like revenge, but it's been too long for someone to take action for something that happened, what? Fifteen years ago?"

"About. Yeah."

"Where's your investigation going now that you know this?"

"Keep digging and hope something turns up, so to speak. There has to be a motive to kill and burn up those two people. I can't help feeling someone was trying to send a message. And Dennis Patton may have nothing to do with it."

"Or making it look like someone is sending a message."

"What do you mean?"

"Creating a red herring to throw you off. What if the person who killed Perry Gardiner and his cousin chose to make it look like a message was being sent? By a drug dealer or some other organized crime figure. That would throw suspicion away from a murder caused by another motive."

"That would be clever, and I've considered that. I checked about a drug connection with Tyrell Williams in Narcotics, and his informants reported Perry was an occasional buyer but only enough for personal use. There's no evidence he was ever a seller."

Destiny took a sip of her wine as she thought, then looked at Joe. "What's that leave? The top five organized crime rackets are counterfeiting, drug trafficking, human trafficking, illegal logging, and fuel theft. Think he could have become involved with any of these?"

"Logging? No, I can't see him hijacking logs," chuckled Joe.

"Seriously. It's a global problem. Cities and countries lose billions in uncollected taxes each year."

"I don't think he was mixed up in organized crime. He wasn't the type. He was mentally unstable when he came back from San Francisco, and organized crime wouldn't deal with someone like that."

"Mentally unstable. You said he was confrontational some time back, right?"

"Yeah."

"You know, if he ran into the wrong persons in a bar or someplace, and he offended them or got into an altercation, it wouldn't take much for them to find him and teach him a lesson. Stuff like that happens."

"Gang members?"

"Maybe. Who knows? Could be anyone with violent tendencies. There's an endless supply of violent, sick people in this city."

At that point, Autumn put her paws up on the couch and looked at Joe. Destiny smiled.

"She seems to have attached herself to you. I think she has a crush."

Joe pulled Autumn up and placed her on his lap. Looking at her, he said, "Is this what you want?" Autumn responded by licking him on the cheek.

"See what I mean. Remind me to kiss the other cheek," said Destiny.

"I guess I have two girls, now, don't I?" He leaned over to Destiny and whispered, "Don't tell Autumn, but I like you best."

"I should hope."

Chapter Thirty-Four

When Joe returned from his morning jog, Destiny pointed to the *Tribune* on the kitchen island. The newspaper was open to a page with the headline "Skeletal Remains Found in Backyard." Joe checked the byline, expecting it to be his contact, Margaret Kummeyer, but was surprised to see the reporter was Jack Waller. That prevented him from calling to find out how word slipped out.

He sat down and began reading the article. Short on detail, it listed the address and reported the remains were found by police forensic technicians at the home of two murder victims. The article went on to state that the Office of the Medical Examiner was handling the identification of the remains.

Destiny set down a cup of coffee in front of Joe and said, "Only a matter of time before the news came out."

"I wonder who leaked it."

"It doesn't matter. I'd be willing to bet the Sun-Times has an article about it in today's edition as well. It's a story with too much of a human-interest angle to go unreported."

"Reporters are going to be all over this."

"You may have to start practicing your "No comment" line," Destiny mused.

Joe looked up. "No comment."

When Joe arrived at work, he went to his desk and logged in to his computer. Sam dropped a copy of the Sun-Times next to him a few seconds later.

"What's this?" asked Joe, pretty sure he knew what it was about.

"Turn to page seventeen. There's an article about our backyard discovery."

Joe found the article and read it. It contained much the same information as the one he read in the Trib, with one exception. This one stated, "Police are not saying if the remains are tied to the two murder victims living in the house."

Joe sighed and handed the paper back to Sam. "There was an article in the Trib this morning, too. Looks like the story's out."

When Sam returned to his desk, Joe pulled out his notebook and got back to the questions he was asking the previous evening. Half an hour into his probing, the phone on his desk rang.

"Detective Erickson."

A man tentatively said, "Uh...I was told you're the one looking into the death of Perry Gardiner. Is that right?"

"That's correct. How can I help you?"

"Well, I have some information that might be of some use to you. I...I don't know how important it is. But I thought you might like to know about it."

"What kind of information are you talking about?"

"I met with Perry at his place shortly before he was killed. And he said some things. Weird things, you know. And then, when I read the article in the *Sun-Times* this morning, it all sorta made sense."

Joe felt this could be something important and wanted to pursue it. "Okay. Could I get your name, please?"

"Sure. It's Bruce, Bruce Canfield. I was a friend of Perry's from high school."

Joe took down Canfield's contact information and arranged a time for him to come in for an interview that afternoon. After he hung up, he told Sam about the call and the interview.

"So, he just called out of the blue?" asked Sam.

"He saw the article in the *Sun-Times* and decided to call in. Said he met with Gardiner shortly before he was killed. Says he has some information that might be important."

"Thank the Lord for good citizens. Hopefully, what he considers important is what we consider important. What time's he coming in?"

"Two o'clock."

Sam returned to his desk, and Joe continued probing when Destiny called. "Hi. What's up?"

"I just got a disturbing message from the Sheriff's Office in North Carolina. They said the NTSB found the engine in Jared's plane had been tampered with."

Joe could tell by Destiny's voice that she was upset by the news. It was certainly something that neither of them anticipated. Because of the cocaine found aboard, all sorts of conflicting ideas began running through Joe's mind.

"Did they give any details?"

"Yeah," replied Destiny. "Something about a loosened fitting on the oil cooler and contamination in the oil. Sounds like sabotage."

"Okay. Let me talk to the detective who's the contact on our end. See if he knows anything else. I'll get back to you as soon as I know something."

Joe walked to Tyrell Williams' desk and waited for Williams to finish a phone call. Joe made his presence known once he ended his call and finished writing a note.

"Hey, Tyrell."

"Joe. You didn't give me any time to call you."

"I assume you've had some updates from our friends in North Carolina?"

"Yeah. As a matter of fact...I had a conversation with the Sheriff's Office about the preliminary findings by the NTSB. Somebody wanted to bring that plane down, Joe. Somebody wanted Jared Harlow dead."

"Destiny got a call from her contact down there, and they told her they found evidence the engine had been tampered with. Is that what they told you?"

"Damn, man! She must have a good source. But yeah. That's what I was told."

"What about the coke? Does this put a different spin on it?"

"Yeah, and it doesn't make sense to me. Why waste all that coke? They're gonna have to sort all that out. We haven't found anything up here to provide a motive or give them any leads."

"I'd guess the sabotage and the coke aren't connected. Two separate incidents."

"That would explain a lot."

"What about Jared's wife?"

"Collateral damage, apparently. Sorry." Williams stood up and stretched. "Did you know they released the bodies?"

"Yeah. Well, let me know if something pops up, okay?"

"You got it."

Joe returned to his desk and concentrated on paperwork from other cases until his lunch break. Then he called Destiny and told her he'd confirmed what she had found when he spoke with Detective Williams. He had not learned anything more than she had.

"Who would have sabotaged their plane? And for what reason?" asked Destiny.

"Tyrell told me they haven't turned up any information here that would have motivated something like that. It sounds like it's in the hands of the authorities in North Carolina."

Joe could hear the frustration in Destiny's voice. "I want to go down there so bad, but I don't think it would do any good. And I don't think they would appreciate it if I showed up and tried to insert myself into their investigation."

Joe needed to do what he could to relieve her frustration. "Why don't you join me for lunch, and we can talk about this."

"I'd like to, but I have a session with my martial arts instructor at one o'clock. I'm sure I'll feel better after I work out some of these negative vibes."

"Okay. I pity the fool."

Joe heard her snicker. "Love you," she said. "Talk with you later."

Two o'clock rolled around, and Bruce Canfield had not arrived for his interview. Finally, at ten after, Joe got a call saying he had arrived. Joe, who believed "on time" was five minutes early, made a mental note about Canfield's lateness and walked to Sam's desk.

"Canfield's finally here. I'll go get him."

Sam got up from his desk. "Okay, I'll make sure the interrogation room's ready."

Joe walked into the public access area and saw a man in his mid-twenties standing with his hands in his pants pockets. He was dressed in khakis, a burgundy t-shirt, and a tweed blazer. He turned when Joe entered.

"Bruce Canfield?" asked Joe.

"That's right," replied Canfield. "Sorry, I'm late. My taxi got stuck in traffic."

"Yeah. It happens. I'm Detective Erickson."

After exchanging a handshake, Canfield followed Joe to the interrogation room, where he was introduced to Sam. Canfield looked around the room, spotting the two-way mirror and the other interrogation elements.

"Am I being interrogated?" he asked, looking at Sam.

"We don't have a lot of visitors, as you could tell by our waiting area, and we aren't set up here with a nice conference room, so we have to make do," replied Sam. "Can I get you anything to drink?"

"Coffee, if you have it."

"We do."

Sam got coffee for Canfield as well as himself, and they all sat down at the table. Joe flipped open his notebook and skimmed his notes from their telephone call.

"You said you had information about Perry Gardiner that we might find helpful. Could you explain?"

"Yeah...Uh...I live in Naperville, and when I heard Perry was back from living in California, I thought I would look him up, you know. We went to high school together and went to the same university for a year. He dropped out and joined the Coast Guard, and I continued on and got a degree."

"How did you hear he was back in the city?" asked Sam.

"His mother spoke to my mother, and she told me."

"Go on."

Well, I drove into the city one day on business, and I thought I would look him up. I didn't know his phone number, so I dropped by the house. It was around five o'clock, and I thought we could drink a couple of beers and catch up, see?"

175

"Did you find him at his father's house?" asked Joe.

"Yeah. I wanna tell you, I was shocked when I saw him. He was always so neat about his appearance, but he looked so shabby—long hair and a beard. He and this girl came to the door and invited me in. I brought a six-pack with me, and we sat down on some old couches in the living room and started drinking beer. I have to tell you…he wasn't the Perry Gardiner I once knew."

"Care to explain that?"

"His language was laced with so many obscenities, it was like every other word was one of the seven words you can't say on television. He never used to talk like that. I mean…I'm not a prude or anything. My dad was a truck driver. I heard him use salty language once in a while when I was growing up. But man…" He took a sip of his coffee.

"Is that what you wanted to tell us?" asked Joe.

"No. After a couple of beers, things got weird. I mean really weird. Perry started talking about how a ghost was haunting him. He wasn't just yanking my chain. He was serious. He said a dead guy from the past was coming to him at night and waking him up. Standing over his bed. Said he couldn't sleep through the night anymore."

Joe and Sam looked at each other. "Did he say who it was?" asked Joe.

"No, he never mentioned a name."

"Did he say anything about doing something? To put this ghost to rest, maybe?"

"No. He didn't say anything specific about exorcising the spirit, that kind of thing."

"Did he say anything else?"

"Well, he said it was like…revenge or something or some crazy thing like that. I dunno."

Canfield ran his fingers through his blonde hair and looked up. "He asked me if I believed in ghosts. If I believed the dead could come back and haunt people. I told him I hadn't thought about it. And he went on to say that I should because ghosts were real. And he couldn't live with it any longer and had to do something to make the spirit rest, but he didn't say what. It got so spooky, I had to leave."

"Did you see much of his cousin, Gina?"

"She never spoke. She sat there listening, staring at me. That was unnerving, too. But when I stood up to go, she went over to Perry, and he said something to her. I didn't hear what it was, but she followed me. And before I got to the door, she stopped me and leaned in and said in this quiet voice, 'Why don't you stay longer?' Then she stepped back and pulled up the front of her dress, and I saw she wasn't wearing any underwear. I about shit! I mean, what the hell was that about? I thought, 'Is this some sick version of the Addams Family here or something?'"

"What did you do?" asked Sam.

"Pushed her the hell away from the door and got out of the place as fast as I could. I drove to a hotel, checked in, and went down to the bar and got hammered. I couldn't deal with the whole thing, what happened to Perry and his weird cousin. Just a nightmare. And then when I heard he was murdered, I thought, 'Wow. This is like something out of a horror movie.'"

Canfield picked up his cup. His hand shook so badly that coffee sloshed over the side. "Christ," he mumbled as he looked at the spill on the table.

"Don't worry about it," said Sam, who pushed a couple of napkins in his direction. "I do that every so often."

Canfield put his cup down and soaked up the spill. "Sorry. It's unnerving to talk about this. Perry and I were pretty close years ago. I thought he was destined to be a writer of some kind. He had what it took. A great mind. He wrote some cool short stories in English class. And he was a likable guy, too. What he became was...a tragedy."

Canfield removed his glasses, reached into his pocket, and pulled out a handkerchief to wipe the perspiration from his face and neck.

"What we've found so far paints a picture of Perry as a disturbed individual," said Sam. "Something happened that changed him after he left the Coast Guard. We may never find out what it was, whether it was a bad experience in the service, drugs, or both, but our main focus is finding his killer."

Putting his glasses back on, Canfield replied, "Yeah. He didn't deserve to die, especially like that. Maybe with psychiatric treatment, Perry could have been helped. Brought back from...Who knows what."

"Is there anything else you can tell us about your visit with Perry?" asked Joe.

Canfield thought for a moment and then said, "I don't think so."

"What about his mother and father?"

"His dad was a nice guy. I never met his mom. She wasn't around. He blamed her for the divorce, but I never knew why. He never said what it was. I saw his sister a couple of times, but I never knew her. She was older and lived with her mom."

"Anything else?" asked Sam.

"Not that I can think of."

Joe rose from his chair. "Thank you for contacting us, Mr. Canfield. Your information has been helpful."

"If you think of anything else, please let us know," added Sam, handing him his card.

Canfield stood and took a final sip of his coffee. "I will. I'm glad it helped."

Sam escorted him out of the building while Joe cleared Canfield's coffee cup and napkins. When Sam returned, they sat down and began discussing Canfield's story.

After taking a drink from his coffee, Sam said, "Sounds like we have a motive for Perry attempting to dig up the body."

"Agreed," replied Joe. "But it looks to me like he stopped for one reason or another. Or someone stopped him and tried to cover up his attempt."

"You think he could have been killed because of what he was trying to do?"

"Maybe."

"But why would Gina have been killed?"

"Maybe she witnessed his murder. Whoever killed him didn't want a witness."

"Mm. That's a thought."

Joe reflected on what Canfield had told them and then looked at Sam. "You know, this doesn't get us any closer to who killed Gardiner and Whitmore."

"Where do you want to go from here?"

"I think we should interview Dennis Patton's brother. He lives here in the city. We need to check him out."

CHAPTER THIRTY-FOUR

"All right. Let's get on that and see what we turn up."

Chapter Thirty-Five

Joe and Sam met the following day to compare notes regarding what they found about Dennis Patton's brother. Dean Patton, who was two years older than his late brother, was not the upright citizen his brother had been.

Dean Patton had a rap sheet for misdemeanors that included domestic abuse, resisting arrest, disorderly conduct, and receiving stolen property. He was only convicted on the charges of resisting arrest and disorderly conduct. Each offense was committed years in the past, and he had no arrests during the last ten years. He was twice married and twice divorced, with two college-aged children from his first marriage.

Patton owns and operates two strip clubs, The Windy City Gentleman's Club and Club 409. Neither club had been cited for any major infractions, and no criminal activity had been found to take place inside either one. The only crime linked to one of his clubs happened two years ago when one of the strippers working at Club 409 was attacked and killed outside her apartment. The offender was eventually apprehended and convicted of her murder.

Joe called the number listed for Club 409, and a female voice answered.

"Club four-oh-nine. This is Brenda."

"Good morning, Brenda. This is Detective Joe Erickson, Chicago PD. I need to speak with Dean Patton. Does he have an office there?"

"I'm sorry, he doesn't. But he does have an office at The Windy City Gentlemen's Club. Would you like that number?"

"I would."

She gave him Patton's office number and said he is usually in mornings after eleven o'clock.

At one o'clock, Joe and Sam drove to the South Loop neighborhood address for The Windy City Gentleman's Club. The entrance door to the red brick, two-story building was locked, so Joe called the number he was given. A woman answered the phone.

"Windy City Gentlemen's Club. This is Barbara. How may I help you?"

"This is Detective Joe Erickson from the Chicago Police Department. We'd like to speak with Dean Patton. Is he there?"

"He is. Could I ask what this is about?"

"His brother."

"All right. Hold, please."

She came back on the line after a couple of minutes and said, "Someone will be down to let you in a few minutes." Click.

Joe looked at Sam and said, "Someone's coming to let us in."

A short time later, a young woman opened the door. "You're here to see Mr. Patton?"

"That's correct," acknowledged Sam.

"If you'll follow me, please?"

Joe looked at the tall, longhaired brunette and wondered if she was employed as one of the strippers. She certainly had the body for it, and her makeup appeared designed for a performance under stage lights.

As they navigated the hallways leading to the back area of the theatre, Sam's question produced an answer to Joe's thoughts.

"Are you one of the performers?"

"I am. I'm Chloe. You should come and see me perform some night."

Before Sam could answer, they arrived at a door with a sign reading "Private." She knocked, and a voice from inside said, "Yes?"

Opening the door a crack, she said, "Two gentlemen to see you, Mr. Patton."

"Come in."

Joe and Sam stepped into Patton's office. The room was a makeshift office improvised from a storeroom. Behind his desk was an archway leading to what looked like a large storage area with metal shelves. Joe noticed a woman walking across the back of that room carrying a small box. The office was neat but utilitarian, with no personal items or artwork on the walls.

Patton rose but remained standing behind his desk, not offering a handshake or a chair to Joe and Sam. His tone was neutral, neither friendly nor confrontational.

"Close the door on your way out, Chloe."

As the door closed, Joe and Sam showed their IDs and introduced themselves. Patton showed no reaction. Walking to a small bar area, he dropped a couple of ice cubes in a glass and poured himself a healthy shot of Jim Beam Black. He took a sip before he spoke.

"What is it you want? Barbie mentioned something about my brother?"

"I assume you were informed that his remains have been found?" asked Joe.

"Yeah. My niece called."

"We have a few questions, given you're the deceased's brother."

"Fair enough."

"Do you know either Bill or Phyllis Gardiner?"

"No."

"What about Perry Gardiner or Gina Whitmore?"

"Never heard of 'em. What's this about?"

"Your brother's remains were found in the Gardiner's backyard."

Patton took a drink. "Okay. So…You know who killed him?"

Joe lied. "Not yet. That's what we're trying to find out. We're also looking into the deaths of Perry Gardiner and Gina Whitmore, who were living in the house shortly before your brother's remains were discovered."

"I don't know anything about that. Sounds like you've got a lot of deaths on your hands."

"One thing led to another."

"So, what do you want with me?"

"We're trying to connect links."

"I'm the victim's brother. There's your one and only link."

CHAPTER THIRTY-FIVE

"You sure?"

Look, are we done here? I don't wish to be rude, but I've got phone calls to make and a payroll to get out."

"Sam?" asked Joe.

"Were you and your brother close?"

"Not really. We didn't associate a lot."

"Why's that?"

"He had this attitude that he was better than me. Because of his job and education. It didn't make for a lot of brotherly love. So, you can understand I didn't care to be around him much. I guess you could say we went our own ways and traveled in our own circles."

"Did he ever come to your clubs?"

"I didn't have either one of my clubs at the time he disappeared. But to answer your question, 'No.' He wouldn't have come if I would have had them. Not good for that squeaky clean schoolteacher image of his to be seen entering or leaving one of my clubs."

"You have a point. Strip clubs and school boards."

"Among other things."

Sam looked at Joe. "I guess that's all I have."

"Thank you for seeing us," said Joe.

"No problem. I take it you can find your way out, gentlemen?"

Sam smiled. "I think we can handle that."

Once the door was closed, Joe commented, "Don't you just love those passive-aggressive types?"

"Yeah. He really warmed up to us, didn't he?"

As they walked down the hall, Sam said, "I don't suppose we could get Chloe to show us the way to the door."

"We could. But you'd need another handkerchief."

"What for?"

"To wipe the drool off your chin."

Out on the street, Sam asked, "So, what do you think?"

"He's a thug. It's no wonder his brother distanced himself from him. Talk about the black sheep of the family."

"I wouldn't put anything past him."

"Neither would I," replied Joe. "Neither would I."

Chapter Thirty-Six

That evening, while Joe was walking Autumn, he thought about Dean Patton as a suspect in the deaths of Perry Gardiner and Gina Whitmore. He felt Patton was capable of murder but was wracking his brain about how he would have found out Gardiner was responsible for his brother's death. It didn't seem logical he could have known. And if he did, would he have cared? So, without further evidence, they would have to eliminate him as a suspect.

After Autumn's walk concluded and they were back inside the house, Joe saw Destiny was on the phone. From the conversation he was overhearing, it sounded like she was speaking to Jacquie. He poured himself a glass of wine and gave Autumn a treat. When she finished eating her treat, Autumn brought Joe her ball.

"So, you want to play now, huh? The walk didn't tire you out?"

Grabbing the ball, which Autumn had dropped in front of him, he rolled it into the living room, and Autumn took off running after it, her tail straight out behind her. She brought it back to him, and they repeated the procedure several times before Autumn decided she was tired of chasing the ball and laid down and began gnawing on it.

Joe got up, moved to the island, and sipped his wine. Destiny finished her phone call and entered from the dining room.

"Was that Jacquie?" asked Joe.

"It was. She was telling me some things she found out about Jared and Liz's estate. It's not what she expected."

"Like?"

"It seemed like half their stuff was leased. His father's real estate corporation owns their house. Jared was renting it. And their cars—their daily drivers—were also leased."

"The cars don't surprise me, but the house? That's unusual. You'd think Jared would have bought it as an investment."

"Jared had a substantial life insurance policy, but he never had the beneficiary changed to make Liz the recipient, so the payout will go to his father."

"Great."

"Well, Liz never had her life insurance changed to make Jared the beneficiary, either. Jacquie's attorney told her that her mother would be the recipient of Liz's life insurance death benefit since she was originally named as beneficiary. People don't think."

"At least her mother is provided for, and it doesn't all go to the Harlows, who are rolling in money and don't need it. Did she find out about their banking and retirement accounts?"

"She didn't mention anything about those."

Joe wondered about Jared's two classic cars, his 1970 Chevelle SS and the 1969 Camaro he was building. He had seen the Chevelle in person and pictures of the Camaro, and he knew they were valuable.

"Did she say anything about his classic cars?"

"Apparently, he owns those. She said she wants to sell the Chevelle but didn't know what to do with the Camaro since it's all in parts."

"Tell her I can help her out with that. I know people to call about selling the Chevelle. It's in great condition and very desirable as a collector car. And I would be interested in buying the Camaro. It's what I've been wanting to build, and I know what he has invested in parts."

"Oh, so you want Jared's Camaro, huh?"

"It's a great opportunity, and since it's disassembled, it'll be hard to sell boxes of parts, much less get what it's worth. I can make her a good, fair deal."

"If you put Jared's Camaro in the garage, your car will have to sit outside."

"I know. But there's enough room to build a carport to protect it from the weather."

"But it'll still be vulnerable to tampering."

"Not if we have a home security system. I think having one would be a good idea, don't you?"

"I've thought about that. Given what we do, we should have one installed. We live in a good neighborhood, but you never know."

"I'll look into it."

"If that Camaro is what you want, go for it. It'll give you something to do besides watch television. You could use a hobby."

Destiny poured herself a glass of wine and then sat down by Joe. "I'm sure Jacquie will be grateful for your help. She doesn't know anything about those kinds of things. Right now, she's feeling like she's been jerked around by Jared's family. The Harlows want to call all the shots."

They made a dinner of pasta with pesto and a baked salmon filet for Joe. Afterward, they adjourned to the living room.

"Jared knew Bill Gardiner, Perry's father. Bill's employed by the same real estate company," said Joe. "He moved from Chicago to Florida to work out of the company's office down there."

"What's he do?"

"Real estate salesman. When I was at Perry's funeral service, I saw Liz there. She was close to me in the receiving line. When greeting the family, I noticed Perry's father had an odd reaction to Liz when she said Jared was in Florida and couldn't return for the funeral service. It struck me odd at the time."

"What happened?"

"As I remember, she gave him her condolences and then said something like, 'Jared's in Florida and couldn't make it back.' And he just responded with an 'Mm.' No 'thank you' or anything. Just a grunt of acknowledgment. Rude, actually."

"You think he was offended that Jared wasn't there?"

"I don't know. Maybe. But his response was strange. I wanted to ask him about it, but I didn't get a chance."

"Maybe the department would pay for a plane ticket to sunny Florida," quipped Destiny.

"Fat chance. Hey. But I need to tell you—I found out we're finally getting a raise in pay. We just found out today. Two whole percent."

"Wow. What will you do with all that money?"

"Oh, spend it on booze and fast women."

"Yeah, and you'll probably squander the rest."

Joe laughed. Destiny could be quite witty when she wanted to be, and her wit could often be as sharp as it was quick.

"Oh, you got me there." He leaned over and kissed her. "You're the best."

"I know," she said with a grin.

Chapter Thirty-Seven

Joe and Sam got called out to a suicide the next morning. They drove to the girl's residence, an apartment on North Broadway in the Edgewater neighborhood she shared with her mother and father.

When Joe and Sam arrived at her parent's home, the ME's van was already on site. The officer at the door had them sign in, and they entered the house and spoke to Officer Clinton, who was first called to the scene. The girl's mother was being consoled in the living room by a woman about her age. Then Joe and Sam walked upstairs to where the ME was already in the girl's bedroom.

Joe and Sam walked down the hallway and met Officer Hill, who was guarding the door to the girl's room.

Joe showed him his ID and stated his name, as did Sam. Joe stepped to the door and saw Kendra Solitsky kneeling, working over the dead girl's body, which was lying on the floor. The body lacked any clothing, and Kendra was making notes on her clipboard.

"Hey, Kendra," said Joe.

Kendra looked up and said, "Hey, Joe. Welcome to my world."

"What do you have?"

"Ebony Atkins. Sixteen. Death by strangulation. She hanged herself with a couple of belts attached to her closet door. There was a suicide note left on the table next to her bed. It cited ongoing bullying online and at school."

"No indication of foul play?"

"No. Pretty clear-cut suicide, in my opinion."

Kendra rose and picked up a plastic sleeve from the bed. She walked it over to the door and handed it to Joe. "Her note. Hopefully, her cell phone messages will tell us more."

Joe took the sleeve, read the note, and then handed it to Sam. "Kids can be so damned cruel."

"Little monsters, some of 'em," said Kendra.

After reading the note, Sam handed it back to Kendra. "Sad. We'll speak to her mother and see if she was aware of her problems."

Joe and Sam left the bedroom area and went downstairs to talk with the girl's mother, who had found her daughter's body earlier that morning. The girl's mother, Kalisha Atkins, was sitting on the couch with another woman. Atkins and the woman beside her were in their early forties and had similar facial features.

"I had no idea anything was going on. Her father and I both have careers, and we have busy lives. Maybe I should have been there more for her."

"You can't blame yourself," the other woman told her. "None of us saw this coming."

"Where is Mr. Atkins?" asked Joe.

"He's in California at a conference, chairing a seminar this morning. He's a professor at the DePaul University."

"Any other children?"

"No, she's all we have," said Atkins, and she began crying again.

The woman comforted her and looked at Joe and Sam with an expression that indicated she wished they would leave them alone.

"Is there anyone we need to notify for you?" asked Sam.

Atkins shook her head no.

"I'm her sister, Jamila Taylor. I'll take care of that."

Sam left his card on the end table and said, "I'm leaving my card. If we can be of assistance, feel free to call."

"We'll be looking into the bullying your daughter apparently experienced, Mrs. Atkins," said Joe. "Bullying's a crime, and we won't let individuals think they can bully others and get away with it."

Joe and Sam remained at the residence and later asked if they could speak with Taylor in private. She knew nothing about any bullying Ebony was experiencing. She suggested coming back to speak with her sister in another day or two when Atkins would be in a better frame of mind and able to give an interview. She did say that Ebony was a student at Curie Metropolitan High School.

When Joe and Sam returned to Area 3, a message was waiting for Joe. The call was from Lainie Maravich, who said she had information regarding Dean Patton. Joe called her back.

"Hello."

"Is this Lainie Maravich?"

"Yes."

"This is Detective Joe Erickson. I received a message you called. Something about Dean Patton."

"Yes, but I don't want to talk about it on the phone. Can we meet somewhere?"

"You can come to our office at Area 3. You know where that is. On Belmont?"

"Okay. Uh...I'm not working today. I don't mean to put you on the spot...."

"Today's fine. Say three o'clock?"

"Okay."

Joe gave her the address and told her to ask for him. The call ended, and Joe told Sam they had a possible source coming in at three o'clock who said she had information about Dean Patton.

"Hopefully, she'll have something helpful. You know who she is?"

"She didn't tell me anything other than her name. Lainie Maravich. I haven't run it yet."

Sam perked up. "Maybe she's one of his strippers."

"Could also be his grandmother."

"I think I'll run her name. She can't be his grandmother." Sam turned and started typing into his computer. Joe smiled and walked back to his desk.

At 2:45, Joe secured the interrogation room for their meeting. Shortly before three, he received a call stating a person named Lainie Maravich was waiting to see him. He walked to the public access area and looked at several people standing. He noticed a tall, pretty redhead who looked like she had just arrived.

Looking at her, Joe said, "Lainie Maravich?"

The redhead said, "Sorry."

Immediately, a dark-haired, middle-aged woman rose from a chair and said, "That would be me."

Joe felt a little awkward assuming she would be one of Patton's strippers, but he introduced himself and thanked her for coming in. He led her to the interrogation room, where he introduced her to Sam.

"Can I get you anything to drink?" asked Joe.

"No, thank you."

"Have a seat," said Joe, indicating a chair.

After exchanging pleasantries at the table, Joe said, "You called me with something you wanted to tell us about Dean Patton. You care to explain how you know him?"

"I work in his office," said Maravich. "I do all the ordering for the club, keep the storeroom organized, and do odd jobs for Dean."

"Were you in the storeroom when we interviewed Dean the other day?"

"I was. I overheard your conversation. There's no door, and the walls are rather thin."

"I see."

"So, you knew what we were asking about?" asked Sam.

"Uh-huh."

"Do you have something to add to that?"

"I do. You asked about the death of his brother. Well, he got a phone call from somebody a while back trying to extort him about where to find his brother's body. The caller wanted him to pay money, and he would give him the location where he was buried."

"And how do you know about this?" asked Joe.

"Dean blew up over it. He started ranting and raving about it to his so-called 'assistants,' if you know who I mean."

"He employs muscle. Is that what you're saying?"

"Uh-huh."

"So, what did he do?"

"He told Chuck, his assistant, he needed to teach some guy a lesson."

"Did it happen?"

"I later overheard Chuck tell Dean he took care of it. Said it was some long-haired creep who drove up an old pickup. Said he wouldn't be a problem anymore."

Joe and Sam sat up in their chairs and focused more intently on what Maravich had to say.

"You think Dean and his muscle are capable of killing somebody?" asked Sam.

"If Dean was threatened...if somebody angered him enough. I think he'd be capable, yeah. Chuck's a pretty scary guy."

"Why did you decide to come in today, if you don't mind me asking? Sounds like there could be serious repercussions if Dean found out you were here," asked Joe.

Maravich looked up from fingering her bracelet and said, "I'm quitting next month. My husband got a job in South Carolina, and we'll be moving down there. I don't care if he does think I ratted him out."

"Aren't you afraid he'll hurt you?"

"My husband used to be a professional wrestler. He quit after he had his knee replacement. Dean knows Jerry would break him in two if he hurt me." She laughed. "I'm not worried."

"Well, thank you for coming forward, Ms. Maravich," said Sam. "I was thinking maybe you were going to be one of Dean's strippers."

"Sorry to disappoint you, detective," Maravich chuckled.

"Not at all," replied Sam. "I think you've got more credibility than one of his strippers."

"Thanks for that."

They chatted for a few more minutes and then concluded their interview. Joe accompanied her to the parking lot where her car was parked. He thanked her again for contacting them and wished her well about her move to South Carolina. Once back inside, he met with Sam in the interrogation room.

"I think we need to pay Dean Patton another visit, don't you?" asked Joe.

"Yeah," replied Sam. "I think we need to bring him in for questioning since he wasn't forthcoming when we first questioned him. We need to put some pressure on him."

"Uh-huh. He could've had one of his assistants make sure Perry Gardiner was no longer a nuisance and had him taken out."

"Makes sense."

Joe looked at his watch. "Tomorrow."

"Yeah. Tomorrow."

Chapter Thirty-Eight

The following afternoon, Joe and Sam traveled to Dean Patton's office to question him further based on Lainie Maravich's statements the previous day. He was uncooperative, and they were forced to arrest him on obstruction charges.

Upon bringing Patton into the interrogation room, he asked to speak with his attorney.

"Okay, if that's what you want," said Joe. "But all we want to know is what happened regarding the extortion call you received about your brother's burial."

"Are you willing to talk about that?" asked Sam.

"Maybe. But I want to speak with my attorney first."

Patton's attorney, Colin Van Buren, was conversing with his client an hour later. After several minutes, Van Buren came to the door and told Joe and Sam to enter the interrogation room.

After sitting, Van Buren said, "My client is willing to answer your questions if you do not charge him for obstruction or any other crime he may reveal during this interview."

"That depends on the crime," said Joe. "We aren't going to overlook any felonies like human trafficking or manslaughter."

"I can assure you he did not commit any serious crimes, detectives."

"Okay. Obstruction is off the table. We aren't interested in any misdemeanors he may have committed."

Van Buren looked at Patton to see if he agreed to Joe's offer and nodded.

"All right. Tell me about the phone call you received about the extortion," said Joe.

"I got this phone call, see," Patton began. "This guy told me he knew what happened to my brother, Dennis. Of course, that got my attention. He told me he'd been murdered and was buried in the backyard of the house where he got shot. The guy gave me the date it happened, so I figured he was legit, ya know? Then he says if I pay him ten thousand dollars, I'd receive the location of my brother's remains."

"So, how did that make you feel?"

"What do you think?" said Patton, who became visibly angry. "It pissed me off! Someone trying to extort me over my dead brother. What kind of sick son-of-a-bitch would do something like that?"

"What did you do?"

Patton looked at his attorney, who nodded for him to go ahead.

"I wanted to educate him, so I set up a meeting where my assistant would hand over the money. But instead of getting money, he'd get a lesson in fucking with the wrong people."

"And your assistant's name?"

"Chuck Nowak."

"You ever hear from this person after that?"

"Yeah. Once. At least, I think it was him. I don't know who else it could've been. I got a note in the mail that said, 'Expect a box of bones, you asshole!' That's all it said."

"And that's the last you heard from him?"

"Yeah."

"And your assistant didn't find him and bash his head in and strangle his girlfriend? Then set their pickup on fire, burning them to a crisp?"

"What the hell are you talking about?"

"Don't say another word," said Van Buren. "My client had nothing to do with the gruesome deaths you're referring to."

"He had motive."

"Is that all you've got?" asked Patton.

"If Mr. Patton can account for his whereabouts on the evening of June 10th, and his muscle can account for their whereabouts on the evening of

196

June 10th, we have no problem."

"I want to confer with my client for a few minutes, please."

Joe and Sam left the room. A few minutes later, Van Buren asked them back inside.

"Have a seat, detectives. My client can produce surveillance video from his club showing he, Mr. Charles Nowak, and Mr. Deiondre Calloway were present on the night in question. In addition, I can produce signed affidavits from several employees who can attest to their whereabouts on the date in question. Would that suffice?"

"We'd like to see that video evidence if you don't mind," said Sam.

"And the affidavits," said Joe.

Van Buren looked at Patton and then at Sam. "We can have that surveillance video for you tomorrow. The affidavits will take a few days."

"Thank you."

"Now that Mr. Patton has fully cooperated with your investigation, may I escort my client back to his place of business?"

"You may," said Joe. "Your cooperation was appreciated, Mr. Patton. We will be speaking with Chuck Nowak and Deiondre Calloway soon."

"I'll make them available to you, detectives," said Van Buren. "I'll be representing them as well. Tomorrow at one o'clock work for you?"

"One at a time. We'll take Nowak first."

"All right."

Joe nodded. "And you'll bring that video evidence with you?"

"Of course."

Patton and his attorney exited the interview room, leaving Joe and Sam looking at one another in silence.

After a few moments, Sam spoke. "So, what do you think?"

"I think Dean Patton is sleazy," said Joe, "but I don't think he would have viewed Perry Gardiner as a threat so great that he and Gina Whitmore needed to be killed and incinerated. He would have seen Gardiner as a mosquito, an annoying pest that needed swatting. So, he had his thug swat him."

"You still want to question Chucky-boy?"

"Oh, yeah. I want to know what he did to Gardiner. Maybe that motivated Perry to start digging."

"Besides the ghost?"

"He did say a box of bones, didn't he?"

The next day at one o'clock, Charles "Chuck" Nowak and his attorney, Colin Van Buren, met Joe and Sam at for an interview. Nowak was an intimidating presence. He stood six foot four, weighed around two hundred forty pounds, and had a face that suggested he possessed Neanderthal genes.

When Nowak and Van Buren sat down, Van Buren slid a can of Dr. Pepper in front of Nowak like a trainer giving his animal a treat. Nowak immediately grabbed it and popped the top with hotdog-sized fingers.

Joe began by stating, "We're not interested in any misdemeanors you may have committed regarding Perry Gardiner. We simply want to know what Dean Patton told you about the person extorting him."

Nowak looked at Van Buren, who said, "Go ahead and tell him, Chuck. They're not going to hold you accountable, and they're not going to go after Dean for this either."

"Okay. Well, you see, it's this way. Dean told me somebody was messin' with him, tryin' to get money from him by sayin' where his brother was buried. Mean thing to do, ya know. Preyin' on a guy's dead brother'n all. So, he sets up this exchange. Money for information thing. Ten grand for where his brother was buried. But Dean wanted to teach this creep a lesson. He tells me to give him a goin' over so he never bothers him again, see?"

Nowak stopped and took a drink from the can of Dr. Pepper in front of him.

"Did Deiondre Calloway go with you?"

"No. Just me."

"So, what did you do?" asked Sam.

"Well, Dean, he sets up this meeting, see. And this guy thinks I'm gonna give him ten grand for the information. What he don't know is, I'm gonna teach him a lesson he won't forget. That night, I pull up to this place we're supposed to meet, and then this old pickup rolls in. I get out of my car, and

198

he gets out of his pickup—long-haired guy with a beard. Looked like a bum, ya know. Anyways, he says, 'Ya got my fuckin' money?' Actin' like a real tough guy. So, I open the trunk and pull out a duffel, and says, "Da boss figures you wanted small bills, so here.' And I toss it down at his feet. He picks it up to take a look and sees it's full of horse shit. And just as he looks at me, I smack him across the jaw. He falls on the ground, and then I kick him in the balls, punch him in the ribs, hit him a few more times in the face and gut. Didn't want to hurt him too bad, ya know? Just enough to send a message. I left him there on the ground cryin' his eyes out. Boo-hoo. Real tough guy. Before I left, I grabbed him by the hair'n says, 'This's whatcha get for fuckin' with the wrong people!' After that, I get in my car and leave." Then Nowak nonchalantly took a drink from his Dr. Pepper as calmly as if he had explained how to tie a shoe.

"Horse shit, huh?" asked Sam.

"I thought it was a nice touch."

Joe looked at Sam, then Van Buren, and back at Nowak. "And he was fine when you left?"

"Oh, yeah. A little worse for wear. But he was fine."

"So, you think he learned his lesson?"

"School of Hard Knocks works pretty good for some people." Nowak smiled and took another drink from his Dr. Pepper.

Joe wanted nothing more than to wipe the smile off this brute's face, but he couldn't. Instead, he asked, "Do you enjoy kicking the shit out of people, Mr. Nowak?"

Van Buren interrupted. "That's not an appropriate question, Detective Erickson. He's been cooperative and told—"

Joe suddenly slid his chair back, an aggressive move that made Van Buren jump. Then he stopped and quietly said, "Excuse me," then he rose and walked to the side of the room.

After a moment, Sam looked back to Nowak and asked, "Was his girlfriend with him?"

"I didn't see no girl with him."

"Do you know what date this was?"

"How should I know? I don't keep a calendar."

Sam glanced over at Joe, who slowly shook his head.

"Are we done here?" asked Van Buren.

"You have any more questions for Mr. Nowak, Joe?"

"No."

"Then it looks like we're done here," said Sam.

After Nowak and Van Buren left, Joe left the room and went to get himself a cup of coffee. Sam followed him, aware of his agitation.

"What's the matter? Looked like you almost lost it in there."

"Nowak rubbed me the wrong way," said Joe.

"He's Patton's stooge, all right. Dangerous guy. You still thinking Patton just swatted a mosquito?"

After taking a sip of his coffee, Joe said, "Yeah. I'd love to nail that thug for Gardiner and Whitmore's deaths. But he didn't do it. I don't think Nowak is smart enough to get away with something like that. And I don't think Patton would have had them killed."

"Where's that leave us?"

"Back to square one."

Chapter Thirty-Nine

J oe and Sam had the next two days off, and Jared and Liz's memorial service happened to fall on the second day. While anticipation of the service was sobering and grew into an introspective look at their own lives, it succeeded in taking Joe's mind off the Gardiner-Whitmore murder case. Destiny's mother, Vivien, drove in from her Winnetka home to attend the service since she knew Liz and wanted to support her daughter.

People gathered at Lincoln Park Presbyterian Church for the ten o'clock memorial service. Joe, Destiny, and Vivien walked up the steps to the entrance to the tan stone building and joined the receiving line to greet Liz's mother and sister, as well as Jared's father, stepmother, and two siblings. It was an emotional moment for Destiny and Vivien when they commiserated with Ruth Lambert, Liz's mother, and Jacquie, Liz's sister. Destiny prepared herself for this moment, but no amount of mental preparation compensates for face-to-face interactions with grieving family members. Tears flowed.

They moved on to Jared's survivors, introducing themselves and offering condolences. Not knowing members of Jared's family, they did not have the emotional connections they had with Liz's sister and mother. Nonetheless, the sense of loss was clearly felt. Jared's father, Edward, a distinguished-looking man around seventy, introduced his wife, Laurie, who looked twenty-five years his junior, and was evidently Jared's stepmother. Jared's two brothers and their wives, all in their mid-thirties, were subdued, choosing only to say 'thank you' in response to their expressions of condolence.

A table with two identical urns featuring framed photographs of Liz and

Jared was beautifully accented with fresh flowers. Destiny stood in front of the table, looking at Liz's smiling picture. Tears ran down her cheeks as she remained motionless, standing between Joe and Vivien.

"She was my best friend. I loved her like a sister."

"I know," said Joe, placing his arm around her.

"She was a wonderful person," said Vivien. "You two were always attached at the hip. You may as well have been sisters. I thought the world of her, too."

Destiny wiped her tears away with her handkerchief and blew her nose. Joe pulled a fresh handkerchief from his pocket and handed it to her.

"You need another one?"

Taking it from him, she smiled and said, "As a matter of fact, I do." And she placed her own in her purse. "I seem to have cried mine out already."

"I have a couple more in case either of you need another one," said Joe.

"Nice you came prepared," replied Vivien. She looked at Destiny and said, "So much for eye makeup today, huh?" Her comment made her daughter smile.

Looking around, Joe saw Phyllis Gardiner in the receiving line to greet Liz and Jared's families. He wondered what her connection was to Liz and Jared and felt he needed to "say hello" to her in an effort to find out once the memorial service concluded.

The memorial service was a sad affair, with friends speaking about the loss of two people so young and full of life taken too soon. The minister, Pastor Janis Westling, gave inspiring, sensitive remarks illuminating who Liz and Jared were, what their lives meant to their families and friends, and how fondly they will be remembered.

After the service, Joe excused himself from Destiny and Vivien and sought out Phyllis Gardiner, pretending he was surprised to see her.

"Hello, Ms. Gardiner. How are you doing?" asked Joe.

"Phyllis turned and recognized Joe. "Oh. Hello, Detective. I didn't know I'd see you here."

"My partner was Liz Harlow's best friend. She's taking her death pretty hard."

"I'm sorry."

Pretending he knew nothing, Joe asked, "Were you related to one of the families?"

"No. But my ex-husband works for Jared's father's company in Florida, so we knew the family somewhat. And Bill was a good friend of Jared's. The two of them used to get together when Jared was in Florida and when Bill came back to Chicago. I'm sure this is hard for him, too."

"Is he here?"

"Julianne talked to him. He told her he wasn't able to get away."

"That's too bad."

"I guess."

"Well…I just wanted to let you know that we're busy working on your son's case. I'm hoping we can make an arrest soon and give you some peace of mind."

"Are you getting close?"

"We're making progress. These things take time."

"I'm glad to hear that. Thank you."

Making an arrest soon. Right. Joe sure as hell wasn't going to tell her they didn't have diddley squat for leads. He parted company with Phyllis and found Destiny and Vivien waiting for him outside on the lawn. He explained who he was speaking with, saying he needed to know her connection to the families.

"It seems you can't get away from work even at a funeral, can you?" commented Vivien.

Joe smiled. "Some days are like that."

"It's part of being a cop, Mom," said Destiny.

Once they arrived home, Joe made lunch while Destiny talked with her mother in the living room. The vegetarian lasagna with a spinach apple salad and a glass of Pinot Noir rounded out lunch. Vivien was impressed and complimented Joe on his culinary skills.

"Thank you, Vivien."

"You can come up to my house and cook for me every day."

"Sorry, Mom," said Destiny. "I already have him under contract."

Following lunch, they started discussing the fact that only Liz had a will, and Vivien told Destiny and Joe that the probate process in Illinois could take up to a year, and that was if there were no challenges to the will.

"So, Jacquie can't sell any of Liz and Jared's possessions until the process is complete?" asked Joe.

"I don't think so," said Vivien. "Not until the estate's been settled."

"So, what happens to their possessions since the house is rented?" asked Destiny.

"Everything must go into storage so the house can be sold or re-rented."

"Oh, man. More expense."

"That means Jacquie would have to find a place to store that '69 Camaro that's all disassembled," said Joe. "That could be tricky. I could volunteer to let her store it in our garage, couldn't I?"

Vivien didn't feel equipped to answer such a question. "I suppose. That would be something she'd have to ask her attorney. Why do you want it here?"

Destiny looked from Joe and then to her mom. "He wants to buy it from her."

"Right," said Joe. "That way, it won't have to be moved when I buy it, and she won't have to pay any storage fees."

"That makes sense. I guess that's between you and her."

Vivien drove back to Winnetka later that afternoon. Joe told her she was welcome to stay over and go back in the morning, but Vivien declined, saying she had a dentist appointment the next morning and did not want to re-schedule it. And she wanted to pick up Otto from the kennel.

That evening, neither Joe nor Destiny felt like cooking, so they had Chinese food delivered. After dinner, they decided to watch a movie, and Joe thought something adventurous and lighthearted might be in order, something to keep Destiny's mind off Liz and the memorial service.

As he scanned his DVD collection, his eye settled on *Butch Cassidy and the Sundance Kid*. He pulled it out and held it up for Destiny to see.

"How about *Butch Cassidy and the Sundance Kid*? I haven't watched it for a long time. What about you?"

CHAPTER THIRTY-NINE

"Neither have I," she said. "Sounds perfect."

They sat on the couch with Autumn watching Paul Newman and Robert Redford as Butch and Sundance for the next two hours. Ten minutes before the end, Joe noticed Destiny had dozed off, but he decided not to wake her, given the nature of the film's conclusion. Once the credits rolled, he nudged her awake.

"Hey," he said quietly. "Hey."

Waking, she looked at him and realized what happened. "Shoot, I fell asleep."

"Shoot is right. It ended the same way."

"Yeah. I know how it ends. Maybe it's good I slept through that part."

Destiny leaned against Joe's shoulder again. "You want to do something?" asked Joe.

Looking up at him, Destiny said, "Uh-huh."

"And what would that be?"

Destiny leaned in, kissed him, and said, "More of this."

Chapter Forty

J oe met with Sam as soon as he arrived at work. Everything had fallen apart on the Gardiner-Whitmore case, and he was eager to start their investigation over from the beginning.

"Where do you want to start?" asked Sam.

"I've thought about this, and I think we should re-start our investigation at the source—the Gardiner house. My gut tells me it's the epicenter of this crime."

"Agreed," said Sam. "I've always had the feeling the victims were killed there, but evidence has been non-existent. Let's go over that place with a fine-toothed comb."

Since the house had been released, they needed to get keys for both the house and the garage. Joe called Phyllis Gardiner, who referred him to her daughter, Julianne Hendricks. Joe left a message for Julianne and received a call back half an hour later. Explaining why they wanted to conduct another search of the house and the garage, Hendricks was agreeable to meeting them there around 12:15.

Pulling up to the house, Joe and Sam saw Hendricks waiting for them on the porch. The front door was open, and she was drinking from a water bottle.

As they approached the house, Joe said, "Thanks for taking time out of your schedule to meet with us."

Hendricks handed him a key. "This key is a duplicate I had. It opens the garage, too. You may as well keep it in case you need to get in some other time. You can return it when you're done."

"I appreciate that."

"No problem. Sorry, but I can't stay to chat. I have a full afternoon and have to get back."

"Thanks," said Sam as she passed by him and walked to her car.

They watched as she drove away. Then Joe looked at Sam. "You want to start on the house or the garage?"

"I already looked in the garage. I'll take the house."

Since the house was already unlocked, Sam stepped inside. Joe walked to the double garage, a much newer building than the house. Unlocking the door, he switched on the light, but it didn't provide much illumination, so he pushed a button on the wall next to the door, and the automatic garage door opener raised the double door. That lit up everything inside so Joe could see the contents more clearly. The garage had a concrete floor that was dirty and stained from old oil leaks and dirt from the cars parked in there. The walls were open studs and outside sheathing browned with age. On the wall next to the door was a workbench with a pegboard where various tools hung from hooks. Rolls of drywall tape and an unopened bucket of drywall compound sat under the bench, something that never made it onto the dining room walls.

Joe slipped on nitrile gloves and began examining hammers and other heavy tools for blood residue. Nothing. Then he moved to the garden tools used for digging. When he examined the spade, he stopped. Bringing it toward the open garage door so he could see it in better light, he saw what looked like dried blood with a few hairs attached on the underside of the kickplate, the flat edge of the blade where you place your foot.

Joe carefully placed the spade back where he found it and called for Evidence Technicians. He examined two shovels but found nothing visibly suspicious. Then he went into the house to find Sam.

"Hey, Sam! Where are you?"

"The basement."

"I found something in the garage."

Sam came bounding up the basement steps. "God, I hate spiders!"

"I know you do."

"Hate 'em!"

"How many did you see down there?"

"One. But it was huge!"

Joe wanted to laugh, but he suppressed it.

"What did you find?" asked Sam.

"A spade with blood and hair on it. I called in Evidence Techs to go over the garden tools and anything else in there."

An hour later, Evidence Technicians Art Casey and Jerry Bristow arrived. They were returning to where they assisted Dr. Maryanne Gillespie in unearthing Dennis Patton's skeletal remains.

"Another buried body?" asked Art, in his usual sardonic tone.

Joe smiled. "Forensic evidence on a spade. I found what looks like blood with hair attached to the underside of the kickplate. Could be the murder weapon in a case we've been working. Other digging tools could have prints and DNA, too."

"All right, we'll check out everything in the garage," said Jerry.

Art and Jerry suited up and began working. Two hours later, they had completed taking samples and fingerprints. They had bagged the spade and shovels and removed them to their van for further analysis in their lab.

"Luminol showed the presence of blood on both the shovel and spade," said Jerry.

"How long before we know about the DNA from the blood and hair?" asked Joe.

"Seventy-five days for the DNA," said Art.

"What?"

"There's a backlog. That's what it's running. Unless you know some bigwig who can push it through."

"Prints will come back sooner. If they're in the system."

"The DNA may be a match from one of the burned bodies the ME's office sent through some time ago. You can check with Kendra. She was the ME."

"Understood," said Jerry. "If there's evidence related to your case, we'll find it."

As the Evidence Techs' van pulled away, Sam looked at Joe and sighed.

"Seventy-five days. How are we supposed to close a case?"

Joe shook his head. "I don't know. This state is so screwed up."

They locked up the house and garage and returned to Area 3. Joe sent an email to Julianne Hendricks saying they found some possible evidence in the garage and that he would hold on to the key to eventually return items taken for analysis by the Evidence Technicians.

When Joe was entering information into his case notes, he felt a tap on his shoulder. Joe turned in his chair to see Detective Tyrell Williams.

"Hey, Tyrell. What's up?"

"You wanted me to keep you updated on the plane crash in North Carolina. They found a fingerprint in the engine compartment that didn't match prints taken from mechanics who serviced the plane. They ran it, and it's not in the system. They also discovered video surveillance of a person who seemed to be working on the plane but was not identified as one of the mechanics employed by the airport. It was the day before the plane took off."

"Was it good enough for facial recognition?"

"No. The person had on a cap and was wearing a medical mask. Looks like he was disguising his face. They have approximate height, weight, and hair color, but that's it."

"Fingerprint isn't much good without a suspect."

"Better than nothin', I guess."

"Thanks."

"How's your case shaping up?"

"Right now, we have to wait for DNA evidence to come back—seventy-five-day backlog."

"Yeah, that's fucked up. Well…duty calls. I'll let you know if there are further developments."

"Appreciate it."

Joe was going to send Destiny an email informing her about the sabotage of Jared's plane. He knew she would want to know, but he was reticent about bringing up the crash, knowing it would probably upset her. He decided it would be better to tell her when he got home that evening.

Chapter Forty-One

Summer turned to fall, and the hot July weather had transitioned into the chilly temperatures of late October. In that time, Joe and Sam closed two cases and picked up three more on their caseload, while the Gardiner-Whitmore case languished with no more leads. While pursuing Ebony Atkins' suicide, Joe identified one boy and two girls responsible for bullying Atkins at school and online. They were arrested and charged with a Class 4 Felony per Illinois law. But that provided little solace for Ebony's parents.

Autumn officially became Joe and Destiny's dog when Jacquie and her mother, Ruth, said they had no interest in taking her. They were both glad because she had become a part of their lives by now.

On Tuesday, shortly after 1:30 p.m., Joe received a phone call from Art Casey, the Evidence Technician.

"We got results back from several DNA submissions. I'm emailing you the results, but given your case and because I like you, I thought you would appreciate a phone call."

"Well, gee, Art. I never knew you cared."

"Consider yourself lucky. I don't like many people."

"Well, I don't know what to say other than…What were the results?"

"The DNA from the blood and hair on the spade proved to be from a close male relative of your victim, Perry Gardiner."

"Male relative?"

"Yes. Father, brother."

"Fingerprints from the spade handle were a match to Perry Gardiner. And traces of blood swabbed from a shovel were also a match to Perry Gardiner."

"Okay."

"DNA from the shovel handle matched Perry Gardiner and one unidentified male."

"What about fingerprints?"

"The shovel handle appeared to be wiped. But we got one partial print from the inside of the shovel handle. We ran it, and it came back to the recent victim of a plane crash."

"Really. Who was it?"

"Jared Edward Harlow."

This was a shock. It took Joe a moment to respond. "You said, 'Jared Harlow,' right?"

"Yes. His prints were in the system because he was arrested on a marijuana possession charge when he was in college. Why? You know him?"

"Uh...casually. My life partner was a friend of his wife."

"Well...Small world, huh Joe?"

"Yeah. You said you're sending your findings over, right?"

"You should have it shortly."

After the call, Joe sat in his chair, staring at his computer screen. He thought about what he just heard. Why would Jared be part of Perry Gardiner's murder? And who did the DNA from the spade belong to? Was it Perry's father? The DNA pointed to him. He's the only male member of Perry Gardiner's family since Perry had no male siblings. At least that we know of.

Joe got up and walked over to Sam. "We need to talk. I got a call from Art Casey with some enlightening information."

The two men walked to get coffee and sat down at a small table. Joe opened his notebook and read off what Art had told him.

"So, we have Jared Harlow and possibly Bill Gardiner at the crime scene? With their DNA and a fingerprint on a potential murder weapon?" asked Sam.

"It looks that way."

"Wow."

"It looks to me like Bill Gardiner was possibly struck with the spade, and Perry Gardiner was struck in the head with something, maybe the shovel. The injury to Perry's skull was determined to be the cause of death. Jared Harlow's print was present on the shovel's handle, so it looks like it's possible he could have been the one who swung it."

"What about Gina Whitmore? She was strangled?" asked Sam.

"That I don't know. But we need to interview Bill Gardiner."

"He's in Florida, isn't he?"

"Yeah."

"Would he have killed his own niece?"

"No, I don't think so."

"Then what do you suppose happened to her?"

Joe began thinking out loud. "What if Perry hit his father with the spade, and Jared picked up the shovel and whacked Perry in the head to protect his father or because Perry was coming after him, too?"

"Okay. Self-defense. But what about Gina?"

"Well...What if she comes out of the house and sees Perry get hit, or what if she sees him lying there on the ground? He's dead, and she tries to call the cops? Jared grabs her, they fight, and he winds up strangling her."

"So, let me get this straight. Jared accidentally kills Perry while defending himself. Okay, got that," said Sam. "And maybe he kills Gina, so the cops don't get involved. Got that. He's running on fear and adrenalin, and things get out of hand."

"That's one possible scenario."

"It's plausible." Sam sipped his coffee as he contemplated these new facts and Joe's speculation. "You're right. We need to bring in Bill Gardiner."

Back at his desk, Joe began researching Bill Gardiner. Then, he suddenly remembered something Phyllis Gardiner had said about her husband. "Bill had gone out of town with one of his Air Force buddies." He was in the US Air Force. What was he assigned to do when he was in the Air Force?

Joe looked up Bill Gardiner's vital statistics but could not see what job he performed when he was in the Air Force. Because he was in the Air Force before the year 2000, his fingerprints would not be in AFIS. He decided to call Phyllis Gardiner to see if she knew what his job entailed.

"Ms. Gardiner, it's Detective Erickson. Sorry to bother you, but I have a question, and I was hoping you could answer it for me."

"Well, I'll try. What is it?"

"It's about your ex-husband. Do you know what his job was when he was in the Air Force?"

"That's an odd question. What's that have to do with Perry?"

"Probably nothing. But something came up, and we were wondering what job he may have done when he was in the service."

"Well, okay. He worked with a unit that serviced planes. Kept up the maintenance on reconnaissance planes."

"That's what I needed to know. Thank you, Ms. Gardiner."

"Phyllis. Please."

"All right. Phyllis. Thank you. I appreciate your time."

Joe walked over to Sam's desk. "Sam. Bill Gardiner was a plane mechanic in the Air Force. He would know how to sabotage a plane."

"You think he was responsible for taking down Harlow's plane?"

"He's got motive. Revenge. If Jared killed his son and niece. And then burned them beyond recognition."

"Yeah, I'd say that's motive, all right. Why didn't he report him to the police?"

"Maybe he didn't witness it. Could have been unconscious. Or maybe because Jared's family is rich and could get him off on self-defense. So, he bided his time."

"How do we get him up here from Florida? We can't go down there."

"Let me think about that," said Joe. "But if we can, maybe we can question him about his son's death. Present him with the evidence. At the same time, we get his fingerprints to see if we can get a match to that print they found on the plane."

"They got one from the plane?"

"One print that's not in the system, and a poor-quality video of someone they suspect could have tampered with the plane. I heard that from Terrill Williams today."

213

"And I suppose Gardiner's prints aren't in AFIS, are they?"

"He was in the Air Force before 2000, so they aren't in the system."

"Okay. I'll let you figure out a plan."

Chapter Forty-Two

J oe came into work the following day with leftovers and an idea. After stashing his food in the refrigerator, he looked up the phone number for Harlow Realty, Inc., and then ran his idea past Sam.

Sam listened and nodded in agreement, saying, "It's worth a try."

Joe set up an appointment with Jackson Hughes, the Vice President of Harlow Realty, for 1:30 that afternoon.

In the meantime, Joe wanted to see if either Jared or Bill may have purchased gasoline to set Perry Gardiner's pickup on fire. It was possible there had been a supply in the garage, but there was a one-gallon container half-full of fuel next to the lawnmower, so gasoline had more than likely been purchased for a another container. He looked up Bill Gardiner's credit card charges and found nothing for June 10th, the night of the murders. But the next day, there were charges in states where he would have refueled on his way back to his home in Florida.

A search of Jared Harlow's credit card turned up a charge on June 10th at an Amoco station for $32.50. More than enough to fill the two-gallon fuel can found at the scene of the fire and to top off his car. Joe called the Amoco station and asked if they had video surveillance. The woman who answered the phone said they did, but it only went back a month. Surveillance video prior to thirty days was automatically erased. Too bad. It could have been definitive if they had a video of Jared filling a fuel can like the one found at the scene of the fire. Joe suspected Bill took off for home, and Jared was left in charge of cleanup at the house. He wondered if Bill knew the extreme measures Jared would take with the bodies. He doubted it. Maybe Bill's resentment was why he chose not to return for his friend's memorial service.

Joe shared the information he found with Sam as they drove to Harlow Realty on West Roscoe Street. They entered the beige stone and glass building and met the receptionist, Tia Carrini, at the front desk. After identifying themselves, they were taken to the office of Vice President Jackson Hughes. She knocked on his door, opened it a crack, and said, "Detectives to see you, Mr. Hughes."

"Send them in," came a baritone voice from inside the office.

Tia opened the door for them, and Joe and Sam saw a thick-set, gray-haired man wearing a white shirt and tie rounding his desk, hitching up his pants. When Joe saw him, he looked vaguely familiar but didn't know where he might have seen him before.

Joe and Sam showed their IDs and said, "Thank you for seeing us. I'm Detective Joe Erickson."

"And I'm Detective Sam Renaldo."

Offering his hand, the sixty-year-old said, "I'm Jackson Hughes, but you can call me Jack. I'm Vice President of Harlow Realty, but you probably know that already." He shook their hands firmly. "Have a seat. What can I do for you?"

Taking a chair in front of his desk, Joe began. "We have an interesting situation with one of our investigations, and I thought maybe you could help us out."

"Well…'interesting,' you say. What exactly do you need?"

"You have an employee named William "Bill" Gardiner who works out of your Florida office. You know him?" asked Sam.

"Bill Gardiner, yes. He's one of our salespersons. Has something happened?"

"We're investigating the murders of his son and niece. Have you heard about that?"

"I know Bill lost his son and niece to violence. Yes. Terrible thing. I attended the memorial service for his son, actually."

Oh, so that's where I saw you before, thought Joe.

"We think it's important to support our employees. Not long ago, our

President, Ed Harlow, lost his son and daughter-in-law in a plane crash. It's been a tragic year."

"We can't go to Florida to question Bill for our ongoing investigation," explained Joe, "and there's a potential problem he may have with authorities down there that could make it difficult for him to travel back here later on. I can't go into that. But we were wondering if you could call him back to Chicago for some reason."

"Problem with authorities? What kind of problem?"

"Like I said, I'm not at liberty to say. But he may be a suspect in an investigation."

"Christ! He's one of our best salesmen."

"Nothing's for sure," said Sam. "But we really need to question him in case things down there...progress."

"So...is there a reason you could call him back here?" asked Joe.

Hughes leaned back in his chair. "Oh, boy. Well...We have a supervisor position opening up, and I could ask him to fly back in order to discuss it with him. He was going to be one of my choices for it anyway, given his performance and years with the company."

"That would be great."

"I can do that. When do you want me to contact him?"

"I'll need to let you know. We have to arrange some things on our end first. But I'll contact you in the next day or two when we're ready."

"All right. That'll be fine. Just let me know."

Joe and Sam had completed what they had set out to do, and they got up from their chairs.

"Okay," said Hughes, rising from his seat. "If one of my employees has committed a crime, he needs to answer for it. I don't want someone unethical on my payroll, and I don't give a damn how good a salesman he might be."

Joe and Sam thanked him and returned to Area 3 to plan what to do after Bill Gardiner returned to the city.

"We need to pick up Gardiner and sweat him about what happened when his son and niece were killed," said Sam. "We have physical evidence, so we can lean on him pretty hard if we have to."

"Yeah. And we need to get his fingerprints so they can be sent back to North Carolina to see if they match the print found on Harlow's plane. He may not have had anything to do with his son's and niece's deaths directly, but he might be the one who sabotaged the plane."

"We don't dare let on that he's a suspect for that."

"Oh, hell no," said Joe. "We have to get his prints off a soda can or coffee cup while he's here. Or maybe from something he drank from during his interview with Hughes. I'll ask Hughes to save whatever he was drinking from so we can dust it for prints."

"We could just arrest him and get his prints that way."

"Arrest him for what?"

"Accessory-after-the-fact. He concealed it."

"We could. But I'd like to use that as a threat to get him to talk. He needs to know we can charge him for not reporting the crime. If we use that as a bargaining chip, we can get him to come clean and give us the facts about what happened. I doubt he killed either one of them."

"I see where you're going. And if he doesn't talk?"

"Then we'll arrest him."

Chapter Forty-Three

Joe called Jackson Hughes the next day and told him he could call Bill Gardiner in for an interview. He also asked him to preserve whatever Gardiner drank from during their interview so police technicians could collect his fingerprints. Hughes agreed to make it available.

Bill Gardiner flew from Tampa to Chicago for his interview three days later. Joe was alerted to the date and time of the interview as well as the hotel where Gardiner would be staying since the company made the accommodations.

The next morning, Bill Gardiner traveled to the Harlow Realty headquarters for his ten o'clock interview with Jackson Hughes. Following his interview, Hughes called Joe, saying Gardiner's interview had concluded and that Gardiner's soda can was sitting where he left it in their conference room. Gardiner drove his rental car back to his hotel, where Joe and Sam were waiting.

In the lobby, Joe and Sam met Gardiner, who was dressed in an expensive blue pinstripe suit.

"Mr. Gardiner," said Joe, showing his ID as he approached him.

"Yes?" answered a surprised Gardiner.

"Joe Erickson, Chicago PD. My partner, Sam Renaldo."

Gardiner turned belligerent. "What the hell is this about?"

"You need to come with us to answer some questions."

"About what?"

"The night your son and niece were killed."

"You can make this easy or difficult. Your choice," said Sam, holding handcuffs for Gardiner to see.

Gardiner paused, looking from Joe and then to Sam. "All right. Let's go."

They left Gardiner in the interrogation room for ten minutes before they came in to question him. When they entered, Joe said, "Sorry about the wait. Something came up."

"Can I get you something to drink?" asked Sam. "Coffee, soda, water?"

"A Coke would be good," said Gardiner.

"Coming up." Sam glanced at Joe before he left. Joe acknowledged and set down his coffee cup as he sat across from Gardiner. Removing his notepad, he turned pages and scribbled notes until Sam returned. Gardiner observed without any attempt at making conversation.

Sam returned with a can of Coke and sat it in front of Gardiner. Then he walked around the table and sat next to Joe.

Looking up, Joe got straight to the point. "Do you have an old injury to your head, Mr. Gardiner?"

"Why do you ask?"

"Because we found blood and hair on a spade in the garage at your house on West Victoria Street. DNA results confirmed the sample was from a close male family member of your son. That would be you. Care to explain?"

Gardiner just sat there, refusing to answer.

"Look," said Joe, "We have enough evidence to charge you as an accessory after the fact in the death of your son and your niece. Now, you can cooperate, and we might forget about charging you, or you can continue to be uncooperative, and we will throw the book at you."

Gardiner paused and then looked up from the table. "Perry hit me with it."

"The spade?"

"Yeah."

"And why did he hit you with it?"

"We had words, and he lost his temper."

"Words about what?"

Gardiner didn't answer. He just stared at the table.

"Was it because you found him digging up Dennis Patton's grave? The man he killed, and you buried?"

Gardiner tried not to respond but was unsuccessful. His nonverbals betrayed him. He was disturbed by what Joe knew. Choosing not to answer, he sat there, turning his can of Coke round and round.

"Mr. Gardiner. We found traces of blood and your son's DNA on one of the shovels. We also found a fingerprint belonging to Jared Harlow on the handle of that shovel. Did Jared Harlow swing that shovel, striking your son in the head, killing him?"

Gardiner stopped turning the Coke can. Tears welled up in his eyes, and he nodded his head.

"Then tell us what happened," said Sam.

A moment later, Gardiner took a drink from his Coke and set it down. After taking a deep breath, he began.

"Jared...He was in Chicago, and he went with me over to the house to see the work Perry was doing on the inside. And when we got there, we found him in the backyard digging up the area where I buried Dennis Patton years ago. I couldn't believe what he was doing. He gave me some cock-and-bull story about Patton's ghost haunting him. Well, I went ballistic and started yelling at him, saying we would all go to prison. And all of a sudden, he swung the spade he was holding and hit me in the head. It knocked me senseless for a minute or so. And when I came to, Perry was lying on the ground, and Jared had Gina down, choking her and yelling over and over, 'Shut the fuck up!' By the time I was able to get to my feet and pull him off of her, she was dead. I went to check on Perry, and...he wasn't breathing. I tried to do CPR, but it was useless. He was dead, too."

He paused as tears welled up in his eyes. A moment later, he continued. "I looked back at Jared and said, 'What have you done?' And he said, 'Perry attacked me with the spade. I had to defend myself.'"

"Why did he choke Gina?"

"He told me she came running out of the house and saw Perry lying on the ground and started screaming and wouldn't stop. He said he had to shut her up, or the neighbors would hear her and call the police." With trembling a hand, he took a drink from his Coke.

"What did you do after that?" asked Sam.

"I...I was numb. I sat down on the back porch steps and cried. I just lost it.

Jared sat down next to me and assured me he would take care of everything. Said he'd make it look like an accident. That I should go back to the hotel and then drive back to Florida in the morning. Not to worry."

"And did you."

"Uh-huh. But I had no idea he'd drive them to a park and burn them up like old newspapers. I couldn't believe he would do that. Just horrible. Why did he do that to them?"

"Did you ask him about it?"

"No. And you know what? The son-of-a-bitch never told me he was sorry. Just went on about his business like nothing ever happened. I swore I'd never talk to him again."

Gardiner picked up his Coke and drank from it. Joe wanted to keep him there until he finished his soda, so he continued asking him questions.

"What exactly was your relationship with Jared Harlow?"

"I work for his father's real estate business. I'm one of his salesmen. Jared was an attorney I worked with occasionally, and we found we had a number of things in common and struck up a friendship. Some friendship."

"What kind of things in common?"

"Guy stuff, you know. Golf, cars, sports. The Cubs, the Bears...."

"Were you aware that Perry had changed after he came back from San Francisco?" asked Sam.

"I was."

"And you let him have the house anyway?"

"He needed help, but I couldn't have him living on the streets. He needed a place to live. I figured if he had a project to work on, if he was away from the temptation of that west coast environment and close to family again, maybe he could straighten himself out."

"But he didn't, did he?"

"Not from what I could tell."

There was a pause while Gardiner looked down at his Coke can, and Joe and Sam finished making notes. Finally, Sam looked up.

"Your explanation of what happened is most appreciated," said Sam.

"I should inform you the statute of limitations has run out on illegal disposition of a body, so you and your ex-wife can't be prosecuted for burying Dennis Patton in your backyard," said Joe.

"That's good, I guess," replied Gardiner.

"And since you've cooperated by giving us the story of your son and niece's murders, we'll overlook the charge of accessory after the fact. I think the deaths of your son and niece have been enough punishment."

"I…uh…appreciate that." Gardiner tipped up his Coke and finished it.

Sam looked at Joe, who nodded. "We're done here," said Sam. "Thanks for your cooperation."

Joe and Sam rose and escorted him out of the interrogation room.

Gardiner looked around for a place to drop his Coke can. Sam said, "Just leave it. We'll take care of it." Gardiner put the can on the table and stepped out of the interrogation room. Joe followed.

"Can I call you a taxi?"

"No, I'll call for an Uber." After accompanying Gardiner to the exit, Joe returned to the interrogation room. When he opened the door, Sam held up an evidence bag containing the Coke can.

Joe drove to Harlow Realty to pick up the container Gardiner drank from during his interview. He met Tia Carrini, who escorted him to a locked room.

"Mr. Hughes told me to keep the conference room locked until you showed up. He didn't tell me why."

She unlocked the room and turned on the light as they entered. Joe spotted a Coke can on the table.

"I can handle it from here, Tia. Thanks."

After Carrini left, Joe slipped on gloves, bagged the Coke can, and brought it back to Area 3 so Evidence Techs could pick up both cans to collect fingerprints.

Holding two items with fingerprint evidence, he walked over to Detective Tyrell Williams, the Chicago liaison for the North Carolina investigation. He explained he may have potential fingerprints for them to compare to the mystery print retrieved from Harlow's crashed plane.

"What makes you think this guy is good as a suspect?" asked Williams.

"He has motive. Harlow killed his son. He had means because he was an airplane mechanic in the Air Force and opportunity—he lives within driving distance and maybe a physical match to the man in the video they have. They don't have any suspects yet, do they?"

"Not that I know of. Let me contact them and see if they're interested. If they have no suspects, maybe they can help us get a rush put on these soda cans," said Williams. "I doubt the FBI labs are backed up like ours are."

Joe returned to his desk and called Gina Whitmore's parents. When he initially spoke to them, he told them he would contact them once he found the offender responsible for their daughter's death. He explained that they had discovered the man who killed their daughter, but he could not be apprehended since he was the victim of a plane crash in North Carolina. Mark Whitmore mentioned something about karma, and his wife thanked him for his kindness in letting them know the truth about their daughter's death.

He also called Julianne Hendricks and provided her with the same information. She was grateful and said she would inform her mother. She went on to thank Joe for his work on solving the case. He chose not to mention anything about her father's involvement on the night of the murders. No sense complicating matters. If Bill Gardiner wanted them to know the truth, he could tell his daughter and ex-wife all about it someday. *Like that's going to happen,* thought Joe.

Chapter Forty-Four

Joe needed to share the break in the case with Destiny, but he didn't know how she would respond to the fact that Liz's husband was the offender who murdered Perry Gardiner and Gina Whitmore. But the truth must be told despite how painful or shocking it might be. And she needed to know how his investigation intersected with the crash of the Harlows' plane.

When Joe arrived home, Destiny was sitting at her computer and talking on the phone. Autumn came running up to greet him, and Joe kneeled and petted her, accepting her affectionate nudges and excited expressions at seeing him.

"Are you happy to see me, Autumn? Are you?" he said as he massaged her ears. That seemed to suffice, and after a few moments, Autumn ran back to be with Destiny.

"You're fickle, Autumn," Joe chuckled. "I'm only good for a treat!"

Upon hearing the word 'treat,' Autumn turned and came running back with anticipation in her eyes.

"I said the magic word, didn't I?"

Rising from the floor, Joe got a doggie treat and tossed it to her. She caught it, ran to her bed, and began chewing on it. Then he got a glass from the cupboard and opened a bottle of Pinot Noir. Letting it breathe for a few minutes, he checked his phone for messages and looked through his mail. One bill, the rest junk. Typical. Then he poured himself a glass of wine and sat down at the island to wait for Destiny to get off the phone. It wasn't long.

Destiny came out into the kitchen and kissed him on her way to get a glass

225

so she could join him.

"How was your day?" she asked.

"Good news and bad news."

"Oh?"

"We got DNA back on the samples taken from the garden tools, and we brought Bill Gardiner, the father of Perry Gardiner, in for questioning. He substantiated what we suspected based on the DNA and fingerprint evidence."

Joe took a drink as Destiny poured from the bottle.

"So, did you find out who the killer was?"

"We did. That's the good news."

Destiny sat down on a stool next to Joe. "So, what's the bad news?"

"The offender who killed Perry Gardiner and Gina Whitmore and destroyed their bodies in the pickup fire was Jared Harlow."

Destiny's jaw dropped, and she was speechless for a few seconds. "What?"

"Yeah."

"You're kidding."

"I wish I was. His fingerprint was lifted from the handle of the shovel we think was used to kill Perry Gardiner. Perry's blood DNA was on the shovel. Perry hit his father in the head with a spade, knocking him unconscious for a few seconds. When he got his wits about him, Perry lay dead, and Jared had Gina on the ground, choking her because he was trying to keep her from screaming. He wound up strangling her."

"Omigod. Omigod," whispered Destiny. Her hand went up to her face, and she used her arm to support her head. "I can't believe it."

"Jared told Bill that Perry attacked him with the spade he used to knock out Bill, and Jared swung the shovel to defend himself and hit Perry in the head, killing him. Maybe he hit him again when he was on the ground, I don't know. Anyway, Kendra said a blow to the head was the cause of Perry's death. Apparently, Gina saw what happened and started screaming and…."

Destiny took a drink from her wine and then looked at Joe. "I had no idea Jared was like that. He seemed like such a nice guy."

"It's hard telling what a nice guy will do under extreme stress brought on by a desperate situation."

"Seeing Perry attack his father may have activated Jared's inner hero, albeit twisted."

"Hero? You're going to have to explain that one."

"Psychologically, his inner hero kicked in to save his friend from Perry's further assaults. He reacted by striking him with a shovel and then silenced Gina to prevent her from causing a scene that could have alerted authorities. His adrenalin caused his attacks on Perry and Gina to be excessive, and they both proved fatal."

"Heroically?"

"In his mind. I'm only speculating."

"Well...I suppose it could explain how a nice guy could flip out."

"Are you sure he was the one who set the fire?" asked Destiny.

"We have a record of him buying gasoline that night. Bill didn't. According to Bill, he was so upset after what took place that Jared told him to go back to his hotel. He said he would take care of things and make it seem like an accident. Some accident. He made it look like a murder. Gardiner said he had no idea Jared would set them on fire like he did. That really upset him. We tracked Bill's gas receipts, and they confirmed he drove back to Florida the next morning."

"I guess that lets him off the hook."

"Not quite."

"What do you mean?"

"I think Bill Gardiner may be the one who sabotaged Liz and Jared's plane. To get revenge against Jared for killing his son and niece."

"Oh my...You sure about this?"

"We won't know for sure until his fingerprints are processed and sent to North Carolina. To see if they match the mystery print they took from the plane."

"You think he could have..."

"It's a possibility."

"Oh, Joe. This whole thing is a nightmare. Liz was just...what? An incidental result of his revenge?"

"Looks like it."

"Unbelievable. It's going to take me a while to process all of this." She took another drink from her wine and then stared off into space. After a few moments, she looked at Joe. "I wonder what Jared's family is going to think. Guilty in absentia for two murders."

"I hate to say it, but they're lucky he's dead."

"What do you mean by that?"

"He can't be arrested and put on trial. Or humiliated in the press. Instead of a news article splashed all over the front page, there might be a short write-up on page ten that no one will read. Harlow Realty and the Harlow family probably dodged a bullet."

"You'll let me know as soon as you find out about the fingerprints, won't you?"

"Of course."

"Because I was just contacted by the police department in New Orleans. That's who I was talking with on the phone. They suspect a serial killer's at work, and they want me to come down there and create a profile."

Joe immediately thought this may not be a good idea coming so soon after the death of her best friend.

"Are you sure you feel up to it?"

"I do. I think it would be good to get away and take my mind off everything that's happened. I told them I'd get back to them tomorrow."

"It's probably a great opportunity," said Joe. "A trip to The Big Easy for a couple of weeks: warm weather, jazz, great food. What's not to like? Who knows, you might run into Emeril Lagasse."

"With what? My car?"

"I hope not."

"I know, it sounds like a great opportunity, and I'll probably agree to work with them."

"Maybe a distraction would be good."

"That's what I'm thinking."

"But I'll miss you, of course."

She leaned over and kissed him. "You'll live, won't you."

CHAPTER FORTY-FOUR

"I usually do."

Chapter Forty-Five

When Destiny was in New Orleans, Joe got word that Bill Gardiner's fingerprints obtained from the Coke cans by the FBI and sent to the North Carolina Sheriff's Office were not a match to the mystery print found on the plane's wreckage. Needless to say, Joe was disappointed. His gut was telling him Bill Gardiner was the one responsible, and his gut was seldom wrong.

Despite the lack of a fingerprint match, two deputies from the Asheville, North Carolina, Sheriff's Office traveled to Florida to question Bill Gardiner since he had motive, means, and opportunity to tamper with Jared and Liz's plane. During the questioning, Gardiner responded to questions about his years in the Air Force and his work as a mechanic servicing planes. They asked him about sabotaging a plane like the one Jared and Liz were flying.

"Anyone with knowledge of how airplanes function could've done it," said Gardiner.

"Did you do it?" asked Deputy Prescott.

"I could have done it. It would've been easy enough. You mess with the oiling system, and you get a catastrophic engine failure. But if I had done it, I can tell you one thing: I wouldn't have left any evidence behind." He smiled, picked up his can of Coke, and looked at Deputy Black. "I doubt you can prove I did it." A hint of a smile appeared on his lips, and then he tipped up his Coke and took a drink.

"We have ways of finding evidence," said Deputy Black.

"Good luck with that," responded Gardiner.

Deputy Black felt like smacking the "arrogant bastard," and Prescott could see that Black was getting pissed. He knew continuing the interview would be a waste of time, so he ended it.

Prescott and Black traveled back to Asheville believing they had interviewed their offender. But the only evidence they had was video footage of an unidentifiable individual with a similar body type to Bill Gardiner, a type that matched a host of other men. They had no other evidence to link Gardiner to sabotaging the plane. The investigation continued, but no other suspect would surface. Eventually, the case went cold.

Not long after his interview, Bill Gardiner sold the house on West Victoria Street as well as his home in Tampa. He resigned from his sales position with Harlow Realty and moved to Belize, where he bought a house with a view of the Caribbean. He now lives there full-time and has no plans to return to the States.

Joe's regular session with his psychiatrist, Dr. Lemke, took place three weeks after they closed the Gardiner-Whitmore murder case. She had a wry smile when Joe entered her office, and her first words were, "Is this going to be a further inquiry into Svengali Syndrome, Detective Erickson?"

Joe chuckled and said, "No, we've closed that case. But thanks for indulging me during that session."

"It's not every patient that brings up such an unusual subject to discuss. That was a new one on me."

"Well, I pride myself on researching my cases."

"That's admirable. I'm glad it helped. What's on your mind today?"

"Failure to see a case closed."

"I thought you said you just closed one."

"This is a different one," said Joe. "I'm afraid it's going to bug me, and the problem is, it's not even my case."

"Care to explain?"

"There's a guy who's going to get away with sabotaging a plane. The crash killed two people, one of them being Destiny's best friend, and now he's moved out of the country, and we'll probably never see him again."

Dr. Lemke paused and considered what he said before she spoke. "There are two things you need to come to grips with, Joe. First, you can't be responsible for someone else's case even though you may have an emotional connection to it. You have to let it go. It's like a wound that will fester and eventually turn septic. And secondly, you know as well as I do that sometimes people get away with the crimes they commit. It's a fact of life, and nothing can be done about it. I'm not telling you anything new. You know this, right?"

"I know."

"So, the sooner you let go of it, the better off you'll be."

"Yeah."

"The best thing you can do is to be there for Destiny as she grieves her friend. Your continuing support will help her heal and feel less alone with her pain. Grief is stressful, so encouraging her to talk about her emotions will help relieve that stress."

"Good to know."

"Physical injuries heal with stitches and a band-aid. Two weeks later, the wound is healed, and the stitches have come out. But grief has no timeline. It's different for everyone. With the appropriate support, the grieving process can be made easier."

"Understood."

"Is she a resilient person?"

"She is."

"Grief is a process. She'll probably get through it. But she's welcome to talk with me if she thinks she needs to."

"Thank you, Doctor."

"Anything else you want to talk to me about?"

"Not really."

"You had any more nightmares?"

"No. None."

"Any feelings of depression or negative responses to loud noises?"

"No."

"And you're taking your medication?"

"Lexapro. Yeah. It doesn't seem to have any side effects that I'm aware of.

CHAPTER FORTY-FIVE

Not like all that stuff Dr. Bunch had me taking for a while."

"At the time, those prescriptions were necessary. But Lexapro, I think you should remain on it for the foreseeable future. You're on a low dose. It's not going to hurt anything. Then, at some point, when you think you're ready, we can look at taking you off of it. See what happens. If you think you need it, we can put you back on it, but if you seem to be getting along fine, you may not need it any longer."

"That would be great."

"Sometimes, patients can eventually go off their medication and go about their lives without any issues. Maybe you'll be one of them. You have any other concerns or questions?"

"No, not really. I seem to be getting along pretty well."

Dr. Lemke put down her clipboard. "You've been seeing me for quite some time now, Joe, and we've been gradually tapering off our sessions. I think we've come to the point where we can suspend them, and you can see me on a strictly voluntary basis from now on."

Joe was glad to hear that. He had come a long way since he had driven himself into a mental breakdown and wound up under Dr. Bunch's care five years ago. Dr. Bunch succeeded in getting him back on his feet and functioning. But Dr. Lemke's recommendation secured his place back on the force and got him feeling good about himself again. And he worked his way back to normalcy thanks to her, Destiny, and his drive to get himself back into good physical and mental condition.

As Joe looked at Dr. Lemke, a thought occurred to him. "When we were done talking, my former Lieutenant Vincenzo would say, 'All right, get outta here.' Is that what you're saying, Doctor?"

Dr. Lemke smiled and rose from her chair. "Yes, Joe. 'Get outta here.'"

Acknowledgements

Joyce Johanson; Detective Timothy O'Brien, Chicago PD; Jolene Grace; J. R. Sanders; Joyce Woollcott; Shawn Reilly Simmons; Verena Rose; and the staff at Level Best Books.

About the Author

Lynn-Steven Johanson is an award-winning playwright and novelist whose plays have been produced on four continents. Born and raised in northwest Iowa, Lynn holds a Master of Fine Arts degree from the University of Nebraska-Lincoln. His four previous Joe Erickson mysteries, *Rose's Thorn*, *Havana Brown*, *Corrupted Souls*, and *One of Ours* are published by Level Best Books. He lives in Illinois with his wife, and they have three adult children.

AUTHOR WEBSITE:
  https://LSJohanson.com

Also by Lynn-Steven Johanson

Rose's Thorn

Havana Brown

Corrupted Souls

One of Ours

www.ingramcontent.com/pod-product-compliance
Lightning Source LLC
Chambersburg PA
CBHW050203120726
47903CB00002B/734